BOUND BY TRUTH

Suzanne Cass

S C

STORM CLOUD
PRESS

Bound by Truth

Storm Cloud Press, Perth Australia

Copyright © 2019 by Suzanne Cass

Edits by Tanya Saari

Cover by Germancreative

All rights reserved.

To all the lost children out there.

CHAPTER ONE

The traffic light turned green. Sierra flicked her gaze right, then left, her hands rigid on the steering wheel, her foot hovering over the accelerator. She could go. The light was green, it was all good. Sweat prickled over her scalp. She checked to either side again. The cars lined up obediently behind the white line at the intersection. It was safe. But still, she hesitated.

The loud blare of a horn sounded behind her, and she flinched and closed her eyes. That was a mistake. With her eyes closed, her head filled with the terrifying sound of screeching tires. Of metal crunching, buckling. Of glass smashing into smithereens. Of screams. Horrible screams.

A horn honked again, this time long and insistent. The light was definitely green, wasn't it? She checked again to make sure. Yes, it was. Green for go. Tightening her fingers around the wheel—and after one final glance to make sure there were no cars speeding toward her—she edged the car forwards.

Clearing the intersection, she released a breath from between pursed lips and increased her speed.

It was stupid. She knew it was stupid. Could a person have a phobia of traffic lights? Not daring to take her eyes from the busy road in front, Sierra fumbled with the door console until she found the button to let the window down. A welcome blast of cool air helped dry the perspiration on her face.

At least this was the last set of lights she'd have to deal with today. The city of Adelaide was behind her, and now she was heading onto the highway that'd take her towards Cape Jervis, and the ferry back to Kangaroo Island. Thank God she lived on an island. Not a single traffic light to be seen anywhere. The idea of spending even one more night on the mainland had her breaking out in a sweat all over again.

Venturing onto the mainland was a necessary evil that had to be endured, although her mother would probably disagree. Aileen Goldstein was always grumbling about how she never saw her middle child, even though she lived closer than either of her other siblings. Her young brother, Logan, was the farthest away, on an island in the Caribbean somewhere, and Kiera was in Hawaii. She did miss her mum, though, and had enjoyed their evening together last night. Mum still lived in their old house in Glenelg. Sierra's heart squeezed tight every time she drove up the driveway to that house. It was always bittersweet when she visited because it reminded her so much of her father. Five years on, and she still missed Dad like crazy.

But even one night on the mainland had Sierra itching to get back to the island. It was quiet there. The wild coastline and the green hills soothed her like nothing else could. Now she was on the road home, she could literally feel the tension leaving her shoulders. The radio was playing a song from the eighties, one of her favorites from the band, The Police. She turned it up loud, and let the wind and the music calm her mind as she drove.

Less than two hours later, Sierra stood at the railing of the boat, watching the mainland dwindle into the distance. The strip of land mixed into the wake of the ferry in the dark, swirling water. She glanced down. Her car was parked on the deck below. She could see the gray roof of the Subaru huddled next to the others, mostly four-wheel-drives, some camper-vans, and a couple of caravans which would belong to the tourists and gray nomads coming to visit the island. The ferry was barely a third full today. Not many tourists were intrepid enough to brave a Kangaroo Island winter. And they were right to stay away. It got bloody cold, windy, wet and just plain miserable out there.

The icy wind whipped past her face, threatening to tear her long, auburn hair from its ponytail. The ocean was rough; iron-gray clouds hung heavy in the evening sky and the wind howled around the ferry. Pulling her Gortex jacket tighter around herself, she drew in a deep breath and released it slowly. Home. She was going home.

A man burst through the door from the inside cabin and took two long strides across the deck to the side of the ferry, only a few feet from where she leaned. White-knuckled, he grabbed the railing and gulped at the sea air.

She crossed her arms and turned her head sideways to take a quick look. His face was pale, and beads of sweat stood out on his forehead. She held back a smile. Whether it was just pure luck, or a strong constitution that stopped her from getting seasick, she'd never know. No matter how rough the water on the Backstairs Passage, she never felt a twinge of nausea. And she'd done this trip many times. But it was always humorous watching big, strapping men like this one beside her succumbing to the roll and pitch of the waves.

"Keep taking slow, deep breaths," she encouraged. "The fresh air will help."

"Really? I'm not so sure about that," he replied through gritted teeth. His face had a green tinge, even beneath the light-brown color of his skin.

"Well, if you really want to feel better, then there's nothing like a good old puke over the side. That works wonders. But will you warn me if you're going to do that, please? I'm downwind." She took a step away from him, arms still crossed over her chest.

"I'm not going to puke," he growled, and she wondered if saying the words out loud was a warning to himself or to her.

"That's good," she replied, still watching him warily.

"No one told me it'd be like this. How long will it take us to get there?"

"The trip is around forty-five minutes. It might take a little longer in these big seas, though."

"Oh, great," the man replied, lifting one dark eyebrow.

She stole another glance at him. Even after ten years on the island, she didn't know everyone who lived there. It was a tight-knit community on the whole, but it wasn't as small as people thought, with a population of nearly four-and-a-half-thousand. She was pretty sure she would've noticed a guy this good-looking before, however. Perhaps a few inches taller than her, which made him around six foot. A thatch of ebony hair, cut short, but not so short you couldn't run your fingers through it. Raven-dark eyes, with a high forehead and expressive eyebrows. At least he was dressed correctly for the climate. Blue jeans—which hugged his impressive thighs nicely—hiking boots, and a thick, waterproof coat. If he was a tourist, he'd come well prepared for the island's infamous weather.

"You sound like you've done this before. Do you live on the island?" He glanced at her quickly, before returning his gaze to the water, taking another deep breath.

"Yeah, I'm heading home."

He nodded. "What's it like? Living on the island, I mean."

"Good. Great actually, if you like life a bit slower. It's beautiful. The coastline is amazing." Sierra let her gaze drift out over the water to mingle with his. She didn't add it also

4

had the power to heal. "Why do you ask?" she added, her interest piqued.

"Starting a job in Kingscote. I'm the new cop on the beat." He glanced up as he spoke, his suddenly shrewd eyes weighing her up.

Well, that answered a few questions about him. The reason for his piercing stare, as if he was trying to delve into her deepest secrets, was now clear. It was a cop stare, intimidating, scrutinizing. And now that he'd said it, she could see his straight-backed stance and athletic, lean body was also a product of his profession. He had to stay fit to catch the bad guys. She had a healthy respect for the cops. The good ones, at least. Was he one of the good guys? You couldn't tell from looking at them, that much she knew.

"Aha. Sergeant Don Coldwater is a decent man. Fair, but firm. You should get on well with him." She didn't add that the Sarge was also a little chauvinistic and old fashioned. Stubborn and single-minded, if he thought he was right. Her dealings with the Sergeant of the island's small police unit were fragmented, at best.

Cops had an ingrained wariness of investigative journalists. Not that she called herself that anymore. But she did the occasional article for *The Islander* newspaper, and had butted heads with Don Coldwater more than once over the truth behind a story. They were polite when they met in public, but there was still an aura of tension between them, as if Don was circling her like she might explode at any moment. Which she wouldn't. Not now. Maybe once she'd been a stick of dynamite, wanting to blow a story sky-high. But now, she was much more circumspect. Life was never black and white. She'd learned that the hard way.

"That's what I've heard," he replied. "I must admit, I'm looking forward to a change of pace. I think the island will be good for me."

"If it gets in your blood, then you'll never want to leave," she agreed.

"Is it really covered in Kangaroos?"

She laughed. "Yes, it really is. You have to be extremely careful when you drive around the island. They like to throw themselves at unsuspecting cars. The tourists usually find out the hard way exactly how many roos there are."

"Damn, really?" He turned to look at her, a grin on his face. The smile lit up a dimple in his chin. Now that he was facing her head-on, she saw his nose was long and defined, and just that little bit crooked, as if it'd been broken at least once. It gave his strong features even more character. Hell, it made him almost irresistible. Not that she was in the market for a man, no matter how tantalizing he might be.

"Where are you from?" she asked, but thought she already knew.

"New Zealand."

Of course, he was a kiwi. She'd picked up his accent as soon as he spoke. That explained even more about him. The lovely treacle-colored skin, the dark, brooding features.

"Have you lived on the island all your life?"

She gave a light laugh. "No. But I haven't come far. I used to live in Adelaide, just over there." She waved her arm in the general direction of the city. If the night had been clear, they might've been able to see the glow of the lights from Adelaide, but tonight everything was covered in glowering clouds. It would be pitch dark by the time they reached the island.

"Funny, I've spent the past eleven years in Adelaide myself. But never once visited Kangaroo Island." He stared off at the disappearing mainland and Sierra pulled her coat in around herself. It was getting colder now the sun was gone.

"Hey," he continued. "I feel better." He tilted his chin. "Thanks for distracting me. I'm feeling almost human."

"Not going to puke anymore?" she asked.

"Nope." He gave her that rakish grin again, the one with the dimple, and something shifted inside Sierra's chest. "My name's Reed. Reed Kapua." He held out a hand.

What else could she do? She took it. "Sierra Goldstein." His hand was warm, much warmer than hers. And strong, with long firm fingers.

"Nice to meet you, Sierra."

* * *

Reed turned the dial on the dashboard as far as it would go, waiting for the engine to warm up enough to start heating the car. Damn, this place was cold. But he'd have to get used to it. Rubbing his hands together, he glanced forward through the windshield of his black Jeep. The car ramp was down now, they'd be giving the signal for the vehicles to move off the ferry soon.

The woman he'd met out on the deck sat in the gray Subaru in front of him. Sierra had offered to show him the way to the Kingscote Police Station. It was the least she could do, she said, to help out local law enforcement. He was to follow her car out onto the main road. He'd been surprised to hear it was nearly a forty-minute drive to the main township. Being an island, he'd thought everything would be close. But Kangaroo Island was a whole lot bigger than he imagined. Nearly one-hundred and fifty kilometers, from end to end.

If he'd had time, perhaps he would've done a little research on the area, but the job had come up, and in an uncharacteristic bout of spontaneity, he'd applied. They'd interviewed him the next day over Skype, and he'd been informed by his Senior Sergeant a day later that he could take the transfer if he wanted it. This was a sideways move, not a promotion. But Reed was happy with that. Life in Adelaide had been growing thin and stretched lately, his days as a cop starting to blend one into another. If he was lucky, this island might even turn out to feel a little like home.

His family had moved to Auckland when he was a teenager, but he'd always yearned to go back to his hometown. Missed the feeling of community and belonging that Hastings offered. Missed the slower pace of country life. Only time would tell if he might find that feeling of inclusion here.

Which reminded him, he should call his father. Nikau Kapua would be keen to hear about his new job. And his mum would want all the details of where he was staying, make sure he was eating enough, have enough warm, clean clothes, whether his new boss was treating him fairly, and all the other minute details. Reed smiled to himself, wondering if mothers all over the world worried about their grown sons as much as Shelly worried about him. Soon. He would call them soon.

A movement from inside the car in front caught his eye, and he watched the back of Sierra's head as she leaned across to look at something on the passenger seat and then sat up straight again, her long ponytail swinging against her shoulders. It was nice of her to offer to show him the way. He continued to stare at her profile, wondering what she did on the island. Now that he thought about it, all their conversation, standing out in the freezing, salty air, had either been about him, or what he could expect on the island. She'd masterfully re-directed every time he asked her a personal question. Damn, how had she done that? He usually prided himself on finagling out the details of people's lives. It's what he did. What he was good at. If he hadn't been so seasick, holding back the violent urge to puke his lunch all over the side of the boat, then maybe he would've been more aware of how she'd played him.

She was arresting; a classic beauty. Dark features, high cheekbones, and a sultry mouth. It was hard to tell exactly what was going on beneath that large Gortex jacket, but from what he could see of her well-toned thighs, sheathed in thick, black leggings, he'd bet his last dollar she had a killer body hidden under there, as well. As they'd parted to get into their respective cars, she'd playfully told him they were sure to run into each other again on the island. And now he found himself hoping her throwaway comment would come true.

Reed blinked. This was the first time in nearly two years he'd actually considered a woman in that way. But then, she probably wasn't the type to do casual, and he certainly wasn't into commitment.

A sharp pain shot up his calf and he eased his foot off the floor, rotating his ankle until the ache subsided. Cold always made his leg worse. But again, it was probably something he was going to have to get used to out here. The only thing between this island and Antarctica was a whole lot of wild ocean.

Anyway, who was he kidding, thinking lustful thoughts about a woman he'd only just met? He wasn't here to find a relationship. He was here to do a job, a good job. Nothing more, nothing less. Better to stop thinking about those luscious lips and waves of silky hair. *Mind back on the job, Reed*.

The cars in front started to move forward and he eased his foot onto the clutch and put the Jeep in gear. It was fully dark now, the sun sinking behind the island well before they docked at the port town of Penneshaw. He flicked on his headlights and eased his car out behind Sierra's. She'd warned him, more than once, not to get too close on the road and to keep his eyes peeled. She wasn't kidding about the roos, they were a real menace, she said.

Just as they drove out of the ferry carpark, a figure stepped toward Sierra's car, and she pulled over to the side of the road. Reed pulled in behind her, letting his car idle as he watched a short man lean in her window, passing her something, while talking animatedly. It was hard to see the man's features in the poorly lit street; all he could make out was the man was wearing glasses, and was thinning on top. Reed waited patiently until finally the guy stepped away from her car and back onto the sidewalk. As he followed her into the main street again, Reed caught a glimpse of the man staring at him as he drove past, no doubt wondering who this stranger was following Sierra around town.

It was too dark to make out much of Penneshaw as they drove through, he'd have to come back and explore it in daylight, so he could acquaint himself with the lay of the land. Once out on the open road, Sierra kept her car well below the speed limit, and he stayed a dozen or so car lengths behind her. Three or four times on the trip to Kingscote, Sierra's brake lights flashed red and he'd had to slow down, watching as groups of kangaroos stared at them from the roadside, before bounding off into the dark, ears pricked forwards, tails held high. By the time they reached Kingscote, he could feel the beginnings of a headache coming on, just waiting for the next set of eyes to appear out of the gloom. This was crazy. One more hazard he was going to have to get used to.

Before he knew it, Sierra came to a halt by the side of the road. She wound down her window as he pulled alongside.

"There you go." Her hand came up and she pointed across the road to a small, squat, white building hunkering on the corner of the intersection. More of a revamped house than a special-built police station. But then, many county stations were exactly that. "Police headquarters on KI."

It took him a second to realize KI was short for Kangaroo Island. He checked it out before turning to answer. The building was lit up with a bright spotlight on the front steps, and all the windows glowed from within.

"Thanks," he said through the window.

"No probs," she replied. "There's a carpark at the side."

He nodded, already having noticed the fenced-off area. There were a series of closed garages at the back, where he assumed the squad cars lived.

"Looks like someone is still working," she said, glancing at the well-lit building.

"Yeah, Don said he'd wait for me to arrive. He's going to take me over to a guesthouse they have lined up for me to stay in, until I can get a place of my own." Reed put his hand in his pocket and stared back at the police station, searching for the feel of his lucky penny, sitting warm, familiar and comforting.

"Good luck," she called, already winding up her window.

"Thanks again," he shouted. It sounded inane and severely lacking. He wanted to say something bright and witty. Tell her he hoped to see her again. But the moment was gone, and she drove off, red taillights fading into the dark.

He stared after them until she turned a corner and the street was empty, still playing with the penny in his pocket. Time to go and meet his new boss. Reed took in a deep breath and drove into the carpark.

CHAPTER TWO

Sierra hummed along to an imaginary tune in her head. Only a few more minutes and she'd be home. Her detour to show Reed the police station in Kingscote had added a good fifteen minutes to her trip, but at last she was nearly there. Her bed was calling. She probably wouldn't eat, just fall in between her sheets and sleep. She couldn't be bothered starting a fire to heat the place. It'd been a long two days. The last fifteen kilometers or so of the road to her house was all dirt, but she was used to driving here now, even in the pitch-black of night. She loved navigating around KI. In the daylight, driving here was like going down a wooded tunnel, sometimes the gum trees hung so close they were just a soft, green canopy over the sky. And at other times, the hills rolled away from the car on either side, a lush green now the winter rains had come. But even when they were a dry, scratchy yellow, burnt by the sun's summer rays, everything seemed more intense out here. More extraordinary. More real. And the sky. It was such a fierce uncluttered blue. She could breathe the sweet, clean air and not feel hemmed in. Claustrophobic. She could forget for a while.

Her phone rang, but Sierra ignored it while she was driving. She chanced a quick glance at the screen. Bloody hell, it was Blake. Again. Eventually, the phone stopped its musical jingle and there was a ping to let her know he'd left a message. Sierra's brow furrowed. Blake was becoming a problem, and she wasn't quite sure how to address it.

Two years ago, she and Blake had dated briefly. Blake was quite a bit younger than her, a visiting biologist on KI to study the Glossy Black Cockatoos. She'd been flattered by his open admiration, and because she knew he wasn't staying, had given in to temptation. He'd been hot, and intense, but Sierra had let out a sigh of relief when he finally left the island to go back to his university and his project. The problem was, Blake had recently returned to KI. He'd phoned her about a month ago, and delightedly told her he'd taken up a full-time position on the island as a local ranger. He was ecstatic with his new job and wanted to take her out to dinner in Kingscote to celebrate. Sierra's heart sunk at the earnestness in his voice, and she'd tried to let him down gently, saying she was busy. It'd been great while it lasted, but she wasn't interested in reigniting something that'd only ever been a fling for her. Blake had phoned her a few times more in the past month, but she'd always managed to come up with a vague excuse not to see him. It was too late to wish he hadn't got the job on KI. It seemed like she needed to get more forceful with him, as he wasn't picking up her subtle hints. She didn't want to hurt the guy's feelings, but if that's what it took, then so be it.

Looking down at her phone once more, to check it really had stopped ringing, she caught sight of the small package Evan had given her. He'd practically jumped in front of her car as she was exiting the ferry tonight. Sierra wondered vaguely if it was a hobby of his, standing on the sidewalk watching the cars disembark from the ferry. He was nearly always there whenever she returned home from a visit to the mainland. Evan ran the local newsstand and post office and he'd asked if she could take a small package out to one of her neighbors. He was a little bit odd, but Sierra felt sorry for him. Living on his own, no wife or kids. So, she always stopped to chat with him.

Lights twinkled through the foliage as she came over the last rise and headed down the incline towards Snellings Beach. It looked like Sam and Debbie were still up. Her closest neighbors were a good quarter mile away. This beach was small and isolated, with only seven other houses in the area. Most of them belonged to Sam and Debbie, who rented them out. Which meant half the time they were empty. Just the way she liked it.

There was also Terry, the artist who lived right at the end of the road. He was pretty much a hermit, hardly ever leaving his property. Sierra sometimes met him and his three dogs on her walks around the bay. He was a tall, spindly man, with a long, Father Christmas beard. Sierra had asked Debbie about him once, and even she didn't know how old he was; she suspected he was in his late fifties. She'd never seen any family come to visit, and his friends were sparse, indeed. Supposedly, his sculptures were quite sought after on the mainland and he sold enough to keep his bills paid, and he was happy with that. There was also the rich middle-aged couple who owned the house next to Sam and Debbie. It was their holiday house, and they came over from Adelaide when they could. Sierra had only met them three times since they bought the place four years ago. And that was the extent of her neighbors.

Stifling a yawn, Sierra turned into her driveway and her house appeared, lit up by the car headlights, a dark shape huddled into the even darker shrubbery surrounding it.

But as she pulled up, a frisson of ice ran down her spine. Something was wrong.

The security light hadn't come on. It was a motion-triggered spotlight that lit up her yard and front steps in a blinding light whenever a car came up the driveway.

That was weird. The bulb must've blown. She'd have to replace it in the morning. Her task of unloading the car just became that little bit harder, now she had to do it in the dark. With a deep sigh, she turned the vehicle off and listened to the engine tick and hum as it cooled down. Other night sounds intruded into her warm, safe space. A tawny frogmouth owl called from a sugar gum near the fence line, it's deep, continuous *oom-oom* sound strangely comforting. A gust of wind rattled the spiky leaves of the grass tree near her front door.

There was no point in sitting in her car all night, so she undid the seatbelt and got out, deciding to go and unlock her door and turn on the hallway light to help her see to unload the car. The frigid night air hit her as soon as she got out, and she pulled her jacket from the front seat and hurried to put it on. Walking toward the steps that led up to her front porch, that eerie prickle of fear came back. Something didn't feel quite right. It was hard to see in the dark, but she was so familiar with her front door she didn't really need to see to fit the key into the lock and turn the handle. That tingling sensation was still there, making the hairs on the back of her neck stand up, and she fumbled with the keys, almost dropping them.

At last, the door swung open and she reached around to find the switch on the wall. Light flooded the entryway, and everything seemed quiet and serene.

Except…

Neither of her cats, Jon and Snow, were anywhere to be seen. Normally, they'd be waiting for her on the mat, meowing for their dinner, rushing past her as she opened the door to get in. But the house was eerily silent. Sierra stood in the doorway, undecided.

Stop being so stupid. She was a grown woman. She wasn't scared of ghosts, or bogeymen, or things that went bump in the night. Squaring her shoulders, she strode down the short corridor and reached for the light switch that would illuminate her large, open-plan living space.

A scream filled the back of her throat.

Her normally simple, but stylish, room looked like a tornado had ripped through it. The coffee table was tipped onto its side, as was the small table at the end of the couch, the lamp smashed on the floor beside it. All the chairs around her dining tabled were also toppled over, and pictures that once hung neatly on the wall were either on the floor, or dangling at crazy angles. Framed family photos and candlesticks had been scattered everywhere.

Her house had been trashed.

What the hell was going on? She cast a jittery glance behind her. Was the person still here? Were they inside? Her stupid heart was beating so loudly in her chest she couldn't hear if anyone was actually prowling around. Taking a deep breath, she tried to calm her pulse and listened carefully. Not a sound. Her house wasn't big, only three small bedrooms, and this large living and kitchen area. Surely, she'd know if someone was still there. On stealthy feet, she crept across the room, sticking to the woolen rugs and away from the wooden floorboards.

As quick as a snake, her hand flashed in and turned the light on in the first spare bedroom. A gust of air flew out between her lips. The room was empty.

But before she could take an inventory of the room, another thought hit her.

Oh no, please let it still be there.

Sierra ran to her bedroom, ignoring the chaos of clothes and other belongings strewn everywhere. The bottom drawer to her dresser hung half-open. She dragged it all the way out, and scrabbled through the contents still left inside.

Sierra exhaled sharply as her fingers closed around the thing she was looking for. She'd know the feel of it, whisper-soft against her hand, no matter what. Holding it up to her face, Sierra breathed in the familiar smell of the pink fleece. Her daughter's blanket.

Thank God the burglar hadn't found it. But then again, why would they? It wasn't like it was worth anything to anyone else.

Sierra sat back on her haunches and took another deep inhale of the baby blanket, still held to her face.

Sierra lifted a finger to touch the scar that ran beneath her hairline. It was barely visible, nowadays. Most people didn't even know it was there. A tear rolled down Sierra's cheek. She swiped it away. Now was not the time or place to get sentimental. She needed to find out if anything was missing. And then she'd call the police. Although, the KI unit only ran one on-call staff member at night, so she knew there was a high possibility they might not be able to send anyone out until the morning. If she called her neighbors, Sam would be over like a shot. Perhaps she'd do that. Most of the time, she loved living by herself. But in this instance, she might feel safer if there was someone else in the house.

Getting to her feet, she tucked the pink blanket under her arm and reassessed the bedroom. Her gaze swept over the top of the dresser. Everything was scrambled and pushed into piles, half of it on the floor. Most of the things she'd had up there were cosmetics, a few knick-knacks and her jewelry box.

Oh no, her jewelry box.

She searched the sea of clothes that littered the floor, finally landing on the wooden box lying upside down with its lid open. She picked it up in a vain hope, but there was nothing inside. All her jewelry was gone. Not too much held any sentimental value, except for her grandmother's antique ruby ring, and the diamond necklace her father had given her for graduation. Apart from the nostalgic value, they were both also worth a pretty penny. She threw the box down in a sudden fit of disgust. How dare someone think they could come in and steal her stuff? It made her feel violated and dirty. And mad. She was getting more furious by the minute.

Then she remembered the cash and turned back to the top drawer of the dresser, hope fading as she saw there was nothing left inside. It was a couple of thousand dollars she kept at home, just in case. Not enough to send her broke, but enough to make her stamp her foot in anger. Bloody mongrels, whoever they were.

She went back into the main room, noting the television was still on its stand, along with the small stereo below it. Her expensive camera hung on its hook in the hallway, and her Kindle reader lay on the floor near the upturned coffee table. Strange, why hadn't they stolen those? Her gaze drifted to the kitchen counter, which was also a mess. Her stack of cook books had been knocked over, and there were utensils strewn everywhere. That was why it took her a few seconds to realize what else was missing.

Her laptop. She'd left it on the bench yesterday morning before she went to the mainland. At first, she thought she might take it with her, but decided she wouldn't have time to do any writing during the day and her mum would want her company all night, so there was no point.

Oh, shit. Her world was on that laptop. All her articles, research notes, files from old stories. Everything.

She dialed the number for the KI police station, barely able to contain her outrage.

"Officer Jones, how can I help you?"

Sierra explained about the break in, but knew even before she finished her account what he was going to say. He was the only one on duty that night. Did she want him to call in the Sarge to come and take a look? The idea of getting Sergeant Don Coldwater out of bed in the middle of the night to drive forty minutes out to her house to check on a few stolen items made her think twice and her indignation cooled. He'd probably see this as a much more trivial offense than she did. She suddenly didn't want to face his dismissive gaze.

After Officer Jones confirmed, more than once, that she was unhurt and didn't require immediate assistance—and that she had a nearby neighbor she could call on—they agreed the Sarge would come out first thing in the morning.

Sierra hung up the phone, and took another look around at her trashed house. The hardest part would be stopping herself from cleaning up the mess before Don got there.

CHAPTER THREE

"This place is out of the way, isn't it?" Reed said, as the squad car came over a low rise to reveal the tiny community huddled around Snellings Beach.

"Yep," Don drawled. "There's lots of these little isolated places on KI. It's the reason some people come here in the first place, to get away from everything."

They were approaching a valley, where a small river flowed down to meet a beautiful pristine beach below them. Puffy clouds covered most of the sky, but every so often a shaft of sunlight made it through, throwing the vista into stark relief.

Reed cast his new boss a quick sideways glance, but didn't reply. Sergeant Donald Coldwater was an interesting man. He must've been heading towards his late fifties. Short and stocky, but all muscle, there wasn't an ounce of fat on him. Short salt-and-pepper hair and a trademark mustache gave him a distinguished air, as did his serious, gray eyes and stern mouth. He reminded Reed of a bull terrier dog. And he had a personality to match. Even after knowing the man for less than twenty-four hours, Reed already understood you wouldn't want to get on the wrong side of Don. He'd heard through the police grapevine that Don and his crew were a solid bunch, loyal, dependable, and good at what they did. Hopefully he could find a way to slot into this tight-knit team.

As Don steered the police car over the rutted dirt road, Reed thought back to the events of the morning. At exactly half-past eight, Reed had reported to the police station in Kingscote. The little guesthouse Don organized for him to stay in until he sorted himself out was only two blocks away, so he'd walked to the station, enjoying the brisk air.

Reed thought he would get there early—the station didn't officially open until nine—but everyone was already there when he entered the building, all clustered in the large, old kitchen sipping on mugs of coffee. Reed hid his surprise. They either loved their jobs a lot, or were perhaps just keen to meet the new recruit.

Don stepped forward and made the introductions. First off was Patrol Officer Eric Jones. Eric was a big man, towering over Reed, and carrying a little extra weight by the looks of the buttons straining to breaking point on his police shirt. But the man was still mighty intimidating. Reed was glad he was on their side as he shook the big man's hand, which engulfed his. Eric's face split into a wide, affable grin as he welcomed Reed to their small unit, and Reed was reminded of the Big Friendly Giant. Then he turned to shake the hand of Patrol Officer Olivia Mettler. Olivia was the complete opposite of Eric, small and petite, with a thin mouth and astute eyes. When she smiled, however, her eyes came alive and her bushy, blonde ponytail jiggled with mirth that belied her stern gaze. Don told him Olivia was their youth and community expert, as well as their liaison with the general public, while Eric was the main patrol cop. But they were also jacks-of-all-trades out here. Their unit wasn't big enough to have them assigned to only one role. Not like the big-city stations.

Reed kept his shoulders squared, and met their eyes with a steady gaze. His new workmates would make their own evaluations. He knew he was good at what he did, but he also knew he'd need to prove himself first, before any of them trusted him.

"Give us a quick run-down of your career so far, if you wouldn't mind," Don had asked, sending him a quick nod of approval. "Ease Eric and Olivia's mind that you know what you're doing."

"Sure thing." Reed took a step back so he could lean against the doorjamb, and put one hand in his pocket. His fingers found the smooth familiarity of his lucky charm. An old bronze penny from the early nineteen-thirties that his mentor at the academy had given him. Reed always carried that penny in his pocket. Cops could be a cynical bunch, but they were also highly superstitious, and Reed never went anywhere without it. Logically, he knew it wouldn't protect him from a speeding bullet, and it hadn't saved him from that terrible car accident that'd scarred his leg, but the human heart wasn't always logical and so he still carried it with him.

"I moved to Melbourne when I was twenty, and did my original training at the Victorian Police Academy in Glen Waverly. After I graduated, I took a job in the rural town of Ballarat, which I know is still a lot bigger than Kangaroo Island, but at least I have some experience working in a country area. We had a team of fifteen officers, and I was in the crime services section. So, my forensic skills might come in handy." Eric grimaced at Reed's words, and he got the impression they didn't have a lot of call for crime scene investigation skills out here.

He continued with his story. "I spent three years in Ballarat, but wanted to experience a big-city station, so took a job in Adelaide. I loved working there, we had a great crew, a great Superintendent." He cast a quick glance at Don, but the man just raised one eyebrow in response. "Then I was involved in an on-the-job car accident, and I left the force for around four years." Olivia gave him a small sympathetic smile. "But once it's in your blood, well, you know...I couldn't stay away. So, I re-joined the force in Adelaide, started almost at the bottom again, but I don't mind. It's the job I love, not the titles. Been back in service for the past four years."

"Sounds like you'll be a good man to have around," Eric drawled laconically.

"I can probably tell by your accent, but I'm going to ask anyway. Where you from, originally?" Olivia interrupted.

"Yeah, you guessed it, I'm from across the ditch." Reed grinned. "New Zealand born and bred."

"I don't have anything against the kiwis. Except when the All Blacks play the Wallabies, then watch out. I'm a huge Rugby fan." Olivia smiled, her ponytail bouncing.

After that, Don showed him around the cottage-cum-station, and Reed dropped his stuff on his new desk—they all worked together in one large room, situated behind the reception area. Then Don sat them all down and gave them the morning debrief, or council of war, as he called it.

Eric had been on-call last night, and he told them he'd received two messages. A woman had reported a burglary around half-past ten last night, but said the perpetrator was long gone, so not to worry about coming to check it out till morning. The second call had been about a disturbance on the beach at Kingscote. When he got there, Eric found a rowdy bunch of kids drinking, and he'd moved them on. Nothing else had been reported, which surprised Reed. But then, he really shouldn't have been shocked; this place was going to be much quieter than his last posting in Adelaide.

"Eric is off-duty in a half-hour," Donald cut in, after Eric finished his report. Reed chanced a quick glance at Eric. Being on-call all night was never fun, and he could see the dark shadows under the big man's eyes. He would do well to go home and get a few hours shut-eye.

"Olivia, I know you still have all that paperwork from the random breath testing we did the other night," Don continued. Olivia grimaced but gave him the thumbs up. "And that leaves you, Reed. You're with me today," Don said. "You can get acquainted with the island on the drive. We're off to check on this burglary."

Nothing like being thrown in the deep end on your first day. "I'm all for that, Sarge," Reed replied.

Now, nearly an hour later, Reed was learning that only the main road that ran from one end of the island to the other was bitumen. Most of the smaller side roads were all gravel, and it made sense as to why all the police cars were Land Cruiser four-wheel-drives. Reed could see a lot of his driving would be done on dirt, and was glad his own Jeep was also a four-wheel-drive. Don turned into a narrow driveway and a cream-colored house, built out of sandstone, appeared, huddled into the native bush. A wooden veranda ran around one side of the house to the front, and three steps led up to a covered porch. Nice. It looked well-cared-for, and had a welcoming air to it. As Reed stepped out of the passenger seat and made his way around the back of the car, the front door opened and a tall, familiar-looking woman came out to meet them.

"Sierra?" The word was out of his mouth before his brain caught up. The shock of seeing her again so soon stopped him in his tracks. She was the person who'd been burgled?

"You've already met, then?" Don cast a quick, shrewd glance back at Reed.

"Yes. We met on the ferry yesterday. Sierra showed me the way to the police station after we docked." Reed managed to regain his composure and put his professional façade back up. He hoped he hadn't been openly gaping at her. Today, she was dressed in black leggings, and an overly-large, dark-blue, hooded sweater. He liked the view the skin-tight leggings afforded of her taut thighs and pert bottom.

"Morning, Sergeant Coldwater. Thanks for coming out," she said to Don. "Morning, Reed. Nice to see you again."

He gave Sierra a quick grin of recognition. As she approached down the steps, he made out the dark rings beneath her eyes, which hadn't been there yesterday.

"Sorry to call you out, but they took my computer, and I need a police report for the insurance," she said, addressing Don directly. She grimaced and put on a brave smile, clearly making out she was fine about the whole thing. "I left the place exactly like it was when I got home, so you guys could see for yourselves. Whoever did this made quite a mess." She glanced at Don and Reed and beckoned them up the stairs. Was it just his imagination, or did she sound a little formal, a little guarded when she spoke to the Sarge? She'd addressed him using his official rank when she'd first greeted them. There was an undercurrent of something going on here, but with his limited knowledge, he'd just have to wait and try and figure it out.

"That's good, Sierra. You did the right thing." Don's deep baritone betrayed nothing of his feelings towards Sierra, good or bad. This was just another regular job, one of many calls the station got every day. "It gives us an idea of the state of mind of a perpetrator, if we can see the crime scene unaltered."

Reed followed his boss's blocky form through the front door and down a short corridor. Stepping sideways, he squeezed past Don and managed to keep his features blank as he took in the large room. Damn, whoever had done this had really gone to town. He wanted to go to Sierra and look her in the eye, to make sure she was okay. But this was his first day on the job and he'd learned enough about his new boss to let him take the lead.

"You see what I mean." Sierra gestured to the room and Reed detected a slight wobble in her voice. Now he really wanted to go over to her. Let her know everything was going to be okay.

"Mmm." Don turned his head slowly, taking in the chaos, face calm and impassive. "Yes." His voice took on an almost perfunctory tone. "This can't have been nice to come home to, I'm sure."

That seemed like a bit of an understatement, and Reed flicked a quick glance at his boss. Surely, Don realized how traumatizing a break-in could be? Reed caught the undercurrent of something else going on here, as if his boss had something against Sierra. Which was odd. He filed that fact away for later.

It was cold in here. Not as cold as outside, where the icy wind dropped the temperature by a number of degrees, but still cool enough for Reed to want to pull up his collar. He turned, and saw a wood-stove hunkered down in the corner of the room, but it was unlit. If that was her only form of heating, maybe she'd been too rattled to light it today.

"No, it did scare me at first. But once I was sure no one was still in the house, then I just got really angry." She squared her shoulders. "I wanted to find whoever did this and give them a piece of my mind."

Reed hid a smile. He could imagine her doing just that, her dark eyes flashing as she let her wrath fly.

"The hardest part was not cleaning everything up. I just want to get everything back to normal."

"I can imagine," Don soothed. "We won't take long, and then you can get everything back to rights again. Okay?"

"That sounds good."

"Do you know how they got in?"

"Yes, they jimmied the window in the bathroom," she said.

"Mmhmm," Don replied, tapping his chin and gazing down the corridor toward the bathroom at the end. "I'll take a look in a sec, check for fingerprints, that kind of thing."

Reed's head came up at the Sarge's comment, but then of course, they didn't have special forensic officers to do things like dust for prints. Don's comment from earlier this morning came back to him, they had to be jacks-of-all-trades out here. Reed would've liked to be the one to do it, with all his training he no doubt would've done a better job than Don, but again, his new status kept him from opening his mouth.

"Can you tell us what's missing? Officer Kapua can take notes," Don said, nodding in Reed's direction, and he belatedly felt around in his police vest pocket for the little note book he always carried, casting a wry glance in his boss's direction. Reed shrugged the small flicker of resentment away. He'd had supervisors like this before. Who liked to do things the old-fashioned way. The Sergeant didn't take notes. Reed was the junior officer, and Don was going to make damn sure he knew his place.

Reed stepped over the lamp, still lying on the floor and made his way to where Sierra hovered next to the kitchen counter.

"Okay. Try and remember everything you can that might've been stolen," he said and started writing on his notepad, catching sight of Don out of the corner of his eye. His boss walked over and peered in the door to what he assumed was Sierra's bedroom. The stocky man frowned, and Reed guessed that room was as much of a mess as this one.

Sierra watched him with wary eyes, arms crossed in front of her chest, a protective gesture. But protecting herself from what, he didn't know. Him? Don?

It seemed odd that someone would completely trash the

place like this. Granted, he'd been to crime scenes where burglars had turned everything upside down to make sure they didn't miss anything. But it didn't seem like they'd taken much here.

"So, my computer was stolen, like I told you earlier." She worried at her bottom lip with her teeth as he noted that down with his pencil. "I need that computer, it's got everything on it. All my work, you know?"

Reed nodded and she fidgeted under his gaze, re-crossing her arms once, and then twice.

"They took all of my jewelry as well. Most of it was worthless, but there were a few valuable pieces. There was an antique ruby ring that belonged to my grandmother." Sierra moved her gaze to stare out the window, a faraway gleam in her eye. "And a diamond necklace. My father gave it to me for graduation." She gave a sad smile, leading Reed to believe it was more than just the monetary value she was worried about. It obviously held a great amount of sentimental value as well.

"And they took a stash of cash I had hidden away for a rainy day. Bastards," she muttered under her breath. "It must've been at least two-thousand dollars."

Reed gave a long low whistle. That was a lot of cash to have sitting around the house. And a lot of money to lose. But something about the whole thing didn't sit quite right. There were a heap of other valuables in her house, like a state-of-the-art-smart TV, and expensive Bluetooth stereo and speakers. Thieves, especially groups of young thugs, often took the high-end liquor, expensive cosmetics, and any prescription drugs they could get their hands on as well. But when he questioned Sierra, she confirmed these items had remained untouched. Why had the burglars left all that? Not wanting to worry her, he kept his thoughts to himself.

"This is probably just the work of some bored kids looking

for something to do, or druggies looking for money. Sorry, I couldn't get any decent prints from the broken window," Don said, returning from inspecting the bathroom, running his fingers down his mustache thoughtfully.

"No." Sierra shook her head. "You're right, I came to the same conclusion last night. Although, I did get Sam, my neighbor to come up and check it out for me. He wanted me to come down and sleep at their house, but I said I'd be okay." Sierra looked a little sheepish, as if she was admitting to a weakness, having to ask her male neighbor for help. Most women wouldn't have even dared stay in the house on their own after something like this. She was much stronger than she knew. "Sam also checked the security light for me as well. Whoever broke in just unscrewed the bulb to make sure everything would stay dark, so at least I didn't have to replace that."

With her hip resting against the kitchen bench, she watched them as they both took one last tour of her house, arms still crossed. It seemed to be her fallback, as if she was constantly on guard, constantly protecting herself from something. Tall and slender, standing on one long leg, the other booted foot balanced on the floor behind her. When she noticed him staring, that bow-shaped mouth tipped up at the corners in a half-smile. He had to physically drag his eyes away from her face. She was absolutely gorgeous, even dressed in her casual attire.

Once more, he found himself wondering about her. A single woman living out here alone. Well, he assumed she was single, there was no ring on her finger, and if she had to be asking her neighbor for help then there was no male person of significance around. She looked to be in her early to mid-thirties, but he could be mistaken. Was she older than she looked? There were fine lines around her eyes he hadn't noticed last night, that hinted perhaps she had more experience in life than he first imagined. But then, who was he to talk? He was thirty-eight already, and he was none the wiser about life, women, or anything else that truly mattered.

He tore his gaze away, and did one last pass through the living area. He was drawn toward the floor-to-ceiling windows at the front of the room. None of them looked like they'd been tampered with or smashed, in fact they were amazingly clean.

"Wow, what a stunning view," he breathed. "Now I can see why you live here." Low, scrubby hills fell away before the house, ending in a hint of yellow sand as Snellings Beach curled away towards the headland. Then there was nothing but ocean as far as the eye could see. The water was indigo-blue today, topped with angry white caps as the wind and stormy weather whipped them up. But he could imagine this view when the sun was shining on a balmy, summer afternoon. It would be pure magic.

"It is gorgeous, isn't it? I know how lucky I am to live here." She came and stood next to him, almost shoulder to shoulder. "This view keeps me sane."

Reed didn't have time to wonder at this comment, as Don called to him from the front door.

"I think we've got everything we need. Let us know if you remember anything else they might've taken, or something that might be relevant."

"Will do. What are the chances of getting my laptop back?" she asked, following close behind Reed, as they went out the front door.

"Pretty slim," he admitted. "Even the most brainless of thieves wouldn't be stupid enough to try and hock it on the island. They'll most likely have taken it across to the mainland by now. Same goes for the jewelry. Our report will go out to the main police stations in Adelaide, so they can keep an eye out for it. But you know..." He shrugged those big, square shoulders of his.

"Yeah, I know," she sighed. "It's lucky I've got most of my stuff backed up on the Cloud. I'll see if anyone has an old laptop hanging around that I can borrow for the short-term. Until insurance pays up and I can get across to the mainland to buy a new one."

"Oh, I nearly forgot, I picked up your mail on the way in," Don said and leaned into the squad car to retrieve the bundle of letters from the back seat. "Save you a trip, eh?"

"Thanks." Sierra took the envelopes and quickly leafed through them, as Don settled himself into the driver's seat. Reed made his way around the back of the car towards the passenger side, wondering at the quirks of living a country life, where the mailboxes were lined up out on the main road, because it was too far for the postman to come all the way to each isolated house.

Sierra's small gasp made Reed stop in his tracks and turn on his heel. She was staring down at one of the letters in her hand.

Her face had gone terribly pale.

CHAPTER FOUR

"What's the matter?" Reed was next to her in three strides. She couldn't hide the shiver that ran through her at the sight of that familiar print on the envelope. The stark fear hovered in her stomach, making it cramp painfully. Why couldn't this guy just leave her alone? And why couldn't she force herself to believe he wasn't an issue? That he was just a crackpot, his words shallow and meaningless? That she didn't shrink a little inside every time a letter or email arrived from him. She blinked and brought Reed's face back into focus. His hand had come up, hovering in the air as if he wanted to take hold of her, but was unsure what was going on. For his sake she pushed the fear away.

"Oh, it's probably nothing. But when I saw this letter...I wonder if the two can be connected?" Could it be? Could he possibly have moved from the fairly innocuous hassling her through the written word, to actually carrying out one of his threats? Why hadn't she considered this last night? No, he'd been doing this for too long now, why would he suddenly change his modus operandi? The wind gusting off the ocean was icy, and Sierra wished she had her coat.

"What do you mean? Connected to what?" Reed demanded.

Where did she start? She'd never mentioned this to anyone on the island before. The cops on the mainland knew about the threatening letters from her supposed stalker. It was all linked to some articles she'd published in the Adelaide newspaper, *The Advertiser*, over twelve years ago now. Back then, they'd done everything humanly possible to find out who was sending her these letters, but to no avail. When she'd moved over here, after the accident, it didn't seem relevant anymore. After the loss of the one thing in her life that truly mattered, everything else was just small potatoes.

"I've got a stalker," she said, lifting her shoulders. "It's a long story, but it all stems from an exposé I wrote for a newspaper twelve years ago. But he only sends letters and emails. He's never done anything physical before. And besides, what in hell would he be doing on the island? As best the police could tell back when all this started, he probably lived out of the state."

"How come you never mentioned this before?" Don's voice held a reprimand, and Sierra bristled at his tone. He heaved himself out of the Land Cruiser and stood beside them on the driveway.

"Because I didn't think it was important. Besides, I've been dealing with this psycho for a long time. He's just an idiot. A deranged idiot. And I haven't had a letter from him in over six months."

"Can I read it?" Reed's voice was gentle, and held none of the air or condemnation Don's did.

"Okay." She went to hand the unopened envelope to Reed, but he stopped her with a raised finger.

"Hang on a second." He dug a hand into one of the large pockets on the side of his police-issue pants and came out with a pair of blue latex gloves.

Sierra eyed the gloves speculatively. It seemed like a bit of overkill.

She opened her mouth to say something along those lines when Reed said, "You can never be too careful. You'd be amazed at what kind of things we can use for evidence nowadays. There might be a crucial clue, a fingerprint, a hair, a fiber, that might give this stalker of yours away."

Wow, she'd never thought about it like that before.

"Why don't we take this back inside," Reed suggested.

Had he seen her shivering? And did he realize it wasn't just from the cold? He didn't seem to feel it himself. He stood there solid and warm, staring down at her with gentle eyes.

"Okay." She beckoned them back up the stairs and into the relative warmth of the hallway. She hadn't lit her fire this morning. But now that she had the go-ahead to clean up, it was the first thing she was going to do. Don squeezed in behind them, and they all huddled in the small hallway.

She stood back and crossed her arms over her chest as Reed carefully pried the envelope open and unfolded the single sheet of paper of neatly typed prose, making sure nothing was caught in the folds. He read it slowly, once to himself, and then repeated it out loud.

Good day to you again, Sierra. Perhaps you thought I'd gone away. Or perhaps you prayed it might be so. It has been a while since our last communication, after all. But no such luck, my dear. I'm still here, and I'm still watching you. It's gratifying to see you keeping to yourself nowadays, like a good little girl. I'd like to think you finally started to listen to me, keep your thoughts to yourself, but I know you better than that. You can't help it, you need to flaunt that vain self-righteousness, that narcissistic need for your voice to be heard. But be warned, I haven't forgotten what you did. And I do mean to make you pay for the lies and innuendo you printed. Perhaps some might say you've paid the highest price of all for your conceit. Perhaps you've already had your judgement day, karma's way of evening up the scales. However, that's not enough for me. How dare you think you're better than everyone else? I know what you're capable of. When you least expect it, I'll exact my revenge. Be afraid, Sierra, be very afraid.

Reed stopped talking and stared at Sierra, his chocolate-brown eyes unreadable. Her guts churned, as the stalker's words repeated in her head. She suddenly wanted to know what was going on behind Reed's careful gaze. What did he think of the stalker's words? Would he think less of her? Was the stalker right, somehow? Had he seen something in her that no one else did? A dark side?

"This guy is completely mad. And completely obsessed. I can't believe you've been dealing with this stuff on your own for so long," Reed finally spluttered.

Sierra let out a breath between pursed lips. Of course, Reed was on her side, why would she ever have doubted him? That stalker *was* completely mad. None of this was her fault. She hadn't asked for any of it. His vague reference to the accident—to her judgement day—made her feel sick to her stomach. The fact he could gloat about such a thing. How dare he? A low pounding started behind her eyes as dismay turned to anger. He was a sick son of a bitch, that was all. She needed to ignore him. Ignore his stupid, ignorant words. The pounding increased until she raised a hand to her temple. Jesus, this was all she needed. Another headache. She had to go and take some medication, try and stop it in its path.

"He's obviously well-educated. He's taken time and care to write that letter." Don cut in, glaring at her over his mustache. "But why would you think this is related to your break-in?" he asked, keeping his professional mask fixed in place. Sierra didn't really want Don knowing about her stalker. And she didn't want him knowing the reasons why she'd moved to the island, either. It was her pain to bear alone; she couldn't stand the thought that someone might pity her. Her relationship with Don was tricky at best, and she wasn't sure she wanted all her dirty laundry to be aired for everyone to see. And she didn't like his subtle, condescending tone. But it was too late now.

"I don't really. It's just when I saw the letter...I don't see how it could be him. Whoever the hell *he* is." It was just a hunch, a feeling. But the fact that her laptop was missing made her skin crawl. Of course, it would be the first thing anyone would steal, it was small and portable and valuable. But there were so many other things they could've taken in her house, as well. Why had they taken it and not the other things?

"Did they get a forensic expert to take a look? Back when this all started?" Reed questioned.

"Yep, they did all that." She lifted her shoulders in a shrug. "Nothing turned up." Squeezing her eyes shut, she willed the pain behind her forehead to go away.

"You okay?" Reed's warm hand landed on her arm, making her jump.

"Oh, yes, a bit of a headache coming on, that's all." She raised a smile and he took his hand away.

"We'll leave you to it, then," Don said, already turning to open the front door. "Let us know if you remember anything else about the break-in, or if anything else turns up in the mail."

Reed hesitated, staring after his boss. He wanted to ask her more questions about the letter and the stalker, that much was obvious. But she needed him gone and maybe he could see it in her eyes.

"Do you mind if I take this with me?" Reed held the letter up in his gloved hands. "I'll give it back once I've taken a closer look."

"What? Oh sure." Sierra didn't really care what he did with it. He could burn it, for all she cared. Tiny pinpricks of light were starting to dance in front of her eyes. She needed to go and lie down. Now. This was going to be a doozy of a migraine, if the pain in her head was anything to go by. A legacy of the accident. Of the brain injury she'd received. The doctor had told her she was lucky to survive with minimal symptoms. But she wasn't sure she was the lucky one at all.

"Are you sure you're okay?" His compassionate gaze held hers, eyes as dark as obsidian. For a second, Sierra wondered what it would be like to have someone care for her. Look after her when the migraines hit and all she wanted to do was go and hide in the dark like some wounded animal. But that life was long gone, now. That life where she deserved to be happy. She lived alone, dealt with the pain alone, and existed as best she could. That was all.

"Thanks, Reed. I just need to go and lie down for a while." She raised her chin to look up at him, stepping back at the same time and crossing her arms. "I'm fine, really. You'd better go, before Don starts hollering for you."

"It was nice to see you again," he said. "Shame it wasn't under better circumstances." He smiled and the dimple in his chin came to life.

She couldn't disagree with him. He pushed the door open and she watched him stride across the driveway to the waiting police car, long legs eating up the distance, shoulders squared and confident. Jesus, he was a good-looking man.

A sharp slice of pain ran through her head and she turned, making her way towards the bathroom to find her bottle of painkillers. It was going to be a long day.

* * *

There was silence inside the Land Cruiser as Don steered it down Sierra's long driveway and then turned right onto the main gravel road. Reed rolled the scene of the burglary over in his mind. His gut was telling him things just didn't add up. He glanced quickly at his boss. What had he thought about it all? Was his gut telling him the same thing? Don had been in the force a long time, perhaps his experience was telling him

Suzanne Cass

something different to what Reed was feeling. Only one way to find out.

"That was an interesting start to our morning. Do you get many of those on the island?"

Don looked startled for a second, as if his mind had been miles away. "You mean robbery and theft, break-ins?"

Reed nodded his head.

"Not too many. It used to be one a month. Two at the outside. But they've been going up lately. Over the past nine months, rates have steadily increased until we've been getting up to ten or so a month."

Reed did a mental double-take. That was still extremely low. Even when he'd been working in Ballarat, there'd been at least fifteen or twenty robberies or trespass and theft every night. The population was nearly ten times that of KI in Ballarat, but still. Crime on the island seemed to be much lower per capita than he was used to.

Don continued. "It normally happens in the main townsites, you know, in Kingscote or Penneshaw. It's unusual for someone to make the effort to come out to the more isolated communities. They'd need a car. Probably more a crime of luck and circumstance than anything premeditated. A bunch of kids out on a joyride, see the house is empty and take a chance, that kind of thing."

"So, you think it was just kids? That wad of cash she had sitting in her top drawer would've been like manna from heaven for them. Could someone have found out she was keeping it at home?" Reed was musing aloud, trying to corral his thoughts into some kind of order.

"It's not unusual for people to keep money in their houses on KI. Cash machines are few and far between out here. It's often hard to get money if you need it quickly. So, it might've just been a good guess on the burglar's part." Don didn't take his eyes off the road, but his frown deepened as he stared straight ahead.

"What about drugs? Dealers and users. Is there a problem on the island?"

"Yes, a growing one, I'm afraid." Don's tone turned bitter, his mustache practically vibrating with indignation. "It's one of the reasons Detective Senior Sergeant Breevant allowed me to hire you. We needed another member to help us deal with the rising crime rate, which is tied loosely to the rise in drug use."

"So, it could be someone out purposely casing houses, looking for easy-to-steal-items and cash?"

"Yes, a definite possibility." Don hesitated and drew in a deep breath. "The strange thing was, there were no fingerprints around the broken window. Not even a partial, or a smudge. But there were glove prints. Latex, if I'm not mistaken."

"The perp was wearing gloves?" Reed's internal alarm went off. This didn't sound right. Your normal criminal usually wasn't smart enough, or prepared enough, to think of wearing gloves to cover their tracks. Something a lot of criminals didn't realize, however, is that with the advent of better techniques in forensics, gloves also left their own unique prints, and could be processed in much the same way as a fingerprint. In some cases, these had been used to make an arrest. But these cases were few and far between.

"Looks like it." Don narrowed his eyes at the notion.

"That seems a little high-tech for a couple of kids, or even a druggie looking for cash, don't you think?"

"Yes, it's unusual."

"And Sierra said they didn't take any of the drugs in her bathroom. Which would've been the first thing a drug addict would've gone for," Reed added. "So, what are your thoughts on this stalker of hers?"

"First I've heard of it," Don growled. "How the hell do

people think we're going to be able to protect them, if they don't tell us important things like, oh by the way, *I've been getting threats for the past ten years from some deranged psycho."* He mimicked a high, squeaky, woman's voice.

On one level, Reed agreed with Don. Police couldn't do their jobs if they weren't given all the facts. But Sierra had been dealing with this well before she moved to the island. Obviously, she thought she had it under control. And she'd said he'd never actually done anything to follow through on his threats. Never made a physical appearance, just mocked her from afar, from the safety of his own living room. An arrogant, cocky bastard who liked to terrify her in a sick attempt to make up for some lack of his own self-worth. Reed made a mental note to look into the articles Sierra was talking about in *The Advertiser*, when he got some free time.

"What do you think that reference to her judgement day meant?"

"Not sure," Don replied. "I have heard stuff through the grapevine about how Sierra moved to the island to get away from a horrific accident that changed her life. But I've never spoken to her about it personally. We tend to talk about strictly professional matters."

"Oh, like what?"

"You know she's a journalist, right?"

"Well, obviously I got that impression when she was talking about the articles she'd written." And it made sense to him now. The way she'd watched him on the ferry the other night. The way she watched everybody, as if more than just a casual observer. Analyzing people and situations, the way a good reporter would. Always looking for the next story, the next angle. A bit like a good police officer. It always paid to be extra observant, extra vigilant.

"I think she used to be some big hotshot when she worked in Adelaide, won an award or something like that," Don said.

Reed's ears pricked up. Could that be what the stalker meant when he accused her of printing lies and innuendo, had she become a target because of the award? Had it put her in the spotlight somehow?

"She does an article for *The Islander* every now and then. You know, our local island newspaper." Reed shook his head and Don scowled at his ignorance. "Don't worry, you'll see one soon enough, they're all over the place."

Things started to click into place at the look Don gave him when he mentioned Sierra's articles. "I gather not all of her pieces are highly complimentary to our little police unit?" he asked.

"No, not always. There've been a few times when we haven't seen eye to eye about certain things." Don's mustache quivered as he spoke, as if admitting even this much physically hurt him. "But that's not really what I meant. She often comes into the station to confirm a lead. Or sometimes it's to try and find out information on the legality of particular things. Sierra's quite involved in the island conservation program. We have a few endangered species on the island, you know. So, if there are any signs of a company not doing the right thing environmentally, then she's on them like white on rice. Or if there are any protests organized, she's usually one of the lead mutineers."

"I see," Reed said. He wasn't surprised to hear any of it. Sierra struck him as a woman with high principles, who didn't like to take no for an answer. Which is how she ended up with a stalker sending her death threats. And why she seemed to butt heads with Don on occasion.

Now, he really wanted to find a copy of those articles as soon as possible. There might be a hint of what this was all about hidden in them somewhere.

On the surface, Sierra came across as a such a strong-willed, determined woman. But it seemed there was a lot more lurking beneath that veneer than he'd first imagined. His heart went out to her when he thought about her fleeing to the island to get away from the after-effects of some mysterious tragedy. He could relate to that himself. He'd quit the force and went off to become a brickies laborer after his on-the-job accident. Pursuing a violent criminal in a high-speed chase, he'd been unable to stop in time to avoid smashing into another car. Even after the scars on his leg had healed, he still hadn't been able to face up to pulling another body from a mangled wreck. It'd taken him four years to recover enough mentally to consider going back to the job he loved. Though he'd been cleared by an inquest of any wrongdoing, the guilt still ate at him. Someone had died and he couldn't shake the idea it was his fault somehow. Not just a terrible accident as everyone tried to convince him it was.

He wondered if Sierra had managed to get over her fear and angst. Or if it was still haunting her even now.

CHAPTER FIVE

Sierra sat out on her front deck, taking small sips of her hot coffee, a blanket wrapped around her shoulders. The wind and stormy weather from yesterday had gone and the sun was making an appearance today. It was still cool outside, but Sierra needed the fresh air to clear her head.

Yesterday had been a doozy. After the Sarge and Reed left, Sierra spent the rest of the day curled up in the cocoon of her warm bed. The triptan her doctor prescribed helped to ease the pain to a manageable level. Without the pills, even the slightest movement caused knives of white-hot fire to shoot through her head, so bad she would sometimes even vomit. But even after the medicine had taken the sharp edges off her pain, her head still throbbed, and any bright light hurt her eyes, so she'd stayed in bed for the rest of the day. Finally, she'd found refuge in sleep, not waking until early this morning, when the sun peeked through her curtains.

Still fragile and achy, at least she was now able to face her first cup of coffee for the day. She liked to swim in the sea most mornings, if the weather allowed. Even in winter, she had a thick wetsuit to keep out the worst of the cold. Swimming and hiking were the two things that kept her fit and trim. She loved the feel of the brisk water as her hands cut through the waves, leaving her mind free to roam. But she couldn't face a swim. Not today.

The view from her front deck was spectacular, and she breathed in the fresh, salty air and the wide-open spaces. The coastline of Kangaroo Island was wild and untamed, the ocean often whipped to a frenzy by freezing gales of wind driven up from Antarctica. But today, it was a gentle, metallic blue, with white, foaming waves curling onto the beach below. She'd loved this house from the first moment she'd set eyes on it and had paid the seller's asking price without a second thought. Every morning when she got up, she was greeted by a different vista of ocean, ever changing with the seasons. She would never get tired of this place. It was her sanctuary, when the rest of the world drove her crazy.

The interior was done in soft creams and natural colors, with warm, wooden floors covered in rattan mats. Pale blues and darker grays were highlighted in the cushions and a throw blanket on the couch, and the paintings on the wall gave a hint of color here and there. The inside was meant to blend seamlessly to the outside through the large floor-to-ceiling windows. The house was a safe haven, a calm place where she could work in peace while still feeling like nature was right there when she needed it.

Jon, her black cat, was curled up in her lap, purring. Snow, who was white—of course—watched from her spot on the table where she could survey her domain.

"A lot of help you two were the other night. Where were you when that burglar broke into our house?" Both cats had clearly done the sensible thing and taken off into the scrub at the first sign of trouble. She didn't blame them for not hanging around. Cats were smart like that. But not the best protection.

"How would you like it if I got a dog instead, huh?" Jon narrowed his green eyes at her and purred a little louder.

Perhaps she should get a dog. Sam, her neighbor, had suggested it the other night, worried about her staying out here, a single woman on her own. Snow got up and stalked over the tabletop until she was level with Sierra's face. The cat gave her a knowing look and proceeded to butt her head up against Sierra's ear, whiskers tickling.

Sierra laughed. "No, you're right, I would never replace you two." And besides, a dog might try and chase the chickens. Sierra had six bantams in a run in her back yard. Initially, she bought them for the fresh eggs they provided, but now she loved them for their quirky company and the way they kept her garden bug-free. They all had names: Cindi, Bindi, Samantha, Blue, Red, and Ruffles. With the large feral-cat problem on the island she always kept them locked up in their pen at night. Which reminded her, she should go and let them out so they could run around the garden. With all the stuff happening yesterday and then her migraine, they'd been cooped up way too long.

Her cell phone trilled loudly, startling Snow, who gave it a disapproving look and stalked away to the other side of the table. Sierra checked the caller ID, hesitated, and then answered the call.

"Jen, hello. How goes it?" Sierra kept her voice bright and perky.

"Same old, same old. How about you?" Jen had a deep voice for a woman, and Sierra let her familiar tone wash over her. They'd known each other a long time; Jen was Sierra's first editor at *The Adelaide Advertiser*. She was now the editor-in-chief, and Sierra knew she was the right person for the job. They'd become steadfast friends after only her first day on the job, even though Jen was nearly twelve years her senior. Jen made a special point of keeping in touch with Sierra after she moved to KI.

Sierra hesitated. "I'm…all good." No point in worrying her

friend. "Just sitting out on the front deck drinking coffee."

"Oh, I love your front deck," Jen sighed. "I'm going to have to come for another visit. Soon." Her friend had visited Sierra many times over the past ten years. At first, it was a regular thing, coming every couple of months, to make sure Sierra was surviving after the accident. But lately her visits had dropped off, and she hadn't seen Jen in nearly twelve months.

"But that's not why I'm calling. I have a bone to pick with you. I hear you came to town and you couldn't even be bothered to pop in and see me."

Sierra winced. Jesus, that woman had her spies everywhere. She'd hoped that her short trip into Adelaide the day before would go unnoticed. But she hadn't counted on the reach of Jen's network.

"Who did you have to bribe to find that out?" Sierra asked, only half-joking. Before her ex-boss could answer, Sierra said, "Never mind. I'm sorry I didn't tell you. It was just a quick trip to pick up a new pair of hiking boots and a few other necessities. And to pop in and see my long-suffering mother," Sierra added as an afterthought. The mention of her family should mollify Jen. The truth was, Sierra hated going into her old office building. It reminded her of Jake. And Grace. And there were still people working there who remembered her, remembered what'd happened. Their pitying looks were almost too much to bear.

"Hmm." Jen didn't sound at all mollified.

"I promise to come and see you next time I'm in town." An idea popped into Sierra's head and the words were out before she had time to think. "Actually, I'll probably be over in a week or so. My computer was stolen, so I need to replace it. Let's have lunch then." *Shit.* She slapped her hand to her forehead. Why had she said that?

Like a bloodhound on a scent, Jen's reply was immediate.

"What? Stolen? How? When? I need the details."

Sierra sighed and sat up straighter. Now the cat was out of the bag, she may as well admit to everything. Jen would find out one way or the other, eventually.

"My house got broken into the night before last. They took my laptop. Plus, all my mum's jewelry and a whole heap of money I had stashed away."

"Bloody hell, Sierra. Are you okay? Have they caught the thief? I'm gonna kill that bastard."

Sierra almost laughed at the overprotective tone in her friend's voice. Jen was African American, and taller than most men. She could just imagine her short, bushy hair standing on end as Jen bristled with indigence. It was one of the many things Sierra loved about her friend, her fierce loyalty to those she cared about.

"Calm down, I'm fine. No, they haven't caught anyone yet. But Jon and Snow are fine, just in case you're worried." Sierra patted the still-purring cat's head. He stretched out a paw and settled himself more comfortably into her lap. "I wasn't home when the thief, or thieves, broke in. They did trash my house, though."

"Oh, thank God." Jen let out a loud, heartfelt sigh. "But hang on, why would they trash your house?"

"I'm not sure. The Sarge thought it was either kids or a druggie. But they didn't take a lot. There was plenty of other things they could've stolen. It was almost as if they took pleasure in turning my house into a complete tip. They even smashed the mirror in my bedroom, and tipped the vase of flowers and water all over my bed. It was odd, very destructive," Sierra mused, almost thinking out loud.

There was silence on the other end of the phone, and she knew Jen was digesting her story, sorting through the details, trying to come up with a motive.

"Have you heard from that psycho lately? That letter-writing stalker?"

Jen's question made her skin crawl. How the hell was that woman so perceptive?

"Yeah," she sighed in resignation. "I got something in the mail the same day as the burglary."

"Bloody hell, Sierra." That was the second time today Jen had sworn, and Sierra knew she must be really worked up. "You have to tell the police about it. There might be a connection."

"I have. The Sarge and the new officer came out to take a look. They were here when the letter arrived. Reed's taken it away for forensic testing. He said even though the police did all that years ago when the letters first started, he might be able to find something they'd missed."

"Good. That's good. It's about time you did something about this guy. I know you tried before...Hang on..." Jen's voice took on an edge of suspicion as she stopped mid-sentence. "Who is Reed?"

Sierra nearly groaned out loud. She was seriously off her game today, letting all kinds of unintended things slip. Well, one thing she definitely wasn't going to tell Jen was that the new police officer was a tempting hunk, with eyes the color of the sky at night, and skin the color of caramel. And that her heart skipped a beat every time he glanced her way. If Jen even got the slightest sniff that Sierra found him remotely attractive, she'd never hear the end of it.

"He's the new policeman on KI, it was his first day yesterday." There, she hadn't given anything away, just the bare facts for Jen to chew over.

"Hmm. And you're already calling him Reed?"

"I met him on the ferry on the way home two nights ago. He'll be a good addition to the team."

"I seeeee," Jen drew the last word out so that Sierra was left with no doubt that Jen knew there was more to the story.

She bit her bottom lip as she willed her friend to drop the subject. The last thing she needed today was a lecture on how it was time she got a good man in her life. The small silence as Jen considered her next words let Sierra know that her ex-boss was dying to ask more questions about the newcomer.

But it seemed discretion won over curiosity when she finally said, "I'll look forward to meeting this new officer on my next trip over." Sierra heard a slight hitch in Jen's voice as it became serious all of a sudden. "But on that note, it reminds me of something else I need to tell you."

"What's that?" Sierra covered a sigh. What did Jen want now?

Jen cleared her throat. "Um, I thought you might like to know that I ran into Jake the other day."

"Oh." It was all Sierra could think to say. Her heart started beating rapidly in her chest at the mention of her ex-husband.

"He was with his...er, his wife."

His second wife, Sierra thought, and then immediately pulled herself up short. It wasn't like her to be spiteful. Jake deserved some happiness. Jake was a photographer at *The Advertiser*—that's how they'd first met—so it wasn't unheard of that Jen would run into him from time to time at work.

Jen gave a small cough; it seemed she was as uncomfortable about this conversation as Sierra was. "Well, there's no easy way to say this, but she's pregnant again."

Sierra's heart squeezed painfully. Jake and his new wife were having their second child. She was glad for him. Glad he could move on after the accident. She was, really, truly glad. It was a silent mantra she kept repeating to herself, and one day, it might actually feel genuine. Just because she was stuck in a terrible kind of limbo didn't mean he had to be as well. It was one of the reasons they'd broken up. Jake had seemed to cope so much better than she had. He'd never blamed her for the accident, either. Which only made her feel even more guilty and more shut off from the rest of society. Everyone coped with grief differently, she understood that. And perhaps her mechanism was to run away and shut people out of her life, so she could grieve in peace. She was reconciled to that fact, if only everyone else could come to terms with it, too.

"That's nice for them. I hope they're happy. I really mean that, Jen."

There was a second's silence on the end of the phone. "I'm sure you do, honey. I just thought I'd let you know, in case you heard it from someone else, that was all."

"Thanks, Jen." Sierra drew in a deep breath. "I know you're only trying to protect me. And I know you think I'm not really over Jake and everything that happened. But you're wrong. I've moved past it now. I'm getting on with my life, and I truly do wish him all the best in the world. He's a good man, and he was a great husband. Sometimes things just don't work out, that's all."

"Yeah, sometimes life just plain sucks," Jen agreed. "But the best of us pick ourselves up and dust ourselves off, then move on."

"Exactly," Sierra said. And in that particular moment, she meant it.

"And talking about the best of us, that brings me to another topic close to my heart," Jen said, and Sierra's heart sank. She knew what Jen was about to say.

"Have you thought any more about my suggestion? About looking into those two missing kids in Adelaide?"

Sierra muffled a sigh. Jen wouldn't let this go, and while Sierra could perhaps see her point, she just couldn't rustle up the same kind of enthusiasm for the project. Jen had a theory that the cases of two children who'd gone missing—feared abducted— three years ago in Adelaide, were somehow linked to two other cases in Port Pirie twelve years ago. The same cases Sierra had run the exposé on. Which is why Jen thought Sierra might be able to help. To pick up on some clue, or hint everyone else had missed. She'd sent Sierra a whole pile of papers and research on the Adelaide cases about six months ago, imploring her to take a second look.

"No, I haven't had time to delve into those reams and reams of files you sent me yet." Which was technically true. Sierra kept herself busy these days, writing articles for *The Islander*, along with all her other conservation projects.

"I know it's asking a lot, Sierra, I do," Jen said quietly. "But you're one of the best investigative journalists I ever met. You won that bloody award for Christ's sake. The highest award given in Australia. It just feels like you're wasting your God-given talent, that's all. And those two little missing girls could really do with a champion."

Sierra had heard it all before, but it didn't stop her annoyance rising. Who the hell did Jen think she was, trying to guilt her into taking on the project? She drew in a breath and counted to five until her irritation subsided.

"I'll pull them out and take a look," Sierra sighed.

"That would be great." The smug tone in Jen's voice said it all.

"But I'm not promising anything."

"Of course not, honey. Just take a look, that's all I'm asking."

"Hmm," Sierra replied noncommittally.

"I meant it when I said I'm going to visit soon. A month, tops, and I'll be over there."

Sierra had to laugh. Jen sure knew how to twist her around her little finger. Sierra realized her friend only had her best interests at heart. "You know I love it when you come over. You're welcome anytime. Are you going to bring Harold with you this time?" Sierra asked, referring to Jen's husband of over twenty years.

"Nah, I like our girly time together. He's one beautiful hunk of a man, but he'd just cramp my style." They both laughed together and said their goodbyes.

As she hung up, Sierra noticed there were two text messages from Blake. He must've sent them when she was bedridden yesterday. She sighed. He was becoming so persistent. And she couldn't deal with him today. Not after what happened.

An idea bubbled at the edges of her mind.

No.

It couldn't be. Could it?

Surely not.

Blake was passionate, hot-blooded, and got fired up about the things he believed in. It was part of the attraction she'd felt towards him. It also meant he had a bit of a temper. Was he angry with her for avoiding him? For not returning his calls? Angry enough to do something violent and unnecessary?

She bit her bottom lip in consternation. Then laughed out loud at her own silliness. With everything that'd just happened, her mind had wandered into territory she wouldn't normally go. There was no way Blake was responsible for the break-in. Or for stealing her laptop. He'd been on the island now for over two months, but he wouldn't do something that idiotic and spiteful, just because she wouldn't go out with him. It was a ridiculous thought, and Sierra pushed it to the back of her mind.

Snow glanced at her as she put the phone back on the table. Now that the coast was clear, the cat ambled back over the tabletop for a scratch between the ears. Sierra stared out at the never-ending blue ocean. She really needed to go and have a long, hot shower, and then perhaps make some scrambled eggs for breakfast. Then she should go and see if Sam and Debbie had an old laptop or computer she might be able to borrow.

But now Jen had put a bug in her ear, she couldn't get rid of the idea. Hell, she may as well go and pull the files out and at least take a quick glance. Thankfully, they were in a box under a pile of her old shoes in her closet. At least that was an item the burglar hadn't been bothered about.

Picking Jon up off her lap, she unceremoniously plonked him on the decking. He gave her that filthy look only a cat was capable of and stalked off, tail held high.

With the blanket still wrapped around her shoulders, she made her way into the bedroom. She'd managed to clean the bare minimum yesterday before she'd collapsed into bed. At least the broken mirror and all its pieces were now in the bin, along with the smashed vase and flowers on her bed. And she'd changed the wet sheets, but the rest of her room still looked pretty much like a cyclone had hit it.

Turning a blind eye to the carnage, she opened the closet door and leaned in. Most of her shoes had been pulled out, but thankfully the slightly dusty box underneath remained untouched.

Sierra sat on her bed and placed the box next to her, lifting the lid and pulling out the top file. It contained the more recent documents Jen had sent her months ago.

There were two more large files in the box. After a second's hesitation, Sierra pulled them out and spread them on the bed in front of her. She thumbed through the first pile. Ten whole years had passed since she'd looked at this file. It was frighteningly thick, stuffed with hundreds of pieces of paper. It was all her research from the series of three reports she'd done for *The Advertiser* twelve years ago, after two children were feared abducted and murdered in the small coastal town of Port Pirie.

Sierra's mind wandered back to that time. When the first child, Emily Newman, was abducted in January twelve years ago, Sierra had only been in the job for three years. It was her second big case, and she went to Port Pirie, along with all the millions of other media, all baying for someone's blood. But after weeks of no leads, she'd returned to Adelaide and her normal duties. It wasn't until the second child, Naomi Chadstone, went missing eleven months later and police were no closer to finding a suspect—or the children—that Sierra felt something else was going on.

She started investigating the police and their role in the two cases. With Jen urging her on, Sierra had uncovered some damning aspects that pointed to police bungling in both cases. It'd taken her nearly a year to assemble all the facts and finally get her report into the newspaper, but it'd set up a storm of resentment against the police, and had them scrambling to halt the media nightmare.

As Sierra flipped through the documents, small fragments of information rattled through her brain. Most abducted children—eighty-five percent—were killed within the first five hours by the perpetrator. This statistic rose to close to one-hundred percent after the first twenty-four hours. Which meant the police only had a very, very small window of opportunity to get a child back alive once they'd been taken. If they screwed it up even the tiniest bit, then there was little to no hope at all. It often came down to just pure dumb luck when a child was recovered alive from a kidnapping attempt. But the cops in Port Pirie had screwed up the initial investigation. Sierra proved they made many basic mistakes in that critical first twenty-four hours. And there had been no going back from there.

A sliver of ice trickled down her spine at the idea that neither child's body had ever been recovered. How did those poor families cope with the not knowing?

There were cases where a child was recovered, though. Not often, but sometimes. Just the other day, Sierra heard a report on the nightly news about a seven-year-old girl who'd been snatched from her mother's arms as they were walking down the street and bundled into a car. The car had been found four hours later in the carpark of a local hotel, and the girl had been recovered and returned to her hysterical mother. But it hadn't been the police who found the car. It'd been the community who rallied around the local mom, an organized church group who'd called up hundreds of their parishioners and found the car using social media. A miracle. A happy ending. But the police had ended up with egg on their faces.

Even now, it still shocked her that there were people capable of such pure evil out there.

The cases Jen had asked her to look in to had happened in Adelaide, around a two-and-half-hour drive from Port Pirie. It was unlikely, but not inconceivable that they could've been committed by the same person. He could've moved his hunting ground to greener pastures. From the relatively small, sleepy town of Port Pirie, to the major metropolis of the capitol city. But then, what had he been up to for all those years in between?

Could Jen be right? Could the two cases in Adelaide be linked to the ones in Port Pirie? When the news broke about the abductions in Adelaide, Sierra watched with muted interest from Kangaroo Island. But she'd moved on from her life as an investigative journalist by that stage, and wanted nothing more to do with it. Which was why she'd ignored the documents Jen sent her, left them shut up in a box in the bottom of her closet.

Until now.

Perhaps now it was time she took a closer look at them.

CHAPTER SIX

Reed stared out the window, contemplating the blue sky. It was Friday morning and he was on duty, manning the station on his own, while the Sarge and Olivia were at the other end of the island, looking into a sheep-stealing charge. Eric said he was going somewhere called Emu Bay to check out a truck for roadworthiness. Something to do with Don's local traffic initiative to make people more aware of the hazards surrounding unroadworthy vehicles. Especially on these gravel tracks the islanders liked to call roads.

Reed was enjoying the solitude. It gave him time to mull over his first week of working on the island. The pace of life was so different out here. People popped in to have a chat with Don about the weather and the price of fresh fruit. They worried about smaller things. There were hardly any major crimes worth mentioning, the last murder on KI had been five years ago. A spate of sheep-stealing was probably the highlight of Don's day. But Reed didn't mind. It was what he was looking for, a way to reconnect with life and people. To destress and get away from the constant strain and demands of a large-city police station. To get away from the unceasing calls for help from domestic violence victims. The growing scourge of drugs—methamphetamines to be precise—where users had to be salvaged from overdosing in the streets, or arrested when they became violent and unmanageable. Of having to pull dead or injured people out of smashed cars driven by a drunk driver. He'd seen humanity at its worst, and sometimes it exhausted his soul.

He'd also encountered personal things in life that'd drained him dry. Grief and despair which hollowed him out, left him an empty shell.

Like losing his unborn son. And then Penny.

Penny. He hadn't thought about her in a while now. The idea surprised him. He and Penny had met when he first moved to Ballarat, just after he graduated from the police academy. They were both young and foolish, twenty-one and invincible. He'd loved Penny's enthusiasm to try everything, do everything, experience everything. She even embraced their surprise pregnancy with verve and optimism. But by then, they never really had a choice. They'd gotten engaged at the age of twenty-two. He'd loved Penny, loved that they had a whole future ahead of them, bright and full of promise, and he'd quickly grown used to the idea he was going to be a father.

Then Penny had gone into early labor at seven-and-a-half months. They'd lost the baby, and Penny never recovered. God knows, Reed had tried to bring her back from the dark place she fell into. But her misery and depression were too massive, and she was determined to destroy herself using any and every drug available.

Penny died of a drug overdose almost a year to the day after their son. Reed suspected the overdose hadn't been an accident, but no one dared bring the subject up near him.

He'd had two relationships since then, each lasting over a year, but when the women started to talk marriage, he'd run far and fast. There hadn't been anyone special for a while. When Carla had stormed out of his apartment nearly two years ago, she'd accused him of having a heart of stone. That he was emotionally unavailable, and only wanted women for one thing, casual sex. She was wrong on the second count, but he couldn't argue about the first. Commitment wasn't for him.

Love was too hard. Life had taught him a valuable lesson. If you let yourself love someone, then all you were doing was opening yourself up for them to hurt you or leave you. Or die. Love wasn't worth it.

His thoughts returned back to his first day on the job, and he wondered how Sierra was getting on after the break-in. She seemed like a person who also liked her own company, didn't tend to want to invite others in. As they were leaving her house after the break-in, he'd asked her if she needed help cleaning up the place. Offered to come back and help her fix anything that might've been broken. But she shook her head and politely declined. Was it a habit of hers, denying she needed help? Keeping herself apart, separate from everyone.

They were no closer to catching the perp. He'd managed to find a spare half-hour yesterday to take a good look at the letter from her stalker. But whoever sent it either knew what they were doing, or had a whole lot of dumb luck on their side. Because there was nothing Reed could find that gave anything away. No prints, no fibers. The letter was typed, not handwritten, and the postmark showed it'd been redirected through the main business precinct of Adelaide, so it could've come from anywhere in the state. Or even outside the state.

He'd been a tad disappointed he hadn't run into her this week. Perhaps she just hadn't needed to come into the main townsite. Much as he hated to admit it, he kept half an eye peeled for her tall, slim figure as he walked down the main street of Kingscote. It would've been nice to see that little quirk she had, where her mouth twitched up in one corner as she smiled. And those full, pouting lips that made him want to trace a finger over them, to see if they were as soft and inviting as they looked.

She certainly was an intriguing lady. He'd managed to find a copy of her newspaper reports online. The ones that'd gained her a stalker, as well as winning her an award. Her series had been an eyeopener, and certainly not very complimentary towards the Port Pirie police in particular, and the South Australian police force in general. He could see why some people might take offense. Especially the policemen and women involved in the initial search for the girls.

A thought occurred to him, and he tapped his finger against his chin trying to corral his thoughts. It was highly unlikely. But the more he thought about it, the more the idea grew on him.

Could Sierra's stalker possibly be a disgruntled police officer?

He wondered if the cops investigating the original letters had ever taken this line of questioning. It might pay for him to see if he could dig into the records. He remembered both the abduction cases; it was just before he moved to Adelaide. The media storm had certainly ignited more than a few heated conversations within the community all over Australia.

He thought back to her reports, trying to recall some of the details. Sierra had accused the Port Pirie police station of having a reputation for not solving crimes. Citing a list of unsolved, violent crimes dating back over ten years. She'd looked into police clearance rates at the Port Pirie station, when someone was charged for a major crime such as homicide, assault, sexual assault, and the reporting rates were abysmally low for that particular station. Her research had many people asking questions. Why was this so? Did the police need more training? Did they just not care? It started accusations flying that the Officer-in-Charge of Yorke Mid-North Local Service Area, Superintendent Shawn Dennison wasn't training his officers properly.

When the first child, Emily, a six-year-old girl, was abducted from her front yard, a person of interest had been brought in and interviewed, but never charged. He lived on the street where Emily went missing and was a registered sex offender, and always remained the prime suspect. The guy flatly denied he was guilty. Said he'd been rehabilitated, stuck to his parole regulations, and was now a model citizen.

Sierra also uncovered the fact that interviews weren't conducted with neighbors and other community members in the vital twenty-four-hour period after she went missing. It seemed there was a mix-up in communication, and the two police teams originally assigned to the case both thought the other team had already done the interviews. Then afterwards, the Senior Sergeant in charge of the Port Pirie station was accused of letting his ego get in the way of the investigation, by dragging his feet and not bowing to the Superintendent's orders to hand over paperwork to other investigators from other stations who'd stepped in to help.

The police defended themselves, stating that thousands of calls had come in regarding the missing girl, some people even claiming they had little Emily and she was safe and well and living happily with them. There were just too many leads for the authorities to follow up, and they'd become bogged down in all the paperwork and chasing false clues.

The second girl, Naomi, was abducted eleven months later on her way home from the park. She'd been a few years older than Emily. Everyone wanted to link the two abductions, including Sierra, but there was no evidence to do so. The two crimes were vastly different, as were the ages of the children, and the police wouldn't say the crimes were connected. Neither of the girls had ever been found, no bodies discovered, and no convictions were made. It was a dead case. A cold case.

Reed stood up and stretched his hands above his head. Sierra sure had stirred up a hornet's nest in regard to police bungling, that was for sure. Even though he was a cop himself, he had to respect the depth of her research, and her terrier-like determination to find the truth. He could see why she'd been awarded the journalistic prize.

Reed had been tempted to look further into Sierra's life. Perhaps even Google her to see if he could find out more about this mysterious accident she was supposedly involved in. But he'd run out of time, and a small part of him thought it was being too invasive. Just because you could find out information about a person, because it was all there on the internet if you wanted to look, did that mean you should?

His leg gave a twinge, and he gave it a shake and took a lap around the room to loosen it up. He'd been sitting too long. And the cold made it ache. Why the hell hadn't he moved to some nice, warm, tropical town up north, instead? He should see if there was a good physiotherapist on the island, that always helped to loosen the tight, scarred muscles. Even a good masseuse would do the trick.

Reed checked the clock on the wall above reception. It was nearly ten. Was it too early for a cup of coffee and a biscuit? He turned to head towards the kitchen, when the phone on the desk shrilled loudly into the quiet building.

"Kingscote police, Officer Reed Kapua, how can I help you?" Reed said, as he picked up the receiver.

"Oh, thank God someone's there," a male voice said loudly on the other end of the line. "Look, it's Mal, from Luxury Rentals over in Penneshaw. We've got a little bit of a situation here." The man sounded panicked and was breathing heavily.

"Okay, sir. Calm down and tell me what's happened." Reed picked up a pen and started writing on the call sheet.

"We've got a family staying in one of our rental properties, and one of their little girls has gone missing." The hairs on the back of Reed's neck stood up. "The father called me this morning, we've been searching for her for over two hours now. We all just thought she'd wandered off and she'd be easy to find. Her older sister said she kept talking about wanting to see the big, furry, kangaroos again. And we thought she'd headed up to the open bushland at the end of the road to see them. But now...I think we need professional help." The man stopped, almost out of breath from his fast-talking explanation.

Reed could sense an edge of hysteria in his voice. He wanted to demand to know why the man had waited so long to call the police, but he kept his voice calm. Berating the guy and the family for not realizing that minutes made a difference would help no one.

"Right, give me your location and I'll be over as soon as I can," Reed said, furiously writing the details down as the man spoke.

This wasn't good. Reed's training kicked in as he went over protocol in his mind. He needed to get to the original site where the girl went missing ASAP so he could safeguard the integrity of it, in case the girl wasn't found. Important clues to the girl's whereabouts could be lost forever if someone was allowed to touch or move something they shouldn't.

Pulling his police-issue coat on, he juggled his cell in one hand as he swiped the keys to the last remaining squad car off the peg board. Cell coverage was patchy on the island, and Reed prayed the Sarge was in a good spot right now as he dialed his boss's number.

"Officer Coldwater." The Sarge answered on the second ring.

"Don, we've got a situation. I just received a call about a

five-year-old girl who's gone missing. Her name's Jessica Walker. It seems her family are tourists on the island and she's wandered away from their rental accommodation in Penneshaw. I'm on my way over there now." Reed had managed to get his coat on one-handed, and was slinging his police belt around his waist as he made for the back door and the garage.

There was a second's silence on the end of the phone as Don digested the news. This kind of thing didn't happen often in this small community.

"Right, Olivia and I are on our way. I'll phone this in and organize a search and rescue on the drive back over. Everyone will assemble at the local fire station in Penneshaw. People should be there to help by the time we get back." Reed could almost hear the Sarge ticking things off in his head, much the same as Reed was doing while he slammed the back door and strode towards the vehicle.

"Have you ever worked a missing-child case before?" Don asked, his tone clipped but soft.

"No," Reed replied. "A couple of missing teenagers in Ballarat. But they were runaways, we found them at a friend's house two days later."

"Me neither," Don admitted. "We've never had to deal with anything like this before."

"I'm going to preserve the scene first. That's critical." Reed said. He was standing beside the car now, desperate to get off the phone so he could jump in and drive.

"We need to find her, Reed. Soon," Don said quietly. "The girl's welfare is paramount, of course. You know as well as I do, the longer these things go on the worse the possible outcome. There's also going to be a media shitstorm if we don't. And I, for one, don't want to have to deal with that."

Reed silently agreed with his boss. "Got it, Sarge. See you in Penneshaw." He ended the call and hopped into the car, hoping he remembered how to get back to the ferry-port town. He'd only done the drive once so far, and that was in the dark, following Sierra's taillights.

* * *

Sierra pulled her car in next to the curb and switched off the engine. Penneshaw was busy today; there were people everywhere in the street, which was a little unusual. She looked down at the list of shopping on the passenger seat, wondering if she'd forgotten anything. It was time to replenish her food supplies, and the local IGA supermarket always stocked her favorites. Mostly local products made right here on the island, like the special sheep cheese she loved, with the wonderful homemade relish to go with it.

It was snug and warm in the car and Sierra wasn't looking forward to stepping into the biting wind she knew would greet her outside. There was no rain forecast today, but the wind alone dropped the temperature by many degrees, even when the sun managed to send down its weak light.

Her thoughts travelled backward, over the past few days she'd spent at home. Days spent poring over the documents Jen had sent her. Sierra made copious notes of her own as she read them, and she also made a few phone calls to confirm something she'd read, or back up hunches on a particular line of investigation.

Her neighbors, Sam and Debbie, had been like angels from heaven when they'd arrived on her doorstep three days earlier, just as Sierra started sorting through the notes. Sam handed over a laptop he said had been sitting around gathering dust in their spare room as he strode in through the front door, and Debbie marched in behind him with a plate full of freshly made scones. After Sierra made them tea and they ate the scones on the front deck, they left, but not before they assured themselves Sierra really was okay after her break-in.

It was an old Apple Mac laptop, but it still worked, even if it was slow, and once Sierra connected it to the internet, she was able to download a lot of her stuff off the Cloud. She was back in business. Sort of.

Sierra would never admit it to Jen, but it felt good to be working on something serious again. It'd take a lot longer than three days to piece together the story of the missing girls and to find out all the information she needed, but she'd made a good start. Had an interesting conversation with one of the detectives who'd worked the case three years ago and gleaned some extra details that weren't in any of the reports she had. Who knew, they could be important. And she'd made some other calls to social workers and journalists who'd either worked on, or followed the case.

Another thing she'd never admit to Jen was the amount of time she spent thinking about Reed. If her mind stopped its machinations about the case for even a few minutes, she'd somehow find him in her thoughts, instead. The way he stood looking out her windows at the ocean. So solid, so assured of himself. The way his hand rested lightly on his gun belt, the other shoved in the pocket of his pants. Those strong fingers, with his honey-warm skin, made her think of how it would feel to have him trace his palm over her body.

A gust of wind buffeted her car, and shook her out of her daydreaming. She grabbed her weatherproof coat from the back seat and slung her handbag over her shoulder, then hopped out of the car. It really was as cold as she'd been expecting.

First of all, she needed to send a letter to Keira. She wished she could be in Hawaii with her sibling right now, or at least someplace warmer. She did love living on KI, most of the time. Keira probably wouldn't answer the letter, she often didn't, but Sierra felt better for at least keeping up her side of the sisterhood.

Keeping up with her younger brother, however, was not as easy. Logan *never* answered her emails or letters. Logan was a lot younger than Sierra. Mum had never said anything, but Sierra suspected he might have been an accident. She had an inkling her parents had been happy to stop at two girls. Then when Logan came along it'd turned their neat, predictable lives on edge. There were seven years between her and Logan, and maybe it was because of this large age gap, but she and her brother never seemed to see eye to eye. Her mum had complained the other day that she hadn't heard from either of Sierra's two siblings in ages.

She jumped up the two steps from the pavement and into the local newsstand. The shop doubled as the post office in this small town. The bell above the door jangled happily as she closed it behind her.

"Hi, Evan," she called breezily to the stocky, bespectacled man at the other end of the shop. He came toward her, a large box in his hands, which he placed carefully on the counter and turned to face her.

"Hello, Sierra. Good to see you again. How did you go with that parcel I gave you the other night?" Evan's voice was deep and gravelly. He kept his red beard neatly trimmed, and his thinning hair precisely combed over to one side. Sierra could only guess at his age, but thought he was on the downward slide toward sixty. He kept in shape for his age, and fitted in well with the small community.

"All good," she chirped. "I gave it to Debbie, like you asked." She didn't mention that she'd been so caught up in the break-in that she'd forgotten all about it until yesterday.

He stared at her for a second and Sierra could've sworn he didn't believe her, but then his features morphed back into their normal affable smile and he said, "Great. Thanks. What are you after, luv? I was just about to close up."

"Oh." Sierra was lost for words for a second. It wasn't like

Evan to close early. Since he'd taken over the ownership of the shop around eighteen months ago, he'd spruced up the place, added some interesting souvenirs to entice tourists, and made sure he was always open. Unlike the previous owner who'd been a lot less reliable. Sierra liked to chat with him whenever she came into the shop. He always seemed interested and attentive.

"Is something the matter? Why are you closing early?"

Evan shot her a sharp look. "Haven't you heard? There's a little girl gone missing. I'm off to join the search. Just about everyone in the street is doing the same." Evan waved towards the front of the shop, but Sierra didn't turn around. Her skin crawled as if there were living things moving underneath it. What had he said? It was as if all the air had suddenly left her lungs.

"Sorry. What?"

"A little girl wandered away from her parents this morning. They're tourists, staying up at one of Mal's rentals. They reckon she's gone off in the bush somewhere and got lost." Sierra concentrated on Evan's serious face, his eyes holding a hint of sorrow as he spoke. He wasn't joking. This wasn't some kind of sick prank. This was real.

"Oh, Jesus," she murmured. She stared at him, almost unable to comprehend. This didn't happen on KI. It was a quiet place, where people came to live a quiet life full of natural beauty, and tourists came to have a good time. That was all. Kids didn't go missing. An insidious little voice inside her head was whispering, *what if she didn't just wander off?*

"I know, luv. That's exactly what I thought. Isn't it terrible?" He laid a hand on her shoulder, which made her flinch. He'd never touched her before, just always been friendly and talkative. It was odd, and it was all she could do not to shrug it off. Evan was staring at her and she realized she needed to pull herself together.

"Yes, it is," she replied, giving him a weak smile. His hand still rested on her shoulder, and a sliver of aversion ran down her spine. She needed to get out of here. Needed to talk to Reed. He would most likely be at the epicenter of things.

"I think I'll join the search, too," she declared, turning away quickly, moving out of his reach. "Do you know where they're setting up HQ?"

"At the Penneshaw CFS. You know, the fire station," he replied, his eyes still not leaving hers. Sierra saw something odd flash over his face, but it was gone in an instant, and she hadn't been able to decipher it.

"Thanks. I guess I'll see you down there soon," she said, turning on her heel and hurrying out the door. She could feel his gaze burning into her back as she left.

Outside, she glanced down, and saw the forgotten letter to Keira still in her hand. She tucked it into her handbag and turned down the street. The CFS was only two blocks away, she would walk.

"Sierra." Someone called her name and she swiveled around, recognizing Sam and Debbie coming towards her. Debbie waved and she stood on the pavement, waiting for them to approach. "Have you heard?" Debbie said breathlessly, even before she'd come to a complete stop by her side.

"About the missing girl? Yes, Evan just told me."

"Poor little lamb, she must be so scared, lost out there in the bush." Debbie's jovial face creased with unhappiness. "We're going to join the search."

"Me too," Sierra declared. "I was going to walk down to the fire station. Did you want to join me?"

"Is that where they're setting up their headquarters?" Sam asked. He was a big man. Broad across the shoulders, with a heavy-set, square jaw. He'd worked as a carpenter before he retired and the hard manual labor had formed him into a tough, fit man. Both Sam and Debbie were in their early sixties, and had moved to KI to set up an Airbnb business with their fleet of growing properties out at Snellings Beach. Her neighbors had become part of the small circle of people she called friends. Even with the age gap, Sierra got on well with them, enjoyed their company.

Kylie and Rhianna were her other two good friends. She'd met both of the women when she'd joined the KI walking group and they'd become close ever since. She wondered if either of them would come down to join the search. Kylie was a single mum and worked in Kingscote, so perhaps not. Rhianna lived out in Emu Bay with her hubby and two kids. It was further to come, out past Kingscote on an isolated headland, and Sierra doubted Rhianna would be here at such short notice either.

"That's what Evan told me," Sierra replied, already setting off down the path. It made sense. Kangaroo Island had a State Emergency Service unit, but it was in Kingscote, and they'd want to set up as close to the disappearance as possible. Debbie hurried to catch up with her, slipping her arm through Sierra's. Sierra didn't mind, it was something her mother might do. Debbie kept up a stream of conversation as they walked, Sam stalking along quietly a few paces behind. Sierra barely paid Debbie any heed, her mind racing. Would Reed be at the station? And why did she care if he was? Because she wanted to see him, that's why. They'd made a connection the other night on the ferry, and then again at her house after the break-in. She was ready to admit that now. It was the first time in a long time—since Blake—that she'd had a physical reaction to a man. Felt a pull toward him, like a fish being tugged gently on a line.

She wanted to see him again. Look into those dark, obsidian eyes and see the corners crinkle up as he smiled.

There was a dependability about him, a trustworthiness that made her feel safe. One question niggled constantly at the back of her mind. Should she tell him about the articles she'd written on abducted children? Would it make any difference if she did? After all, there could be no interrelation at all. Could there? But she knew she needed to tell him. To make sure he understood she wasn't hiding anything. To keep the air clear. If this girl wasn't found soon, a whole horde of media would descend on the island and then everything about her past as a journalist was sure to come out. For some reason, she wanted Reed to hear it from her own lips.

But it was more than that.

She wouldn't go as far as calling it a premonition. More like a churning in her guts, warning her something wasn't right. As soon as the words had come out of Evan's mouth about the little girl, a heavy weight settled in her chest. And she instinctively knew it wouldn't go away anytime soon, as if a dark foreboding was hanging right over her head. As if this girl had something to do with her past. Was perhaps connected. She knew it was a ridiculous assumption, crazy and way off-base. Of course, this had nothing to do with the other missing girls. But this heavy, dragging apprehension wouldn't leave her.

They rounded the corner, and a mass of milling people came into view. As they got closer, Sierra could see it was organized chaos. Sergeant Coldwater's voice could be heard bellowing orders through a bullhorn from the middle of the crowd, which parted as they walked up, revealing Don in his dark-blue police uniform, looking serious and ever so slightly harassed.

"I know you all want to help," he said to the gathered crowd. "But you need to give us a bit of space to work." He dragged his hand down his face, stroking his mustache in annoyance.

Officer Olivia Mettler was there also, hovering behind a large table that'd been set up out the front of the building, covered in stacks of paper, clipboards, hand-held GPS units, and a box of high-vis vests. Two other men also lingered around the table, both wearing the familiar bright-orange uniform of the SES team. One of them she recognized as Tom, a fellow member of the KI walking group she and Kylie and Rhianna were part of. Sierra cast her gaze around for Reed, but disappointment sat heavy in her stomach when she couldn't see him.

"Tom Hubbard is the head of the community SES here, and he's going to brief you all in a second," Don said, projecting his voice once more through the bullhorn. The quietly murmuring crowd went silent.

Tom Hubbard was a burly man, with a thick, bushy beard, and bright beady eyes. He was often gruff and prickly, not an easy man to talk to. When she first met him, she'd been surprised to find out he was involved in the SES, and even more surprised he was the leader. But as she got to know him and broke through that gruff, outer shell, she could see a man who was eager to be a valuable part of society, who wanted to help, to be liked. He just didn't have great social skills. But he was damn good at organizing, at marshaling people, telling them what to do with his loud voice and take-no-nonsense attitude. People listened to him.

"We need to keep this search as organized as possible, so we don't have random people going off in random directions," Don continued.

As Don spoke, movement attracted Sierra's attention, and she turned to look behind her. A police Land Cruiser pulled up in the background at the edge of the fire station car park. Sierra shaded her eyes to see better, and then her heart kicked in her chest as Reed got out of the car. He was here. Don continued to expound on the necessity of following the SES team-leader's instructions, waving his hands around in time with the bullhorn. Sierra returned her gaze to the Sarge, but the back of her neck prickled with the need to turn around to get another glance at Reed. As if on cue, he materialized by her side.

"Hi," he said quietly.

"Hi," she replied, allowing herself to enjoy the feeling of him standing close beside her for a second or two. But it was now or never, so she bit her lip and drew in a breath.

"I need to talk to you," she said.

His dark gaze landed on her face as he studied her for a moment. "Well, I need to talk to you, too," he replied.

CHAPTER SEVEN

"I asked them to put you with me," Reed said to Sierra. "That way we can talk and search at the same time. Come on." He beckoned her toward his police car. She gave him a startled look, then turned and waved in the direction of an older couple—they might be the next-door-neighbors she'd mentioned the other day—then, with high-vis vest in hand, almost had to run to keep up with his long-legged strides. Reed had spoken quickly to the Sarge, given him all the information he'd gathered so far, and asked permission to take Sierra with him. Things were not looking good; it'd been over four hours since the girl first went missing and he was itching to get back and start searching.

He jumped into the driver's side of the Land Cruiser as she hopped into the passenger seat.

"Where are we going?" she asked.

"We're going back to the rental property where the girl was staying with her family. It's called Lofty Rest, right on the edge of Penneshaw, backing onto the bushland. I want to see if I can find some kind of clue as to which way she might've gone." Reed scowled at the road through the windshield. He was driving too fast, taking corners at speed, but he couldn't seem to slow down. Sierra hung onto the safety bar above her head but only nodded in quiet acknowledgment. "The SES will organize everyone else into teams, and they'll start combing the bush and coastline around the town."

"Good. That's good," she replied. "Oh." Sierra covered her mouth as an idea seemed to strike her. "I never even considered, there are cliffs down to the left along the coast. You don't think she could've..." She trailed off and he could tell she was imagining the little girl's body lying crumpled and still at the bottom of one of these cliff-faces. He knew, because he'd imagined the very same scenario.

"Anything's possible. We have to cover all avenues," he said, a little more brusquely than he intended.

She stared at him, face pale, hands clenched together in a tight fist in her lap. Her beautiful lips were pulled down into a serious line, eyes dark and thoughtful. Then she sucked in a deep breath. "I have to tell you something. I wanted to tell you before you hear it from someone else and get the wrong idea."

He had a pretty good idea of what she was going to say, but he let her continue.

"So, you know I used to work as an investigative journalist back in Adelaide. I told you when I got that letter from the stalker." She kept her eyes trained out the front window, not looking at him. "But we didn't get to the part about the articles themselves and why the stalker has been harassing me." He remembered he'd wanted to ask her at the time, but she'd said she had a headache coming on, and she'd looked so frail and sick he'd let it go. Should he let on that he'd already looked up her articles?

She continued before he could open his mouth to interrupt. "I reported on a couple of cases of missing children. Abductions. And I ran a series of articles about them. So, when I heard about the missing girl this morning, I was shocked, of course. But I also felt sick to my stomach. I know firsthand there are evil people out there, who commit evil deeds." She glanced at him and for the first time he could see the fear and revulsion leaking out of her. "I guess what I'm saying is that I have direct experience with this kind of thing. And if you think…" She stopped and swallowed hard before continuing. "Do you think there's any chance this could be more than just a girl who wandered off and got lost? I mean, I know this is a small island, a backwater, if you like, and nothing like that ever happens here. But…"

"I think it's too early to speculate at the moment, but like I said, we have to keep every option open."

She returned her gaze to the front, her body tense and rigid in the seat. "I can't explain it, Reed. But for some reason…I don't know why…this feels like it's more. I can't tell you anymore than it's a hunch, a gut feeling. Something's not right about this. And I felt I had to tell you. Ask you if you thought there could possibly be a connection?"

What was she talking about? Why would she think there was a connection? Sure, she had experience with these kinds of things before, but it was way too early to start making assumptions. Like the girl had been abducted, not just wandered away. Wasn't it? So then why had he taken all the precautions, preserved the crime scene as if that was indeed exactly what happened? Because it was protocol, he reminded himself. And because he'd had the same feeling of foreboding she was talking about. Maybe the foreboding was completely misplaced, he was thinking the worst because he'd only just finished reading her articles and they had him contemplating child abductions and pedophiles and all the kinds of things that could go wrong in a hurry on a case like this.

Reed pursed his lips. "Thanks for telling me, Sierra. But I have a confession to make, too. I've already read your articles, I looked them up the day after your break-in." He gave her a sheepish glance. "I thought it might be important to know more of the story, as I was trying to analyze the letter," he added. Although why he said that, he wasn't entirely sure; he didn't need to justify himself to her. "It's one of the reasons I brought you along. Like you said, you might have experience with this kind of thing. Possibly more experience than I do. And I need every little bit of help I can get right now. *We* need the help," he qualified.

Don had disagreed with Reed when he'd asked him earlier, if he could take Sierra with him. "She's just a civilian, Reed. I don't think we should involve her," Don had said, lowering his eyebrows. "And more than that she's a journalist." Don didn't elaborate, but Reed knew what he meant. That Sierra might try and use her position here, on the island and in this search team, to her advantage. If she wanted, this story could be a huge scoop for her. Perhaps even kick-start her career again. She was the first journalist on the scene, and she had a hotline directly to himself and the Sarge.

"Ever heard of the saying, *keep your friends close, but your enemies closer*?" Reed had asked.

"Humph," Don had grunted. "Well, just make bloody sure you keep an eagle eye on her." And then he'd turned back to answer a question from Tom Hubbard. Reed hoped he wasn't severely misjudging Sierra's character, but she didn't strike him as that kind of person. For now, he needed to trust her and take any help she offered.

In one of her articles she'd mentioned that she was *bound by truth* to get all the facts out there, so the public could make up their own minds. He was struck by the words. And struck by the sentiment behind them.

If only he wasn't so distracted by her all the time. Even with everything going on, with him driving at break-neck speed, part of his subconscious was still acutely aware of her as she sat only a couple of feet away. Aware of the tiny frown that marred her forehead. Aware of her long, sensual fingers clasped in a fist. Aware of how good she smelled, warm and slightly tangy. Tempting.

He came to an intersection and dragged his mind back to the here and now. "I was also hoping you could do us a huge favor. Word of this missing girl will get out soon, I know we won't be able to stop that. But I was wondering if you could possibly be a liaison between us and them? The media, I mean. Perhaps stop them hounding us mercilessly so we can get our jobs done?"

"Keep them off your back?" She gave a hint of a smile, the first he'd seen all day. "I think that might be an impossible task."

"If anyone can do it, you can." And he meant that with all due respect. She had a certain tenacity about her.

"Okay, I'll try, but you can't avoid the media completely. The best way to keep them from hounding you day and night is to give them the information they crave. I can help you organize press conferences, that kind of thing. Let's just hope it doesn't come to that."

Reed nodded. It was the best he could hope for right now. He'd been involved in other cases before where the media had gotten in the way, hindered the investigation. He just hoped that wouldn't happen here.

"Are you bringing in help from the mainland?"

"Yes. Another two police units will arrive tonight, they're coming over on the evening ferry. And a dog unit will be arriving on a chartered flight in a few hours' time. But we're on our own till then. Olivia and Don will canvass the neighborhood before they get here. See if anyone saw the girl this morning. Eric is guarding the house, keeping the family calm."

He turned a corner and slowed the car. Up ahead was the rental house where the missing girl's family were staying.

Four or five cars were clustered in the road next to it, and a small group of people was milling around in the front yard. Reed shook his head in disbelief. Damn, he thought he'd made it clear to Eric the house needed to be kept sterile, that he wasn't to let anyone near it. Reed wanted to get out and yell at the other man, tell him that this case needed to run like clockwork. Just because they lived in a small, hick town, didn't mean they needed to run it like a small, hick investigation. But he knew he wasn't going to yell at a colleague he'd only been working with for less than a week.

Reed clenched his teeth as he stopped the car well up the street from the house.

"Are you okay?" Sierra asked.

"Not really," he growled. "Let's see what's going on up there."

* * *

Sierra tried to be inconspicuous as she waited on the curb, not listening as Reed talked in low tones to Officer Eric Jones. But it was hard not to overhear Reed's hushed words as the two men stood not two feet away from her in the gateway to the house.

"You shouldn't have let them in here," Reed said, gesturing to the small crowd of people who now hovered around the front yard of the house. The rental property was a quaint three-bedroom cottage that'd been renovated and updated with all the modern luxuries. It was a favorite of the tourists who came to stay on KI. Especially because the view from the front verandah was straight across into the rugged bushland that edged the small township. It felt almost rural, but still with all the comforts of town.

"They just want to help," Eric replied, chin jutting defensively. "Everyone's first priority is to find this little girl. That's all that really matters right now."

Sierra could see by the way Reed clenched his teeth he was

holding back what he really wanted to say. Sierra was acquainted with Officer Jones and she liked him, found him easy to get along with, affable, but also prepared to do his sworn duty when required. The way Eric was glaring at Reed right now, however, made her revise her judgment of him. She added resentful and defensive to his list of traits, something she'd never experienced before. All this alpha-male dominant thing always made her smirk. Men could be so predictable sometimes. Sierra guessed Reed probably had more experience in working these kind of crimes than Eric would ever see in his lifetime. But Reed was also the new recruit out here, and he'd have to be careful what he said if he didn't want to alienate the rest of his team.

"I agree," Reed said patiently. "But the Sarge said we need to keep the crime scene sterile. At least until forensics get here. The last thing we want is those mainland boys accusing us of shoddy policing." Reed lifted his hands in the air in an imitation of a self-effacing shrug and Sierra was impressed. He'd handled the situation well. "At the moment, this job is more important than being out there, searching with the others."

Sierra turned away to hide a small smile. He was good.

Her gaze landed on the two people standing up on the veranda staring down at them. The murmur of Reed's conversation faded into the background. A woman was holding a girl's hand. The girl looked to be around nine or ten. They had to be the mother and sister of the missing girl. Reed had said there was an older sister. She couldn't see anyone who looked like they might be the father, and surmised he was probably out searching. Sierra blinked and looked away. She couldn't bear to see the naked, haunting fear in the woman's eyes. It went straight to Sierra's soul. She knew how that mother felt. Knew the raw anguish that'd be scouring her insides, turning them into a barren wasteland. A lump formed in Sierra's throat, and she crossed her arms over her chest, taking a step away, as if to escape from the horror of poor woman's despair. This was a bad idea. She shouldn't have come. Perhaps she should get Reed to take her back into town and then she could get in her car and drive home. Where it was quiet and safe.

A warm hand landed on her shoulder, making her jump. "Right, let's get started." She pulled herself together enough to nod her agreement.

He gave her a hard stare, and she thought he might be going to ask if she was okay. Those astute black eyes bored into her. But then they clouded over, became preoccupied, and he said, "I talked to the parents earlier. The last time they saw Jessica was at breakfast, around seven A.M. The mother was busy tidying up—they were supposed to check out this morning—and the father was in the shower." Reed walked as he talked. "The mum, Heather, sent the two girls off to the living room to watch TV while they packed up the house. But the older sister said Jessica kept talking about wanting to see the kangaroos one more time before they left. Supposedly she was obsessed with them. Taylor, the older sister, said she ignored Jessica and started watching some cartoons on TV. That was the last time she saw her."

They were almost back to his squad car now. She could hear voices coming from the surrounding bushland, people calling Jessica's name. And there were more people walking up and down the road, poking into bushes and looking in ditches. The place was overrun with people trying to help.

"Grab your high-vis," Reed said as he unlocked the car. "Do you have water?"

"Sorry, I came in such a rush when I heard," she apologized.

He didn't answer, but dug around in the back seat of the car and came out with two plastic bottles of water, handing her one and opening his and taking a swig.

"So, if you were a five-year-old girl who was obsessed with kangaroos, where would you go?" His question surprised her. But then she glanced back down the street toward the house, where Eric was finally ushering the well-meaning people out of the front yard. The house sat toward the end of the street nearest to town. She swiveled around and faced the other way, where the street kept going for around a hundred meters or so, before taking a sharp, right bend. Where the road bent right, the bushland opened up into a flat, grassy plain. The perfect spot for kangaroos to graze, although she couldn't see any there at the moment. All this activity had probably scared them away.

"That way." She pointed to the clearing.

"I was thinking the same thing," Reed said adamantly. "Shall we start down there?"

"As good a place as any," Sierra agreed.

"Do you mind staying behind me as we walk, until we get to the clearing?" he asked. "I know it's probably useless, lot of people have already tramped up and down here. But I just want to keep an eye out for anything that might be a clue."

"Sure," she acknowledged. "I'll keep my eyes peeled as well." As long as she could keep her eyes on the road and away from his backside, that was. Away from those nicely-shaped thighs she'd first noticed on the ferry, that were just as agreeable now she saw them encased in the dark-blue pants of his uniform. *Concentrate, Sierra.* This was not what she was here for. Lowering her gaze, she stared at the gravel along the side of the bitumen. At least it hadn't rained in the past twenty-four hours. Any signs should still be preserved. She wasn't sure exactly what she was looking for. Footprints perhaps? What else would a little girl leave behind? She trailed behind Reed as he walked, head down, concentrating on the ground around the edge of the road. They stopped level with the open field. A wire fence cut the road off from the open area. Would the little girl have been able to climb though that fence? Perhaps she just went up to it and peered through, pushing her forehead up against the wire, to see the kangaroos feeding. Reed stepped gingerly closer to the fence. Sierra stayed by the roadside, not wanting to interrupt him. While she waited for him to conduct his surveillance, she cast her gaze around for anything out of the ordinary.

That's when she saw it.

A discarded candy wrapper.

On the ground by her feet. Right at the edge of the road.

"Reed," she called, not sure if she should bother him. When he lifted his head, she said, "I don't know if this is anything, but do you want to come and take a look?" He turned, and she lowered her gaze back to the wrapper, scared it might suddenly disappear.

Reed crouched down to get a better look at her find. He snapped a shot of it on his phone, then pulled out a pair of latex gloves and put them on before he gingerly picked it up. "This wrapper is fresh. Not wet or covered in dirt. Which means it could've been here for a day or two. No more."

"Is it..." She didn't know how to finish her question. Could it be related to Jessica? Or was it just coincidence? People dropped candy wrappers all the time, threw them out their windows. There had been people traipsing up and down the road all morning. Could one of them have dropped it? It was a wrapper from one of those chewy caramel candies. Sierra knew it well; it was commonly sold in all the local stores.

"I don't know," he replied. "But I'll bag it up and keep it for evidence. Document where you found it. Every little bit helps. I'll ask the mum later if her daughter had access to any of these kinds of candies."

Sierra stared at him as he stood up next to her.

"You've got good eyes. Observant."

She shrugged. "I guess it comes with the territory when you're a journalist. Sometimes it's the little things that count the most."

"Ain't that the truth." Reed gave her a quick smile before he began to rummage around in his police vest pockets, finally pulling out a zipper-lock bag. He'd taken his police cap off in the car and hadn't bothered to put it back on. Now his head was lowered in front of her, his thick, black hair dark against his skull, a few tufts sticking out above his eyes, where he'd run a restless hand through it. She watched his shoulders move beneath his jacket, broad and strong. And she felt that tug again. The same one as on the ferry. A physical magnetism toward this man. As if something were drawing her slowly in.

Reed glanced up and caught her staring. He raised an eyebrow, and she knew he understood what she'd been doing. That she liked what she saw. Was drinking him in as if she was a woman dying of thirst. Heat rose up her neck and she was thankful he wouldn't see the tell-tale red behind the high collar of her coat.

"What do we do now?" she asked, moving away to stare out over the green field, crossing her arms over her chest.

"We keep looking," he said. "I think this area is still our best bet. I'll get Tom to organize a team to come and search this open ground. You and I will skirt around to the left and search just inside the edge of the bushland."

Sierra decided Reed's instincts were right. This felt like it might well have been where the little girl had come to see her precious kangaroos. But his notion relied on the fact Jessica walked down here on her own, and was now lost or injured somewhere. It didn't account for another theory.

That someone had seen Jessica walking down the road. Or found her standing in this very spot, looking for a way to get through the fence. And taken her.

CHAPTER EIGHT

Sierra's feet ached. She hadn't realized she would be tramping through the bush all day when she'd left the house this morning. If she had, she would've put on her hiking boots and a proper pair of light-but-tough walking pants. As it was, her Converse sneakers had done the job, but were now pinching her toes painfully, and causing a blister to form on her left heel. Not that she cared. If it meant finding the little girl, she'd keep walking all night in these shoes.

It was now well after dark. Her stomach rumbled painfully, but she ignored it. The cold was seeping through her thick Gortex coat now the sun had disappeared. But she ignored that, as well.

"Time to call it a day." The familiar voice came through the thick bushland. Tom Hubbard was leading this team, as well as organizing all the other teams. He'd said he couldn't just sit back at HQ and watch on while everyone else searched. Sierra could understand that sentiment completely.

But were they really calling the search off? The thin stream of light from her flashlight bobbed along the track in front of her, as she made her way towards the team leader. Reed had given her the light out of his car before he left a couple of hours ago to report to Don, and she joined up with the SES volunteers in this group. The other police teams would've arrived from the mainland by now and he and Don had to bring them up to speed. Reed said no one was on dispatch in the office at the moment, as all hands were needed on deck for the search. That made it harder to communicate with his other officers, especially as cell phone reception was so patchy on the island. He'd hated to leave the search, but the debriefing couldn't wait.

Sierra made her way into a small clearing where other volunteers were gathering around Tom. Her flashlight lit up their bright-orange high-vis vests, and for a second, they looked like a multicolored pack of brightly plumed birds all flocking together. She stumbled over a small log as she entered the clearing and held back a curse. Her legs ached, and she could feel exhaustion creeping in. But she would've kept searching until dawn if she had to.

"Is everyone here?" Tom asked, his voice broadcasting over the top of Sierra's head into the surrounding scrub. There were a few muffled replies as the last of the stragglers arrived, the light from their flashlights or headlamps mingling with the growing glow around the huddle of humanity.

"Sorry, folks, but it's SES protocol. We don't search after dark. We can't put the lives of our volunteers and professionals at risk."

There were a few grumbling complaints from the back, and Sierra echoed their dismay in her head.

"I know, I know," Tom placated. "I've heard it all before." He sounded tired and Sierra looked up to catch a glimpse of his lined face in the bright lights of everyone's flashlights. There were lines around his eyes, she could see them clearly even though his shaggy hair and bushy beard. This thing was taking a toll on him, like it was taking a toll on everyone. She'd have to see if she could catch him later and have a quick chat. Let him know they were all in this together.

"But we're not giving up. Those of you who are up to it, we'll re-assemble back at the fire station in Penneshaw at five A.M. sharp. We're going to keep looking until we find this girl."

Sierra's shoulders slumped. She knew he was right, there were good reasons to call off the search. One of the most important ones being that a vitally important clue might be missed if they continued to search in the dark. So why did it feel so much like defeat?

She only half-listened as Tom continued, "If you hike out to the road, a bus will be along shortly to pick you up and take you back to Penneshaw. Go home, get a hot meal and a good night's sleep. We need you all back tomorrow."

There was a rustling sound and Sierra's mouth began to water. She'd recognize the sound of a bag of candy being opened anywhere.

Tom's voice boomed out over the top of the surrounding crowd. "I know it's not much, but everyone is welcome to grab a candy for the trek back to the bus."

Sierra joined the queue filing past Tom, who had an extra-large bag open in his hand. But just as it was her turn to put her hand in and grab one, she noticed the label and flinched away.

It was the same brand as the wrapper she'd found at the side of the road this morning. She shook her head and kept walking, Tom giving her a confused look as she went. But how was she supposed to explain that?

Was there a connection? Should she tell Reed? Those candies were for sale in all the supermarkets, they were common and easily available. Surely it was just a terrible coincidence?

Sierra followed a group of three other people out along the narrow track, her mind whirling with questions. Uncertainty mixed in with the horrible cold lump that'd been sitting in her chest cavity all day, ever since she'd heard the news.

"Hi, luv. Is that you, Sierra?" a voice called from behind. She stopped walking and turned around. A thickset figure emerged out of the gloom. She caught a glint of reflected light from his glasses and immediately knew who it was.

"Evan. Hi. I didn't know you were with this team."

He fell into step beside her, and she could hear by the rasp in his breath he was working hard to keep up with her, so she slowed a little. "Well, of course I came straight out here. I want to help find that poor little girl." Sierra couldn't see his face properly in the flickering lights of everyone's torches, but it was enough to know he looked much like a beaten basset hound. Which was how she felt as well. How they all felt. Hollow and defeated.

"It's just so terrible, don't you think?" he continued. "That poor girl's family. I saw her, you know. Yesterday. The whole family came in to buy a postcard. They were so lovely together." Evan was rambling, almost stumbling over his words in his haste to get them out. "I gave the two little girls a candy each, and the little one, she was so happy when I gave it to her. The older sister, she wouldn't take it until her mum said it was okay. Smart girl that one. But I can't believe what's happened. What do you think, luv? Do you think she just wandered off?"

What was it today? Every time she turned around someone was talking about candy. It must be all a huge fluke, she was reading too much into it. Sierra didn't feel like chatting to anyone right now, least of all the well-meaning, but interfering, Evan. She gave a resigned shrug of her shoulders. But he wasn't deterred and kept up a constant stream of one-sided babbling as they made their way back to the road. She gave a grunt every now and then by way of reply.

The bus was waiting for them as they emerged from the

bush, a bright bubble of light in the dark night. As they went to get aboard, Evan grabbed her arm and she flinched at the strength behind those plump fingers.

"You are coming back to search tomorrow, aren't you?" His eyes bored into her from behind his spectacles. "I mean, we need all the help we can get to find little Jessica." He was still gripping her arm, and she had to resist the urge to shake it off. What was it with this guy and touching her? His sense of personal space was seriously off, all of a sudden.

"Of course, I am," she agreed.

Finally, he let go of her arm. "Good. That's good. I'll probably see you then," he said as he followed her up the stairs. She chose an empty seat next to an older lady up the front and after a second's hesitation, Evan moved off, farther into the back.

Nearly an hour later, Sierra parked her car in the main street of Kingscote, right out the front of the local fish and chip shop. She was starving, and the thought of a pile of steaming-hot chips and some freshly grilled fish had her mouth watering. But the dilemma of what to do after she'd eaten was still swirling around her mind. It was another thirty-minute drive out to her house. Perhaps she could give Kylie a call and see if she could stay at her house tonight. It'd save a lot of time if she didn't have to drive home and them back again tomorrow morning. She sometimes stayed over after a girl's night at the Queenscliff pub. Other times they get together at Rhianna's place in Emu Bay, and Sierra would often spend the night there afterwards as well. But Kylie's place would be the obvious one to stay at tonight. Kylie might also have a spare pair of boots she could lend her so she could keep searching tomorrow. Sometimes it was a bonus, having a friend with the same-size feet.

It was a good plan. She'd buy herself some dinner then give Kylie a call.

The fish and chip shop was warm and bright, a stark contrast to the cold street outside. Sierra noted the queue of people waiting to be served. Obviously, she wasn't the only one who was hungry and cold after the search. In her periphery, she saw a person detach themselves from the crowd and come towards her.

Reed.

Her heart did a little flip-flop at the sight of him. What was he doing here? He smiled at her, lighting up that dimple in his chin and the lump that'd sat cold and hard in her chest all day melted a little.

"Looks like we had the same idea," he said, coming to stand next to her at the back of the line.

"They do the best fish and chips on the island. Perhaps even in the whole of South Australia," Sierra said.

"Wow, big call." He grinned, showing off straight white teeth.

"How did the rest of the afternoon go?" she asked.

His full lips pulled down and he scowled. "Not good. Still no sign of the girl. The mainland cops are already pointing fingers and trying to take over. Don's not happy. He's told us all to go home and get a few hours' sleep and some food, and then come back in early tomorrow." He said this in a low voice, so as no one else in the lineup could hear. Her momentary happiness at seeing Reed again turned sour.

"I'm going to need to call in that favor from you tomorrow morning. The media have gotten wind of the situation and they've swarmed onto the island."

Sierra could just imagine. It would be like a feeding frenzy at the zoo, with everyone vying for the latest scoop, the best sound bite, the most sensational photo.

"Where were you planning to eat?"

She was surprised by his change in topic. "Probably just in my car," she admitted. At least it would be warm in there and then she could call Kylie afterwards.

"Come to my place. I'm at the guesthouse a few streets back. I've got a little self-contained flat out the back. It'll be warmer than your car. More room. And I'd love your company, if you can spare it."

"Um…" Sierra hesitated. Was that really a good idea? To be alone with him, even for a short while? But then, what could the harm be? She was a big girl, and just because she was physically attracted to him didn't mean she wasn't in full control of her own urges. She'd love to find out more about the search, see if they'd found any more hints as to where the girl might be. "Sure, why not?"

"Great." His smile came back, the one with the dimple, and hit her full force. She felt like she'd been shot with a bolt of electricity.

* * *

Reed turned the key in the lock and opened the door into his little one-bedroom flat, Sierra following close on his heels. He dropped his parcel of fish and chips on the kitchen counter, then went over to flick the gas heater on. It was cold inside, but the little heater did a great job, and the room would soon warm up. He picked a dirty shirt off the back of a kitchen stool and bent down to clear a mug and bowl from the coffee table. Then he caught himself. Why was he acting like a nervous teenager? Sierra wasn't a date, she wouldn't mind that his place wasn't spotless. It was a spur of the moment thing; he'd never thought Sierra would ever come and visit him here. Not that it wasn't a nice surprise when she had agreed to come.

"Make yourself at home." He gestured to the couch. "I'll get us some plates. What would you like to drink? I've got beer, soft drinks, and water."

"Water will be fine, thanks. I need to re-hydrate. Don't worry about a plate, I'll eat it straight from the wrapper."

Reed hesitated, about to grab himself a beer from the refrigerator. He should drink water, too. Even though it was cold on the island, with all the walking he'd done today, he knew he hadn't drunk enough. He took off his uniform jacket and unstrapped the heavy belt from around his waist, and laid them both on one of the kitchen stools.

When he returned to the living room, Sierra already had her meal unwrapped and spread out on the coffee table. She'd taken her Gortex coat off, and hung it over the back of the couch. Her long legs were stretched in front of her as she sat on the floor to eat. He couldn't help but notice how firm and muscular they were, sheathed in black leggings. Nicely shaped thighs tapering to slim calves. How would they feel wrapped around—

"Sorry, I'm starving," she said through a mouthful of grilled fish, interrupting his train of thought. Which was lucky, because his mind didn't need to dwell on how it might feel to hold her against him. It was the last thing he should be thinking about.

The smell of the hot food made his stomach growl. It'd been a long time since breakfast this morning. He sat down on the couch near her, and opened his parcel of food. His leg was aching like a bitch after all the walking and standing he'd done today. It would need to be iced tonight, if he had any hope of not walking with a limp tomorrow. Which was the reason he chose the couch instead of the floor; he didn't think his leg could handle that kind of strain of being stretched out for too long. The injury had damaged his calf muscles, and he didn't have the flexibility to sit with his legs out straight for long periods anymore without it cramping up.

As he sat, he flicked the TV on and turned the volume right down, to see if there was anything on the late news about the missing girl. All the news channels originated from the mainland, and he wanted to know what information they were broadcasting. They both sat in silence for the next few minutes while they assuaged their hunger. It was nice to have someone in the flat with him. No, scratch that. It was nice to have Sierra in the flat with him. He liked the feel of her presence as she sat next to him. Warm and reliable and real. Their silence was companionable, not awkward.

Sierra was the first to speak. "So, what's the news? Is there anything new you can tell me now we're away from public ears?" She glanced up at him, her smile drawn as she pursed her lips. "I mean, you don't have to tell me anything if you're not allowed to talk about it." She popped a hot chip in her mouth and chewed as she waited for his answer. His gaze caught on her sultry mouth and he had to physically pull his eyes away as her tongue came out to lick away a grain of salt. They were oh, so tempting. *Behave.* It was the second time he had to rein in his libido. This was not what tonight was about. Corralling his thoughts, he turned his attention toward the TV, so he wouldn't be distracted by her lips.

"There's been no more sign of Jessica, but I guess you probably knew that. There was one interesting thing I learned tonight at the debrief meeting. You know how I told you they were bringing in a tracker dog to see if they could follow Jessica's trail?" He risked another glance at her.

She nodded, a fascinated look on her face as she chewed slowly on another chip.

"The dog supposedly picked up Jessica's scent. Followed it down the road toward that open field where the kangaroos graze. The same direction we went in."

Sierra sat back, eyes wide. "And...?" she prompted.

"You'll never guess where the dog lost the scent again."

Sierra shook her head slowly, but he could see understanding growing in her eyes.

"Right where you found that candy wrapper."

"Oh, God," she said on a breath. The silence hung heavy between them. "What do they think it means?"

"No one wanted to say it, they wouldn't even speculate, just kept talking about how there were lots of reasons for a dog to lose a scent and how they're going to try again tomorrow morning. So, in the end I threw it out there. I asked the question. Was it possible she was abducted? Don went ballistic, said this was an island of good, law-abiding people and things like that just didn't happen out here."

Sierra sat completely still as she took in this new development. He could see her mind turning it over. He liked her sharp wit, her intelligence. It was stimulating. And she didn't try and hide it, either. He wanted to get to know this woman better. The thought appeared in his head, startling him. It wasn't just her body he found attractive, although that was pretty darn smokin' hot. It was the way she saw the world, her direct manner. There was no artifice about her.

"They're not even considering the idea of an abduction?"

"Yes, they are, but only because I forced the issue. Once I brought it up, one of the mainland detectives, Stanly Moman, agreed with me and said he was already writing that up as an option in his report to his Senior Sergeant."

"Have they come up with a list of suspects, yet?" She tapped her chin as she spoke, and again, it was as if he could see the cogs of her mind turning, and he almost knew what she was going to say next. "Have they checked the sex offender registry?"

"Yes, Olivia is doing that tonight. She'll let us know if there's anyone we need to look at tomorrow."

"Jesus, I can see why the Sarge doesn't even want to admit the possibility. This is a fairly small community. It would certainly put a rip in the fabric of island society if people thought there was a monster living in our midst." Her eyes glazed over, and she seemed to drift off into thoughts of her own. Dark thoughts, if her heavy frown was anything to go by.

Reed wondered how much she knew about this particular topic. How far had she delved into the depths of human depravity, into the soul of a pedophile, to write her exposé on the missing girls so long ago? She definitely knew her stuff. Had it affected her, that knowledge? Was that one of the reasons she'd moved to KI? To get away from corruption and viciousness found in normal society? Don had mentioned she'd fled Adelaide to get away from the effects of an accident, but that didn't feel like it was the whole story. There was more to this woman, much more. And he wanted to find out what emotions, fears and joys ran in the deep waters of Sierra's mind.

"Are you going to hold a press conference tomorrow morning?" she asked, interrupting his musings again. "Is that why you need my input?" When he nodded, she said, "That's good, you need to keep them informed. I'll help you draft some answers to the questions I know they're going to throw at you. If they get a sniff that this might be more than just a little girl lost out in the woods, they'll be like hounds baying for blood. I can give you some tips on how to tackle them, try and damp down the hysteria."

"Good, that would help a lot." Reed was glad he'd asked for her help; she might make the difference between them looking like cops who cared, who knew what they were doing for a change, rather than officious bastards who never gave a straight answer and just alienated the media, instead. For the next ten minutes or so, Sierra talked tactics. What questions the media were likely to ask, how to answer them. How to come across as compassionate, yet also professional and proficient. He enjoyed talking to her, almost as much as he enjoyed the closeness of her. The way her shoulder bumped up against his thigh when she turned to look at him.

The thought he should join her on the floor occurred to him, but then if he moved, that delicious contact might be broken, so he stayed seated on the couch above, looking down on the top of her head.

"Wow, it's getting warm in here." Sierra undid the zip on her hoodie and pulled it off. All she had on underneath was a skin-tight sweater. It was the first time he'd seen her without the bulky tops she liked to wear, and her figure was just as spectacular as he'd imagined. The sweater highlighted her slim shoulders, straight back, trim waist and generous breasts. Reed had to pretend to look at the TV so as not to get caught staring at her curves. He'd seen hints of her breasts beneath the overlarge hoodie, but now the soft fabric draped suggestively, showing them off to full advantage. The sight sent a shot of heat straight to his groin, and it made him stir uncomfortably on the couch.

There was a lull in the conversation and he suddenly needed to fill the silence. Reed was struck by the fact he barely knew anything about this woman. "Tell me about your family."

"What?" Her delicate brows drew together as she glanced up at him.

"I'm interested, that's all." He shrugged, because he couldn't add that he was interested in where she came from. Who and what had formed her dark-auburn hair and equally dark eyes, her seductive mouth and slightly olive skin?

She hesitated, and he thought perhaps she wasn't going to answer. Then she said, "My father was Jewish. My mother is Irish. Quite a combination, really. A Jew and a Catholic." She smiled, and it was clear by her expression that the union had been a volatile one. "I got my looks from my dad, but I get my stubbornness from my mum."

Reed picked up on Sierra's inflection. "You said, your father *was* Jewish?"

"Yeah, he died about five years ago. Had a heart attack."

"Sorry to hear that."

"It's one of those things none of us can avoid. Death and taxes." She began to bunch her food wrapper up into a ball, but then stopped and stared at nothing in particular. "He was a tenacious man, my dad, he made sure my brother and sister and I all grew up with a strong sense of who we were."

Ah, so that answered his question as to whether she had any siblings. He let her keep talking without interrupting.

"He encouraged me to travel to Israel before I started my degree at uni. I took a gap year, and stayed with my grandparents for nearly nine months. It was definitely an eye-opener. Made me even more determined to become a journalist when I got home. That country is such an enigma. There are so many good things happening there, but at the same time so many hurtful, morally wrong things, as well. So many individuals with so many stories that need to be told. I liked being able to tell people's stories." The faraway look remained on her face, but again he picked up her inflection. She *liked* telling people's stories as if she didn't, or couldn't do that, anymore.

"I can tell." She obviously missed her dad, even though she'd been flippant about his death. "Does your mum still live in Adelaide?"

"Yeah, she stayed on in the family home. But she's started spending three or four months of every year back in Ireland, visiting all her aunts and uncles and cousins. If I wasn't still in the area, I wouldn't be surprised if she moved back to Ireland for good. She says it's always felt like home, even though she's lived in Australia since she was four years old."

Reed listened to the sound of her voice, enjoying the timbre of it. She had a deep tone, a little raspy for a woman. But it was nice, like syrup flowing over soft sand. And he liked to watch her lips move as she talked. Her mouth had an almost hypnotic affect. From where he sat, he could see the crown of her head, when she wasn't tilting up to look at him. Her ebony hair was pulled back into a tight ponytail, but after her day spent walking through the scrub looking for a lost girl, strands of hair had pulled loose and were hanging untidily around her face. She looked windswept and windburnt from her day searching. A purely natural beauty, without any pretense or vanity. It was refreshing. Reed had to resist the urge to reach out and smooth down a few of those flyaway tendrils.

Sierra stretched her feet out and then pulled her knees into her chest and stood up in one fluid movement. "Floor's getting a little hard," she said, almost apologetically. "Mind if I join you?"

Reed patted the cushion next to him by way of invitation. But he didn't move over. If she wanted to sit on the couch, then she'd have to do it right next to him. He was already in the middle of the couch. It was a test, of sorts. If she didn't sit next to him, then he had his answer. But if she did…

Her dusky eyes bored into him as she looked first at him and then at the small space on the couch, as if reading his mind. Damn, was he that transparent? Then she sat, settling her nicely-shaped butt into the suede fabric of the cushion. Her knee brushed up against his as she wriggled into place. Was it on purpose? His leg tingled at the touch. His whole body was suddenly aware of just how close she was now. He needed to do something to distract himself. What had they been talking about?

"I take it that your brother and sister don't live around here, then?" It was the first thing that popped into his head.

"No. My sister, Keira, ended up in Hawaii. She was a bit of a gypsy, traveled all over the world for a long time. But she finally met a guy on the Big Island, got married and settled down. And my little brother, Logan has also been traveling the world. I think those two got all the wanderlust genes in the family. I seemed to have missed out. Or else, I'm the only sane one. The only one who stayed at home." She laughed lightly. "I heard Logan was currently in one of the Caribbean Islands, but you can never be sure with my little bro. He's a wildcard, that's for sure." Sierra grinned and caught his eye, and their gazes locked. He couldn't look away, and it seemed, neither could she. The grin faded on her lips.

This was not the right time, or the right place, but he couldn't help himself. Someone, or something had taken over his mind, was directing his body. He was no longer in charge of his own actions. He had a beautiful woman sitting right next to him, and he wanted to kiss her. So badly it made his lips twitch.

He leaned towards her.

She didn't pull away. Just watched him with those dark, impervious eyes. But now they weren't quite so impervious. Now, there was a hunger glowing in their depths. Her lips parted ever so slightly.

Reed brought his hand up to cup her cheek in his palm. She continued to stare at him.

Then she leaned in and met him halfway. Their mouths collided.

CHAPTER NINE

He tasted salty from the chips, and his mouth was warm and inviting. His lips crushed down on hers. This was no hesitant, tenuous kiss. He wanted her. And, surprisingly, she wanted him. Her cheeks were hot beneath the gentle touch of his thumb. And her own hands came up, her fingers burying themselves in his dark hair. It really was as thick and lush as it looked.

It'd been a long time since Sierra had kissed a man. Since she'd even wanted to kiss a man. But her body hadn't forgotten how to do it, as she feared. Instead, it was like she was making up for lost time. She was burning up inside, as if Reed had set a fire in her mouth and the volcanic heat was flowing down her throat and into her veins. It was almost embarrassing, the way she responded to him, but now that they'd started, she couldn't stop.

His tongue explored her mouth, and she wanted to melt with the pleasure of his lips on hers. One hand drifted down from the nape of his neck, over the sharp edge of his shoulder blades and followed the ridged muscles of his back. He was just as powerful and hardened beneath his shirt as she'd imagined. A shiver of anticipation rolled through her. What would he look like without his shirt on? She had a sudden, crazy urge to rip the buttons open and tear the shirt from his body, like some wanton woman from one of those bad historical romances she sometimes read. Instead, her fingers found the waistband of his pants and she began to tug at the shirt, untucking it until she found the skin she was craving, letting her fingers absorb the heat of him.

She had to see what was under his shirt. She fumbled with the buttons of his uniform, finally undoing the last one. Then she slowly spread the garment apart, pushing it down over each of his shoulders. The broad planes of his chest were revealed, and the corded muscles of his neck and shoulders tensed as he shrugged the shirt all the way off. And then his glorious pecs and abs were revealed, his biceps bulged as he strained and moved to rise above her. She swiveled so she lay along the couch, with him stretched out beside her. He was one of the most drop-dead gorgeous men she'd ever seen. All that honey-colored skin, soft like velvet over the hardened muscles of his torso. To top it all off, a large tattoo spiraled over his left shoulder and down onto his pec. It looked to be a tribal design, something to do with his Maori heritage, perhaps. It made him look dangerous. She had to touch him. Her hand was on his neck, running over his collar bone, tracing the lines of the tattoo. Down his chest, then hovered over one hardened nipple.

Reed groaned at her touch and her throat tightened at the sound. Closing her eyes, she tipped backwards so her head rested on the arm of the couch. Now she could feel the weight of his chest pushing down on her and her nipples peaked as she savored the sensation. He ran a hand up the side of her chest, his palm grazing the edge of her breast and she wanted to arch into him. Wanted him to do it again. His mouth left her lips and trailed hot kisses down her neck, so searing it felt like he was branding her. Was this what it used to be like with Jake? She couldn't remember. And at the moment she didn't really care.

Reed's phone rang loudly, and they both jumped at the unexpected sound. Silently, selfishly, she hoped he wouldn't answer it.

"Damn," he whispered, his mouth moving against hers.

She didn't want this to end, and her hand clasped the back of his neck tightly as he hovered over her.

"I'm sorry." He lifted his head and caught her gaze, regret showing in every line on his face.

"Me too." Sierra put a hand to his naked chest and pushed gently.

He untangled himself from her legs and walked over to the kitchen to answer his phone, picking up his discarded shirt on the way. Sierra sat up and rearranged her clothing, drawing in a quiet breath as she did so. Reed had his back to her as he answered the call, and she watched the muscles of his deltoids ripple beneath the tattoo as he shrugged into his shirt. She could watch that view all day. What was it about a topless man that was so bloody sexy? Perhaps the phone call had been precipitous after all. The saying, *saved by the bell* echoed through her head. This had been getting out of control. She'd kissed a few men since she'd divorced Jake, been on a few dates, but her heart had never been in it.

Of course, then there'd been Blake. She'd met him because she was heavily involved in the Friends of the Glossies, a volunteer group that wanted to help preserve the large, beautiful, endangered birds. She'd been chosen to show him the protected nesting sites. It'd been a brief but intense encounter and she was almost glad when it ended. If only Blake had kept it that way, instead of becoming demanding and just a little bit creepy when he'd moved back to the island. For the hundredth time, she wished he hadn't taken that job as an island ranger. Which reminded her, she still hadn't returned his phone calls.

But her fling with Blake didn't even begin to compare with these few minutes she spent kissing Reed. Her lips still tingled from where his mouth had crushed down onto hers, and she had to stop her fingers reaching up to touch them. To make sure it'd all been real.

Reed's voice became louder, and she finally returned to reality and began to listen to what he was saying. He was striding over to the TV, turning up the volume. The late-night news was on. An image of KI flashed up on the screen, and then an image of the missing girl, Jessica, was overlaid onto it. Looked like the news had already broken on the mainland. Reed covered the phone with one hand as they both listened intently to the program. The news anchor gave the facts about when Jessica had last been seen and then showed footage of the SES volunteers in their orange uniforms searching and calling through the bush. Just as Sierra thought that might be the end of the report they flashed back to the anchor, who said, "Police are still treating this as a case of a child who wandered away from her family. But some people are already asking the question, is there more to it? Could this be another abduction case in the making?"

"Damn," Reed said for the second time.

"Yes, but I'm not surprised," Sierra said quietly. The mood in the room became somber as they were both reminded why they were really here.

"I should go," she said. Reed needed to get some rest. And so did she.

"You could stay here." His eyes were hopeful, but they both knew what her answer was going to be.

"Thanks, but I've got a friend in Kingscote, I was going to ring her and see if she could put me up for the night." And that reminded her, she needed to phone Sam and ask him to feed her cats and put her chickens back in their pen before it got too late. Sierra stood up and grabbed her hoodie from the floor, pulling it on over her head.

"Are you sure?" He came and stood next to her, close. She liked the fact she had to tilt her head a little to look up into his face. Her gaze traced the outline of his jaw and up his strong cheekbones, then settled on his slightly crooked nose. She wanted to reach out and run her finger down that nose, to feel the bumps and ridges. Ask him how he'd come to break it.

Instead she nodded and picked up her coat from the back of the couch and forced herself to walk toward the door.

"See you tomorrow. I'll meet you early, at the fire station? To help you prep for the press meeting?"

"That would be great," he replied. But he wasn't a coward, like her. As she turned to walk out the door, he grabbed her around the waist and pulled her in. He stared down into her face for many unreadable seconds, then kissed her, a comfortable, familiar kiss. Letting her know he wasn't going to apologize for what'd happened between them. Then he let her go.

CHAPTER TEN

Reed drew in a deep breath. Then another. In through his nose and out through his mouth. Calm. He needed to stay calm. For Don's sake, as much as anything else. He could see Don was seething, but holding it in, nonetheless.

The press conference had just ended, and Reed, Don, and Sierra retreated to the safety of the fire station to collect themselves, while the media packed up their equipment and moved on. They were in the kitchen area of the CFS, and he leaned his hip up against one of the laminate benches. It was after nine in the morning, and Reed was chafing to get back out and help with the search, but he'd been caught up with his boss, helping him field the media frenzy. Eric and Olivia were already out there doing their job, along with the extra four officers from the mainland, and it galled him that he was stuck here. Reed wanted to be there when the tracker dog went back to the family house, to see if it could pick up the trail again. But this was a necessary evil, and at least Sierra had agreed to help them.

"Those fuckers, how dare they imply we're not doing our job properly?" Don couldn't hold his outrage in a moment longer. "How dare they say we don't care about that poor little girl." Don's face was turning an interesting shade of purple.

"I know, Sarge, but Sierra did warn us." He turned and flicked a quick glance at her. She was standing with her back against the wall, out of the way, perhaps letting Don get rid of some of his temper.

"Yes, and thank God she did." Don snorted, but seemed to lose some of the heat from his temper. "I'm sorry, Sierra, but that was a pack of vultures out there. Hyenas out for blood, and they didn't really care whose. I know it was a long time ago, but how could you possibly have been a part of that?"

Today Sierra was dressed in long hiking pants, with a pair of weatherproof hiking boots on her feet. Imminently more suitable for continuing the search through the bush. She must've borrowed them from her friend last night. She still had on the bulky hoodie from yesterday, and Reed's pulse spiked briefly as he remembered what she looked like without that large covering. Her slim shoulders and the shape of her collarbone.

"They're just doing their job, Sarge. You have to remember that. They want the truth as much as we do." Her voice was quiet and measured. Clearly not wanting to enter into an argument with the police chief.

"I'm not so sure of that," Don huffed. "But I do owe you thanks. If you hadn't prepped me on how to answer some of those questions, I might've looked like a bit of a fool out there. It's been a while since I last did a press conference."

"You did a good job," Sierra said soothingly.

Actually, Reed had been surprised at how good a job Don had done. He'd remained cool and determined, showed just the right amount of sincerity and compassion. Sierra had remained inside the fire station, out of sight. But Reed stood behind his boss as he faced the wall of microphones and cameras outside, and even he'd felt a little intimidated by it all. By the barrage of questions, and the aggression of some of the journalists. He couldn't reconcile that mob out there with what Sierra confessed to do. It wasn't the same thing at all, in his mind.

"And we'll have to do it all over again this evening," Don complained.

"Hopefully we'll have some good news to give them by then." Reed sincerely wished they'd have something a little more concrete by tonight. If they didn't, then perhaps the accusations from some of the journalists that they weren't doing their jobs properly might actually hold some weight.

Don's phone rang, and he walked over to a corner of the room to answer it. Reed went over to where Sierra was hovering in the corner.

"I'd like to add my thanks to Don's. You were a good help." He stood close, mainly because he liked the feel of her presence. He caught a whiff of something floral, shampoo perhaps. It was a cheerful aroma, vital and alive, like her.

"What?" Don's loud exclamation made Reed look up sharply. "Are you sure?" They both stared at Don, wondering what was going on. "Where did you say this was?" Don's body-language had gone from rigid and angry to rigid and alert. He stood in profile, and Reed could see his mustache quivering with reined-in exasperation. They listened as Don asked a few more questions, then he gestured for Reed to bring him a pen and paper. He hurried to hand him his own small note pad and pen he always kept in his police vest. "I'm sending Officer Reed Kapua over right now. Wait for him to get there. And please don't touch anything. And don't go near the area until the officer gets there."

Reed stiffened. An icy sliver of fear filled his gut. *Oh, no. Please no. Let it not be that.* Sierra tensed beside him as they both stared at Don, terrified of what he was going to say.

"One of the search teams just found something. Bones. They think they might be human," Don said.

Reed expelled a loud breath. Damn, he'd been thinking the worst—that they'd found the little girl's body. But bones meant the body had been there for a long time, way too long to be little Jessica. He glanced at Sierra and saw relief wash over her face, as well.

"Bones? Human bones?" said Sierra, as if repeating the words might make them more real. "Here, on the island?"

"Yes, I believe so," Don replied, the irritation plain in his voice. "Which is just what we didn't need. Another complication. Shit, what's going on here?" Don's last question seemed to be rhetorical, and he began to pace to and fro at the end of the kitchen.

"Where?" Sierra asked the question on the tip of Reed's tongue before he was able to utter it.

"Over by the Glossies nesting area." Don waved the small piece of paper in the air, where he'd written down the instructions.

"Do you mean the one on Binney's Track?"

"Yes, that sounds about right." Don turned to Reed. "I need you to get out there now, and I'll need your report ASAP. If it is human bones, and not just some dead animal, then I'll need to get that forensics guy they sent over from the mainland to take a look. With all this hysteria being stirred up by a missing girl and talk of abductions, I wouldn't be surprised if it's just a dead sheep or a fox." Don grimaced and narrowed his eyes. "But I know you've got some skills in that area, so I trust you to handle it for now."

"Right away." He was surprised by Don's words of confidence. Less than a week ago, Reed had thought he might have a long road ahead to get his boss to trust him. He was the new guy on the block, and it was human nature for Don to want Reed to prove himself before he became an integrated part of the unit. But this sudden nightmarish turn of events was putting the squeeze on them all, and perhaps it was forcing Don to accept him much quicker than he once would. The Sarge was correct, this was a huge complication, one they didn't need right now. It'd take the focus off the search for the missing girl. But someone needed to get over there and get the situation under control.

"I'll show you the way, if you like." Sierra stepped forward. "I know where it is. I've worked with the Glossies before."

Reed hesitated. Was that a good idea? Getting her involved in a search for a missing girl was one thing, but if they were human bones? That was a whole other level. And the implications were far-reaching. It could mean there was a killer on the island.

Don's phone rang again, its urgent tone cutting through the silence.

"Yes, yes, take her with you." Don waved in their general direction. "Now get going. I've got to answer this, it's the Senior Sergeant looking for an update, and he's going to be pissed when I give him this news." Don turned his back on them and effectively dismissed them both.

It looked like Reed had no say in it, Sierra was coming whether he liked it or not. "Right, let's go."

Sierra grabbed her coat and backpack from the bench as he led the way past the two big fire trucks, hunkered in the large garage area and out the back door, to where the police Land Cruiser was parked in the rear lot.

"Which way is it?" he asked as she hopped into the passenger seat beside him.

"Take a right out on the main road, I'll direct you from there."

"Got it," he replied, steering the car out of the carpark.

"Do you really think it's human bones?" Sierra worried her bottom lip as she stared out the front windshield.

"We won't know till we get there. Why?"

"Because the more I think about it, a Glossy nesting area would be a great place to hide a body."

"Okay. First of all, what's a Glossy?"

"A Glossy Black Cockatoo. They're an endangered bird, native to the island. I volunteer for the Friends of The Glossies. We record all of their nesting sites, make sure they stay protected."

"So why would it be a good place to hide a body?"

"I'm sure there are lots of great places to hide a body, if you wanted to, on the island. There are a lot of isolated tracts of scrub that've never seen a human footprint. But we try and keep the Glossy nesting area's a secret; the less people who know where they are the better. We need the birds to remain as undisturbed as possible. We often put up signs warning people to stay out." She held up a hand as he started to protest. "I know that doesn't always work, but most tourists respect our signs and our wildlife."

Reed was more than skeptical, but he held his tongue.

"And sometimes, if we get the funding and the time, we erect fences around the area, as an extra step to keep people and predatory animals out. This is one of the sites that has a fence around it."

"So, you're saying someone could've chosen to bury a body there because you're almost guaranteed no one will go in there?"

"Something along those lines, yes." Sierra looked decidedly unhappy about that scenario. "The Friends of The Glossies only go in there once a year, during breeding. And even then, we try to make as little impact as possible. The rest of the time the place is left untouched.

They drove the rest of the fifteen minutes it took to get to the site in relative silence, with Sierra giving him instructions when necessary. Having Sierra sitting next to him in the car, it was almost like a re-run of yesterday morning. And he was just as aware of her presence as he'd been yesterday. Even more so now he knew what she tasted like. That kiss kept replaying in his mind, even as he followed Sierra's instructions and pretended his whole body wasn't pulsing with the need to do it again.

His phone rang loudly in the silence of the cab.

"Do you want me to answer that for you?" Sierra queried, reaching for his phone in the middle console.

"Check who it is, first," Reed replied. He really needed to sort the Bluetooth connection out in this car, so he could easily answer his phone.

"Caller ID says, Dad," she said, glancing up from the screen.

"Leave it. I'll get back to him later."

She gave him a quick, curious look, then replaced the phone in between their two seats. Silence descended again.

He really should call his folks. He'd promised he would as soon as he was settled. But who would've guessed things would get quite this crazy on the island? It was because of his father, and the things he'd sacrificed in his life, that Reed was able to become a police officer. He owed his parents, even if they'd never acknowledge it.

His father, Nikau, had worked hard, taken a safe, dependable job as a plumber and put in long hours to make sure his family, his sons, had the best childhood he could give them. Nikau was a leader amongst his culture, people looked up to him, and he gave back to the community with both hands and a strong heart in many different cultural projects, to make sure his people's heritage was preserved. And he'd instilled that same strong sense of belonging to their Maori heritage in both Reed and his brother, Seb.

One of the hardest things his father had ever done was to move his family away from their home near Waikaremoana, where his tribe, the Tahoe came from, to the big city of

Auckland. He'd done it to get Seb away from the growing influence of the Mongrel Mob and the scourge of alcohol and drugs that went along with it. The boys hated the big city at first, and hated their father for uprooting them and sending them to some public school where they knew no one, had no friends. But now with hindsight, Reed could see it was the best thing Nikau could've done for his boys. It freed them to find their full potential, had taken them away from the trap of being stuck in a small town, with nowhere to go but down.

Nikau always encouraged Reed to follow his passion, to fulfill his potential. And he'd been the first to cheer Reed on when he got into the Academy in Melbourne.

He would call him just as soon as he got home tonight. Right now, he needed to focus elsewhere.

Every now and then, they passed signs of the search for Jessica. A flash of an orange uniform off the side of the road, as another team searched a grid area. A local couple parked by the side of the road, handing out hot tea and coffee to the searchers. A sign noting a rally point for a particular team, telling them where to meet. The camaraderie from last night was gone now, replaced by a sense of foreboding. Reed wanted to ask Sierra if she'd received anymore threatening letters from her stalker. But by the look on her face he knew she wouldn't appreciate it, so he let the topic lie. For now. It did need to be addressed, however. She couldn't continue like that, never knowing when another threat was going to land in her mailbox. He would make sure this was properly looked into. As soon as he had the time. He wished they could go back to that easy time last night, when the apprehension and disquiet had retreated for a few special moments. Go back to kissing her.

Sooner than he thought, they were on Binney's Track, then Sierra pointed to something in the distance. A group of people hovering around the edge of the road, most wearing the bright orange high-vis vests given out by the SES search teams. Reed pulled off the road and parked the car.

"Oh, that's Sam and Debbie." Sierra pointed to an older couple coming toward them. "My neighbors," she clarified when he gave her a confused look. Of course, now he remembered. Sierra jumped out of the car to greet her friends, and he followed. She embraced the gray-haired woman, and the tall man patted her back in a fatherly gesture. It was nice to see Sierra had someone who appeared to care about her. Up till now, Reed had thought she'd seemed quite alone. He was glad that wasn't the case.

"This is Officer Kapua," she said, and the tall man, Sam, held out his hand to greet him.

"I've heard about you. The new cop on the block is hard to miss," Sam said gruffly. "Sad to meet you under such circumstances, though."

A car approached down the dirt track, driving fast, straight toward them, stopping all conversation. It was a white four-wheel-drive with a green National Parks and Wildlife sign on the side.

"Oh, shit," Sierra said softly as a young, blonde, good-looking man stepped out of the car. She ducked her head and moved behind Reed. Was she hiding from this guy? He had on a dark-green weatherproof coat and khaki pants, and he was pulling on a cap with the same Wildlife logo as the car as he strode towards them.

"I'm Blake Tendall, the ranger in charge of this area." He extended his hand toward Reed. "I just heard the news over the two-way. I came over as fast as I could, to see if I can be of any assistance." He cast a quick glance around the rest of the small gathering, his gaze stopping when he came to Sierra, eyes widening with surprise.

"Sierra?" Blake seemed to blurt out her name without conscious thought. Reed watched the interplay with interest.

The guy looked as if he'd been caught off-guard.

"Blake," she said, acknowledging him with a nod. She was polite, but aloof. There was definitely something going on here. Something he needed to find out about. Later.

The kid had his mask of efficiency back up in place within seconds.

"What can I do to help?" he asked.

"I was just talking to Sam and his wife, Debbie." Reed gestured to the older couple who'd also been watching the interplay between Sierra and this new guy with as much interest as he was.

"Yes, we were the ones who found the bones. Shall we show you?"

"Yes, lead the way, Sam. Can you three please stay behind us?" Reed asked. "The rest of you, please stay where you are," Reed said to the gathering crowd. "We need to keep the scene as clean as possible." Some of them nodded in agreement, but most of them stared at him speculatively. Weighing him up. The new cop. Reed slipped his hand into his pocket as they followed a barely-there trail into the dense scrub by the edge of the road. His fingers found the warm shape of his lucky penny. He let the worn edges slip though his fingertips. It calmed him, as it always did. Reminded him things would turn out the way they would, but there wasn't a hell of a lot he could do about it. Stressing about things he couldn't control wouldn't do him any good at all.

He was glad Sam was leading the way; he would've been lost in the first few minutes. The bush was thick and dense, overhung with the high branches of the towering eucalyptus trees above. It took them less than five minutes to come up against a wire fence line. How the hell were they going to climb this? Now he understood Sierra's comments about it being one of the least likely places to look for a body. How would a killer get the body over this fence? He glanced back and saw Sierra, her face pinched and unhappy, with Blake following silently behind her. What was going on between those two?

"There's a gate around here." Sam indicated the direction.

"Yes, but not many people know about it, we like to discourage everybody from going in here," Blake called out from behind them. Trying to be helpful or trying to exhibit his knowledge? A bit like a peacock fluffing up his feathers. Reed couldn't decide. But he was definitely getting the vibe the ranger was here to prove a point. He was young and enthusiastic, but maybe he was taking his job just a little too seriously. Either that, or he was showing off for Sierra's sake. By the look on her face, she wasn't in the least bit impressed. Reed followed close behind Sam as they circumnavigated the fence.

"We almost didn't go in," Sam conceded. "But then Deb said what if the little girl had crawled under the fence? Or got through one of the holes. Wombats sometimes dig under the fence, and they can leave a hole big enough for a child to climb through. Deb said what if she was lying in there, hurt and couldn't move, and we bypassed her because we didn't want to disturb the Glossies? But I was really doubtful. I mean how would a little girl even get all the way out here?"

"I said we were told to search every square inch of our area, and that's what we were going to do," Deb interrupted. But we wouldn't have found the bones if we hadn't been searching in the grid pattern, either." She looked at Reed. "You know what that is, of course, the grid pattern?"

He nodded. It meant each person in the team searched in a long line, all keeping parallel and at a designated distance from each other. The gap between searchers changed depending on who or what they were looking for and the type of terrain. He guessed in this case they were probably less than ten meters apart.

"Because I was holding my line," Sam said. "I stepped over a log, rather than going around it, which is what I would've done if I'd been out walking normally. That's when I saw them, poking out from beneath the log." He gave a visible shudder as he spoke. "My heart nearly stopped beating for a second. Then I yelled for Deb to come and look."

"What did you see?" Sierra spoke for the first time.

"Fingers. A hand. I saw a hand poking up out of the ground." Sam's face went pale at the memory. "I think something had been digging around beneath the log. You know, like an animal. Because the earth had been disturbed. Perhaps whatever it was uncovered the...body."

"Did you touch anything? Disturb the site?" Reed knew his tone was too curt, but he needed to know.

"No. I knelt down to get a better look. But as soon as I saw what it was, I backed the hell away."

Reed could sympathize. Most normal people never got to see a dead body. And when they did, they were completely freaked out by it.

"Here's the gate." Sam stopped next to a section of the fence, but Reed couldn't see anything at first. Then as Sam's fingers went to work unhooking loops of wire he began to make out the cleverly camouflaged gate. If you didn't know it was there, a person would've been hard pressed to find it with the naked eye. Now he knew it was here, he could see the grass flattened around the entrance, where the search group had gone through.

"Who knows about this gate?" Reed asked.

"Only a select few," Blake replied, as Sam was still busy unwiring the gate for them. "Us, the Park Rangers, of course. And all of the Friends of The Glossies." Blake indicated to Sam and Debbie. "Plus a few others, mainly people interested in the birds or the habitat."

Reed's mind went into overdrive as he digested this fact. If there really were human remains inside this enclosure, then it might narrow down the field of suspects considerably. Sam finally got the gate open, and Reed followed him through the narrow opening.

"It's over here." Sam motioned for Reed to follow him. The undergrowth was thick in here, coming up past his knees. And the towering trees—Sierra had told him they were sugar gums—grew thickly as well, their large trunks making for an obstacle course as he wound his way between them. One of the trees had fallen and now lay sprawled ahead of them. The large, dead log was almost too big to step over, and now Reed suddenly understood what Sam had meant about wanting to go around it. Sam walked along the length of the log, peering over it at times, until he found what he was looking for. He stepped back and pointed. A chill ran down Reed's spine at the look of grim distress on the older man's face.

Sierra and Deb stopped a few feet away, but Blake followed. Reed waved a hand to make sure he kept well back. The last thing they needed was more boots trampling all over the place.

He nodded at Sam and stepped gingerly over the log a few feet down from where he was pointing. His eyes raked the ground on the other side of the dead tree. Long grass curled up around the base, and vines and other undergrowth tangled along the side. But there was an area where the growth wasn't as thick. As if the ground had been broken up a while ago, and the plants were only now coming back. Then Reed saw the spot Sam described. Damp earth, dark and loamy, had been dug up. Clods of soil and grass were scattered around and a dark space opened up beneath the log. What kind of animal had done the digging? Reed couldn't be sure. A fox, perhaps, looking for a tasty meal? Or one of the many large, feral cats who prowled the island.

And there, in an open patch that'd been uncovered by the

digging, Reed could indeed see something sticking up. He took out the little Maglite torch he always carried in his vest pocket and shone the flashlight on the area, hunkering down on his haunches to get a closer look. It was gloomy and hard to see in the dank undergrowth.

Damn, damn, damn. The bones were definitely of a human hand poking up out of the dark soil. Reed moved the beam of light over the area. It came to rest on a smooth, rounded lump a little farther under the log.

Reed swallowed hard as his gut roiled at the sight. Part of a human skull was looking back at him.

This was his worst nightmare.

Not only were the bones definitely human, but if he wasn't completely mistaken, they were also of a child. They were too small to be an adult. But there was no way this could be little Jessica. These bones had been here for a year, at least, to get to this level of decomposition. Jessica had only been missing for twenty-four hours.

It was another child.

This case had just taken another, much more sinister, turn.

"Oh, Jesus," Blake said from behind him. "I think I'm going to be sick." He stumbled away into the bush, and Reed heard retching sounds from behind a large tree. Poor kid, it must be the first dead body he'd seen. Reed felt a sliver of callous amusement go through his gut. Served him right for wanting to poke his nose in. Perhaps he wouldn't be so quick to be overzealous with his authority next time.

CHAPTER ELEVEN

It was hard to see her mailbox in the dark, even with her headlights directed at the row of boxes for the Snellings Beach population, all lined up along the roadside. Sierra counted three from the end and lifted the flap, then gingerly put her hand in to retrieve her mail. It'd be just her luck if a large huntsman had taken up residence in there again. But there were no hairy, arachnid legs running over her hand tonight, and she breathed out a sigh of relief as she withdrew the bunch of envelopes from inside.

There were three letters today, and Sierra flicked on the internal cab light of her car as she settled back in the driver's seat.

Her breath froze in her throat as she rifled through them. The last one in the stack was the familiar bland white envelope with the sterile, black print on the front.

Another letter from her stalker.

Sierra bit her lip and stared at the letter. Then she threw it down on the passenger seat. She couldn't deal with it right now. It'd been a shit of a day and she was exhausted. She had a pretty good idea what the letter would say, anyway. More of the same threats and diatribe.

Putting the car into gear, she turned down the road toward

Snellings Beach. It was late, after ten P.M. already. But she'd decided she needed to come home tonight, even though Kylie had offered up her spare bedroom again if she wanted it. She needed to check on her cats, and the chickens. Kylie had been such a sweetheart about her staying last night, and they'd sat up chatting for over an hour after she arrived from Reed's place. They'd cracked open a bottle of red and talked about the only news anyone on the island was discussing—the missing five-year-old girl. Of course, Sierra hadn't mentioned where she'd had dinner, but she did tell Kylie she needed to get up early, as she'd offered to help Sergeant Coldwater with the news conference in the morning. Sierra was glad she'd stayed at her friend's house last night. It'd helped ground her again, after that impetuous kiss with Reed. Bring her back down to reality. Got her mind off Reed and his lips. Hot, sensual lips, that had set her body aflame.

Even so, Sierra had been looking forward to seeing Reed this morning. Couldn't stop the nervous butterflies bouncing around in her belly when he'd strode into the fire house, flashing her a knowing grin, with the dimple dancing. But the day had quickly descended into dark madness. Finding those bones had really rattled Sierra. And Blake turning up. That'd rattled her, as well. She'd made sure to try and avoid him all day, which'd been fairly easy, as he'd been too busy being overly-helpful to Reed, and the rest of the cops who'd showed up later. But Blake had cast her more than one curious glance when he thought she wasn't looking. And sometimes, there was more than mere speculation in those glances, sometimes she thought she saw a hint of resentful spite.

She was feeling a tad guilty that she still hadn't returned his phone calls, or his texts. But then she reminded herself she wasn't about to start pandering to him if he was going to act like a sulky child. For some reason, she couldn't completely rid herself of that little nagging voice in the back of her head that kept prodding at her. There was no way he could be responsible for the break-in at her house. It was stupid to even consider it. She'd tried to let him down easy, but he'd have to man-up and accept she wasn't interested in him anymore. End of story.

Consciously moving her mind onto another topic, she remembered the look on Reed's face when he'd confided to her that the bones belonged to a child. His regretful grimace and gray pallor told her he was just as shocked and saddened as she was. He said they'd been buried for at least a year, by the looks of it. But he could be wrong, they'd have to wait for the coroner to confirm before they could make it official. Sierra's internal alarms started to jangle. Immediately, the documents spread out on her bed had jumped into her mind. Those two missing girls. Surely, they couldn't be related. Could they? Those girls and these bones? Surely it was too much of a coincidence? Then why couldn't Sierra rid herself of this terrible feeling of disquiet?

As Sierra turned into her driveway, she made a decision. Reed had told her they'd have to wait for DNA evidence to prove who the bones belonged to. But that could take weeks. Tonight, the media had started asking the hard questions after the discovery of the bones had been made public. Demanding to know if the police thought Jessica had been abducted and wasn't just lost. The whole island community was becoming scared and outraged. Asking whether it could be one of their own who'd done this? Or was it some off-islander who'd come over on a day trip for a thrill-kill?

She decided to delve more deeply into this case, use her own contacts to find out more. Because if they were connected...Well, wouldn't that open up a can of worms. And perhaps Sierra might be able to help find the killer.

Sierra glanced nervously at the front of her house as she

drew up. Then let out a whoosh of air when the security light flashed on. she smiled as her two cats got up off the front door-mat and gave her that cat-stare that said *Where the hell have you been?* Even though Sam had fed Jon and Snow for her last night, they would've been most displeased at having to spend the night without her comfy bed to curl up on. At least everything seemed to be back to normal tonight at her house.

Sierra got out of her car and unlocked the front door. The cats rushed past her into the house, another good sign that all was well. She needed a glass of wine, some food, and a hot shower, in that order.

She'd spent most of the rest of the day with Reed, as he waited for the forensics officer to arrive. They roped off the area with police tape, and he'd got the names and addresses of everyone in the search team, as he wanted to interview them all later. Eventually, Don put in an appearance after lunch, chaperoning the man from the state coroner's office, who'd come to retrieve the bones. Reed had finally taken Sam and Debbie back to the police station to get their official statements and dropped Sierra back in town around mid-afternoon, where she'd re-joined the search for missing Jessica. But the mood of the searchers was somber and restrained. Word had already got around about the discovery of human remains. And there was still absolutely no sign of the missing girl.

Tom Hubbard had once again been in charge of her search group. This time she'd managed to get him alone for a few minutes at the end of the day. He hadn't said much, had let her do all the talking. But he looked even more haggard and under pressure than before. Sierra felt sorry for him and she'd disregarded her silly anxiety from the day before about the candies he was offering around. She almost regretted mentioning them to Reed last night. But she knew that sometimes even the smallest clue could be important, no matter how much she thought it was of no consequence.

Evan had been nowhere to be seen this afternoon. He must've joined another search group. She doubted he'd given up, not after his fervent speech yesterday about how desperate he was to help find the little girl. She didn't want to admit it, but she was almost thankful. She couldn't put her finger on exactly why she was glad not to have run into Evan today. Perhaps it had something to do with how he'd seemed a little too zealous yesterday. It'd spooked Sierra for some unknown reason.

Even though the day had been hard to get through, and even though the sight of that small, helpless hand sticking out of the soil would probably never leave her, a small part of Sierra had enjoyed working with Reed. Enjoyed being by his side. She'd liked watching him at work. He was calm and unruffled. Had an aura around him that made everyone want to trust him. And, holy hell, didn't he look good in that police uniform. Strong and tall, masculine and rugged. And now that she knew what those lips tasted like, what a killer body he had under that uniform, she had to stop herself reaching out to touch him on more than one occasion. The hot flash of desire that shot through her at the sight of his biceps bulging as he shifted some heavy debris away from the crime scene had been inappropriate and ill-timed, but she couldn't stop it.

She shook her head to rid it of images of Reed Kapua. First thing tomorrow morning, Sierra was going to start making some more phone calls. There'd been two contacts who'd been either unwilling or unable to take her calls earlier in the week. Sierra was going to call in a favor from Jen. Perhaps her friend might be able to lend some of her editorial weight behind a second request to speak to these men. One of them was the first officer on the scene when the original girl was taken. He was still on the force, but had moved to another unit in Adelaide. And the next was the detective in charge of the second case. She had some questions she wanted to ask about what sort of evidence had been found at the scenes of both missing kids.

Which meant she really needed to get to bed sooner rather than later. Sierra always left her fireplace set and ready to light, so all she needed to do was strike a match to the tinder and then close the door. The house would soon heat up. She pulled a tin of baked beans out of the cupboard and tipped them into a saucepan to heat, and popped some bread in the toaster. Not a gourmet meal by any means, but hot and filling. While she waited for the beans to heat, she grabbed the flashlight she always kept under the kitchen windowsill and went out to check on her chickens. Even though it was late and they would all be asleep, with their heads tucked under their wings, she wanted to make sure they had food for the morning, and that Sam had secured the door to the chicken run properly when he'd closed it up last night.

She switched on the rear veranda light and followed the beam of her flashlight down the gravel pathway to the chicken run. All was quiet and serene, as she flashed her light through the doorway into their little roosting house. One of them—probably Cindi—gave a few low clucks at being disturbed, but the rest of them continued to slumber on peacefully. Sierra opened the metal box next to the chicken run and filled a plastic container with grain, scattering it over the dirt floor of the open area of the run. The girls had laid two eggs for her, which she would add to her baked-bean dinner. Happy that all was good in the world of her bantams, she went back into the house.

The beans were bubbling on the stove, and the smell of warm toast filled the kitchen. Quickly adding the eggs to a small frying pan, she put two more logs of wood on the fire, and then poured herself a glass of red wine. By that time, her simple meal was ready, and she took it to the dining table to eat. The laptop she'd borrowed from Sam and Debbie sat on the table, reminding her she needed to follow up with the insurance company to see if they'd paid out on her claim yet. When they did, she'd have to go to Adelaide for the day to buy herself a new computer.

She may as well check her emails while she ate, to see if anything new had come in from Jen. Spooning beans into her mouth with one hand, she fired up the old computer and waited. And waited. It was amazing how quickly she'd gotten used to her lightning-fast Mac laptop, and now she became impatient if something took more than a few seconds to load. It was only a few years ago that she'd owned one of these clunkers. The world had become so impatient now, expecting everything to happen instantaneously, including herself.

Finally, her emails loaded and she began scrolling, sifting through the mostly junk mail.

Oh, shit.

There was an email from the stalker.

Which was unusual. He seemed to prefer the old-fashioned letter in the mailbox method. But he had sent her a few emails over the years. She knew it was the same person, his prose was unmistakable.

Should she open it? The white envelope was sitting on the hallway table, unopened. This was highly unusual. He'd never sent her an email and a letter at the same time. And this was the third contact in a week. Up till now, she hadn't heard from him in over six months. Had even dared to hope he'd gotten tired of harassing her and stopped sending his vile hate mail. Was he upping the ante for some reason?

Sierra clicked on the email and took a sip of her wine as she read the words on her screen. She'd expected to see more of the same old verbal haranguing she was used to, and it was definitely there, but there was also something different about this one.

If you knew what's good for you, you'd stop trying to resurrect your journalism career. I know what you're up to. It's all about vilifying more innocent police officers, who are just trying to do their jobs, isn't it?

It was almost as if he knew she'd begun investigating the missing children case. But that would be impossible. Wouldn't it? The only people who were aware she was even looking into it were her and Jen. And the few police and other professionals she'd contacted for her research. Unless this stalker somehow had an informant. Or unless he was one of the people she'd contacted. Could her stalker possibly be one of the people on the inside of this case? The idea raised goose bumps on her forearms, and she had to put her wine glass down as her hands began to tremble. Could it really be possible that she was getting closer than she thought?

But her stalker had appeared after those articles she'd published twelve years ago, about the girls from Port Pirie. Why would he be worried about her investigating this new case? Unless they were somehow linked. And if they were linked, was it because he was still trying to protect someone or something from the first case?

Sierra had often wondered about her stalker. Who he was and what his motives were. He'd always been decidedly vague as to what it was about her articles that upset him the most. Was it just the fact that he hated all journalists, and had zeroed in on her as a target for his fury? She knew of journalists with similar stories, of a nutcase who'd held them personally responsible for a story they'd filed in a newspaper.

You are merely a purveyor of lies and innuendo. All you do is twist the truth to suit yourself. Why do you believe you're so much better than everyone else? Your shit stinks just as much as the rest of us. You should look in the mirror, Sierra. Hold yourself to the same scrutiny you subject others to.

Which was all a complete load of hogwash.

You have no right to persecute the police the way you do. They are only doing their jobs the best way they know how. You'd better watch your back, Sierra, or someone might just start persecuting you.

Not for the first time, Sierra considered whether this stalker was perhaps in the force, or at least had been, at some stage. The cops at the time had never been able to pin it down to any one option, and even though Sierra thought that perhaps they hadn't tried all that hard—hadn't taken him seriously—after the accident she'd tended to agree with them. There were more important things to consider than one unstable person sending her deranged letters. She'd decided to try and ignore him and get on with her life. His threats were meaningless and mindless. He could never possibly hurt her as much as she'd already been hurt.

But now, here he was, getting back up in her face again. And it didn't seem like a coincidence anymore. If that was the case, she had to find out how her stalker was related to this newer case. She really needed to talk to Jen about this. First thing in the morning, she was going to call her.

But right now, she was going to get some sleep. If, indeed, she'd be able to sleep with all of this going around in her head. Leaving the dishes in the sink, Sierra tamped down the wood stove and made her way to her bedroom. Tonight, for some reason, her large, king-sized bed looked cold and uninviting. She walked over and pulled out the bottom drawer of her dresser. The pink bunny blanket was nestled there at the bottom. She picked it up and held it close to her chest. Maybe having this near would help her sleep. Hold the memories of her baby girl close, and perhaps banish thoughts of evil pedophiles and stalkers.

* * *

Sierra stretched and yawned. It'd been a fitful night of broken sleep. Neither of the cats was on the bed with her, which was unusual. The night had been full of noise as the wind got up and whipped the trees into a frenzy. She still had the pink bunny blanket wrapped around one hand. Carefully unwrapping it from her fingers, she folded it neatly, leaving it on her pillow. Time to get up and get moving; she had a lot to do today.

As Sierra padded through to the kitchen on her slipper-shod feet she saw both cats sitting at the back door glaring at her as if affronted it'd taken her so long to get up because they wanted out. One of these days she was going to install a cat flap, then they could come and go as they pleased.

"All right," she grumbled and went to the back door, then was surprised when they both skittered outside like the devil was on their tails. Silly things. The wind was still strong, but not as gusty as it had been last night. She went and stood on her back veranda to stare out at the gray ocean. Should she go for a swim today? She hadn't been out in over a week now. But winter always put a damper on her ocean swims. Even with her thick wetsuit, it would be icy and rough out there today.

Movement in her back yard caught her eye and she glanced down towards the chicken run huddled in the far corner near the fence.

A drift of feathers floated over the lawn.

Sierra realized she couldn't hear the normal contented clucking of her six girls as they pecked in the open area of their run. As she looked carefully, she noticed there was a dark lump in one corner of the pen.

She put a hand to her throat. Her heartbeat suddenly sounded loud in her ears.

Spinning on her heel, she ran down the steps towards the chicken enclosure, not caring she was still in her pajamas. *No.*

No. Please let her girls be okay.

But they weren't. She could see even before she came to a complete stop outside the wire fence. They were all dead. Little lumps of brown feathers lay in motionless heaps around the pen.

What had happened? Had a fox got into the pen? A feral cat? But the pen had been built to withstand these kinds of predators. She slipped in through the gate to take a better look.

And that's when she saw it.

The chickens hadn't just been killed. They'd been murdered.

All of them had their heads cut off.

A sob escaped Sierra's throat.

Who would do something like this? Why?

Sudden understanding grew in her mind, and her head sprang up as she searched the bushes. She needed to get back inside and lock the door. Sprinting for the back door, she nearly slipped and fell in her stupid woolly slippers. But she made it and slammed the door behind her, peering through the glass pane to the outside to make sure no one was there.

CHAPTER TWELVE

Reed rubbed a hand across his eyes. They were gritty and heavy, and he felt like he could sleep for a week. The three hours he'd managed to grab last night wasn't nearly enough, but he'd just have to keep pushing through. Things had gone completely bonkers on the island since they'd found those bones yesterday morning. Three more police units—teams of two—had arrived yesterday afternoon to help in the full-scale homicide investigation. And the media. Damn, Reed didn't even want to think about that insanity. They were ceaseless in their pursuit of a story, and their numbers were growing to plague-like proportions. You could hardly move on the island now without tripping over a swarm of them. He was on his way back to Penneshaw from the Kingscote station, going to meet up with the mainland officers and take them all out to the gravesite.

The saddest part was, they still hadn't found any trace of the little girl, Jessica.

His phone buzzed on the seat beside him. Sierra's number flashed up, and his pulse thumped in his neck. Even with all that'd been going on yesterday he still found his thoughts often circling back to her. Wondering what she was doing, was she managing to get some sleep, if he would see her again today. He pulled over to the side of the road and punched the Answer Call button.

"Reed, it's Sierra." Her voice was high and breathless, and his internal alarm bells went off.

"What's the matter?" he demanded. Even from those few short words, he could tell she was scared.

"They're dead. They're all dead." Sierra's voice hitched on a sob. "I tried to call Sam and Debbie, but they must be on their way into town to keep searching. They didn't answer their phone. Which is why I called you." She wasn't making any sense and Reed's heart lodged in his throat at her garbled words.

"Who's dead, Sierra?" Reed asked carefully, using a low but firm tone to try and break through her near-hysteria. His hands gripped the steering wheel until his knuckles turned white, as his mind went into overdrive. Dear God, not more dead bodies.

"The chickens. They're all dead."

"What?" It took his racing mind a few seconds to understand what she'd said. He'd been conjuring up dead children's bodies strewn all over her house. But chickens? What the hell was she talking about?

"My chickens. I went outside this morning to check on them and they're all dead. Murdered. Reed, someone cut their heads off." Sierra moaned as she said these last words.

Reed swallowed as a sour taste filled his mouth. He sat very still, digesting her words. Shit. His brain finally began processing what she'd said, and then the uneasiness and fear crept in.

"Someone's sending me a message, Reed. A very powerful message."

"Are you okay?" he barked, his police brain taking over.

"Yes, yes, of course. I've locked myself in the house, but I'm pretty sure whoever did this is long gone."

Reed went over the layout of Sierra's house in his mind, and he wasn't happy with what he remembered. Snellings Beach was an isolated spot on its own, but then Sierra's house itself was hidden in a small dip in the land, sheltered by large trees and not visible from the road or any of the neighboring houses. A perfect spot for a criminal to carry out his deeds unseen, if that's what he was planning. The house also had lots of glass windows; easy to smash if someone really wanted to get in. Reed put the Land Cruiser in gear and was about to turn the car around when he caught himself. He wanted to get out there, to protect her. But he was duty-bound to meet these mainland cops.

"Damn, Sierra. I want to come out there. To help you. But..." His mind raced with scenarios. Could he get someone else to take these guys to the site? But then he was the one who knew most about it, he'd been first cop on the scene. His input might be vital to help them find a clue to nail the killer. And he did want to talk to these new guys, get their take on the situation. A fresh pair of eyes and opinions could often help see something everyone else had missed.

He heard her take a deep breath over the phone, as if drawing on some previously unknown strength. "It's okay, Reed. I know how busy you are. This is such a terrible time."

He could imagine her standing in her kitchen, tall and slim, her shoulders hunched and arms crossed defensively as she held the cell to her ear. Those dark eyes of hers staring out the window towards the ocean. She was a tough woman. A strong woman. At least that was the façade she projected. But everyone needed comfort at some time or another. And he sensed this was one of those times. His fingers twitched with the need to take her into his arms. But there was little he could do over the phone. He wanted to get out there and see her for himself. Make sure she was truly alright.

"Give me a few minutes, Sierra. I'll call Don and see if I can

—"

"Don't, Reed. Please don't let me take you away from work. I'm almost sorry I called now, my problems seem pretty insignificant in light of the missing girl and now the bones. I just needed someone to talk to, that's all."

"Stop being silly. Your problems are not insignificant. And of course, I'm worried about you. If I could, I'd be out there in a flash." His brain was still working overtime, trying to come up with a solution. "You need to come into town, Sierra. Where it's safe." Yes, that would be better. He would feel much better if he knew she was somewhere he could keep an eye on her.

"I was going to come back and help search some more," Sierra admitted.

"Good. Let me know as soon as you hit town. You can stay at my place." His mind was already coming up with plans of what to do, how to keep her safe. Then he remembered the letter still sitting in the station. The one full of threats. His hands went suddenly cold and clammy. His instincts had told him there was something going on there. And it seemed they might be right.

He didn't like to ask, but the question was a burning one. "Do you think this has anything to do with the letters? With your stalker?"

There was the slightest hesitation before she answered. "I'm starting to think it might. I got a letter and an email yesterday."

"Well, if it is him, we need to figure out what's got him so riled up all of a sudden." Why had this guy suddenly ramped up his aggression? And why, after ten years, had his threats gone from the fairly harmless written word and tipped over into more hard-core physical attacks? If it was the stalker, then Reed needed to act quickly. It meant the guy had been on the island. Could still be on the island.

Or the most bone-chilling thought of all: the stalker actually lived on the island.

What the hell was going on here? This place had gone from a sleepy, small-town island to one full of child abductors, possible pedophiles, killers, and deranged men who stalked women. And he thought he'd moved here for a change of pace.

"I might have some idea what's bothering him. I've started another investigation," Sierra said carefully. "But I'll tell you everything I know when I see you. It's a long story."

"Okay. Please just get out of there, Sierra."

"I'll leave soon," she promised. "I'll call you when I get to town."

He wanted her to come now, not *soon*. He still fretted, itching to turn this damned car around and drive straight out to her house. Then he looked at the clock on the dash and swore under his breath. He was already running late to meet the other cops. Time to get his head back into the game, start to see the bigger picture again. A little girl's life may depend on how they handled this investigation. On how well he did his job. But even as he continued down the road toward Penneshaw, his mind refused to concentrate on what he needed to do next. Instead it kept drifting, seeing Sierra's face, pale and lined with worry, staring out the big, glass window of her house toward the unforgiving ocean.

* * *

Sierra hurried from the front door of her house out to her car. It was now two hours after she'd talked to Reed, and she needed to get into town. She typed out a quick text to let him know she was leaving now and slammed the car door shut.

She'd spent the last few hours making phone calls, interspersed with periods of peering out the picture windows at the front of her house and constantly checking that her doors and windows were all still securely locked. Common sense told her whoever had committed that abhorrent act in her back yard wasn't still lurking around. They were long gone. Her nerves had slowly settled as she talked on the phone, and her confidence grew with each call she made. That, and the idea of seeing Reed again soon had her almost back to normal. But she hadn't dared go back outside. Her poor girls. Their little feathery bodies would have to lie there in the dirt until she could get the courage to go out and retrieve them. Give them a proper burial.

Bastard. How dare he hurt her innocent pets. What a fucking coward. Her blood had begun to boil the more she thought about his gutless act.

At least that rage had given her the impetus not to take no for an answer when she finally made the phone calls. And she thought she might have found something important. A breakthrough, perhaps. A tiny bit of information from the cop who'd been first on the scene when the girl had disappeared three years ago. Something that wasn't in any of the reports she'd read so far. But it had been filed away as evidence, even though the cop thought it was probably useless. She couldn't wait to hear what Reed thought of the new information.

In the end, she hadn't needed to call Jen, which was a good thing, because if she found out about the chickens then she would completely freak out. And that was the last thing Sierra needed at the moment. She'd packed an overnight bag, not sure if she wanted to come home tonight. But also not sure where else she might go. Sam and Debbie hadn't answered her frantic phone call, which probably meant they were in an out-of-range spot on the island, already out searching for the missing girl again. She wished she didn't have to rely on the older couple quite so much. The isolation and beauty of this area was what had attracted her here in the first place, but she was now seeing it also had its drawbacks.

She started the car and set off down the driveway. As she

picked up speed along the gravel road out of Snellings Beach, she noticed a strange vibration in the steering wheel. Bloody hell, her car might need a wheel alignment, or perhaps there was something wrong with her shock absorbers. It was a good thing she was heading into town today. The vibration remained as she turned onto the main highway toward Kingscote, but it wasn't getting any worse, so Sierra decided to keep going. Her mind was swirling with all the implications of what the guy on the phone had told her, and all she wanted to do was get to town. Talk to Reed.

There was a sharp bend in the road coming up, so she slowed the car and dropped down a gear, driving on autopilot, her mind still engaged elsewhere. But as she came out of the bend and headed down a steep hill on the other side, the car began to shake violently. What the hell was happening? She touched the brake, and suddenly she was no longer able to control the car. The steering wheel wasn't responding at all. The car bucked and bumped. She tried to yank the car back into a straight line, using all of her brute force against the unresponsive wheel, but it was no use. Strangely, she didn't panic. Instead, a kind of calm descended over her, and it was almost as if she could see herself from outside. Still holding on to the wheel with one hand, she began to quickly shift the car down through the gears, slowing the car's headlong flight. Thank God this part of the road had straightened out, but the car was still drifting toward the gravel edge. She knocked it down another gear and then gingerly tried pulling on the emergency brake.

The car was definitely slowing, but she had no control over where it was headed. The left wheel dropped off the bitumen and into the gravel. This part of the island was sheep country, and as such, the road was edged by low, rolling hills of pasture. Scrubby bushes flew past the passenger window, getting closer and closer. But at least there were no large trees edging the road. If she hit a tree at this speed…

A large drainage ditch opened up in front of her, but there was nothing she could do except scream. The car nose-dived into the large trench and came to a crunching, bone-shattering halt. Glass from the broken windshield flew through the car. Air bags deployed all around Sierra as she was thrown forward, and her seatbelt bit painfully into her chest. Then everything became dark.

Sierra lifted her head and opened her eyes, dazed and confused. It was eerily silent. She thought she might've blacked out for a few seconds. Her head hurt. She did a mental scan of her body, checking for injuries. The dashboard was jammed up against her right knee, but she could still move, even though it hurt. And her chest and shoulder ached, probably from where the seat belt had cut into her.

She needed to get out of the car. The urge was overwhelming, and she scrabbled for the door handle, suddenly desperate. Her hand shook so much she had to pull the handle three times before it gave. But the door wouldn't open. It had to be warped by the impact. Jammed shut. Panic flooded through her. She was trapped in here. A scream rose in her throat. She rammed her shoulder against the door. Once. Twice. Then with a screech of metal on metal it gave way, and Sierra tumbled out onto the ground. The mud was cold against her cheek, but she welcomed the feel as she lay there, collecting herself.

Gingerly, she levered herself up onto her knees, wincing as pain sliced through her leg and then her chest. Using the car to grab onto, she pulled herself to standing and surveyed the mess in front of her.

The hood of her poor car was crumpled beyond recognition, the windshield completely shattered. The front right-hand wheel was hanging off at a ninety-degree angle. If she didn't know better, she would've sworn a couple of the lug nuts were missing from the wheel. Had her car been tampered with? A shiver of pure fear ran though her. Could the same person who killed her chickens have actually gone that far? Surely not. That would be murder. She suddenly felt extremely cold. *Stop it.* She shook her head to dislodge the terrible thoughts. She was alive. She was okay. And it could've been so much worse. If she hadn't managed to slow the car down or if the road had been lined with trees when she veered off, she could've very easily died.

The sight of the destroyed car and the idea someone had meant her harm was too much and she had to sit down in the grass by the side of the road before she fell. Her whole body was shaking now, and even though she knew it was the effect of the adrenaline leaving her body—she was probably going into shock—she felt useless and helpless. Tears rolled down her cheeks and she couldn't even find the strength to lift her hand to wipe them away.

As she sat there, memories from a day ten years ago overwhelmed her. Memories of the last time she'd been involved in a car crash. Sierra wrapped her arms around her body, trying to stay focused, but the impressions came howling back.

Grace was singing. The babbling, high-pitched warble only a nine-month-old was capable of. The Wiggles were on constant repeat in Sierra's car, and they were both belting out Grace's favorite, the Hot Potato song. Sierra's heart lifted at the sound of her daughter, happy and giggling.

The girl at daycare had told her that Grace had a fairly good day and it seemed her little girl might finally be settling into the new routine, after Sierra had returned to work last month.

The traffic light was red, and as she waited for it to go green, Sierra did the actions from the song while Grace giggled in the back seat. The music was turned up loud, and

Sierra didn't care that other people in the cars around her might overhear her terrible crooning. As long as her daughter thought it was funny, then that was okay with her.

A car flashed through the intersection in front of her, going way too fast, and Sierra turned her head to watch it for a second. Stupid idiots, speeding through the intersection, they were going to kill someone. But Grace wasn't to be distracted and so Sierra took up her singing again a few seconds later.

The lights went green. Sierra put her hands back on the steering wheel and moved off.

Her world turned into a sudden, blinding, crunching sphere of pain and deafening sound.

Sierra didn't remember a lot after that. She knew she screamed and screamed, a wild animal sound, until her throat was hoarse. People ran from all directions and huddled around her. She kept screaming for her daughter.

The doctors told her she'd almost died that night. And sometimes she wished she had. Had taken the place of her daughter. If only she could've given up her life to save Grace, she would've done it in a heartbeat.

But nothing could bring her daughter back. She had to live with that reality every single day.

She'd been put into an induced coma for nearly two weeks. By the time she woke up, her husband, Jake had already arranged Grace's funeral. She didn't even get to say goodbye to her beautiful daughter.

Tears were streaming freely down her face now, accompanied by snot and saliva too, as Sierra howled in anguish. She hadn't cried like this since the day she'd found out her daughter was dead. Instead she'd kept it all bottled up inside. This crash had brought it hurtling back to her as if it happened yesterday. She sat in the long grass, crying and wailing, beating the ground with her fist, over and over. It wasn't fair. Life wasn't fair. She missed her daughter so much.

Sierra didn't know how long she'd been lying there on the cold ground. Her grief had finally run its course and now she gave the occasional, hiccupping sob, but the tears had abated. She felt completely washed out. Scoured and raw. Empty. But also clean. Like a blank page. As if this breakdown might actually have been a breakthrough.

She put one leaden hand on the soil beneath her face and levered herself up to a sitting position. Out of the corner of her eye, she could see her hair was festooned with leaves and sticks from where she'd lain on the ground. With a superhuman effort she pushed herself up to standing, swaying for a second until she regained her balance. She probably looked horrific. But there were more important things than wiping the snot and tears from her face. She needed to get out of here.

Sierra took an unsteady step back and cast a glance up and down the road. Not a car in sight. But that wasn't unusual, this end of the island was isolated. Sometimes, only a handful of cars used this road on any given day. She might be waiting quite a while for someone to come and rescue her.

Limping around to the other side of the car, she managed to pull the door open. The contents of her handbag were scattered all through the front of the car. It took her a few seconds to locate her cell phone. The glass front was cracked and for a second she panicked until she hit the button and the screen lit up.

Hallelujah, there was reception. It was weak, but it'd be enough to make the call. There was only one person she wanted to talk to. One person she trusted enough to come and rescue her. Reed. She dialed his number and let out a gasp of relief when he answered.

CHAPTER THIRTEEN

Reed held the door open and ushered Sierra into his little flat. She limped past him and went straight to the couch and sat down. His pulse still raced whenever he thought about her phone call two hours ago. Telling him she'd crashed her car. And he was still berating himself for not going out to her earlier this morning, when she'd first called him about her chickens. It was stupid. He'd known something was off, could feel it in his gut, yet he'd let his brain and work dictate his actions. Had thought she'd be okay.

"Thanks, Reed. For everything." She grimaced, as she re-adjusted her position on the couch. The doctor said it was only bruising on her chest and ribs, from the seatbelt. Nothing was broken. "I didn't expect you to take me to the ER, but thank you anyway."

"You needed to get checked out. What if you had a broken rib and it punctured your lung? Or internal injuries you didn't even realize were there?" He didn't add the part about his own culpability. How, if he'd come out to get her, this would never have happened. He'd driven her straight to the hospital in Kingscote. Which wasn't so much of a hospital but a small health clinic, run by a couple of nurses and one doctor. But they'd been efficient and professional, arranging

X-rays and other tests to make sure Sierra was fine. Her knee was also bruised and possibly twisted, so they had strapped that and told her to keep it iced for the next twenty-four hours.

"Well, thank you again." She lay her head back against the couch and he saw a flash of vulnerability cross her face as she closed her eyes. A small cut split her eyebrow from where the airbag had violently inflated, which the doctor had covered with a couple of butterfly-strips to hold it together. And her temple and brow above the cut were starting to turn gray with a bruise. The doctor had asked her about the scar just beneath her hairline as he was dressing the cut. He'd lifted her hair to take a closer look, but she'd shut him down, saying it was nothing, really, just an old scar that didn't bother her anymore. Reed had stored that bit of information away for later. It was obvious to him at least that it wasn't *nothing*, and he meant to ask her about it when the time was right.

Her normally lush, vibrant lips were pulled together in a thin line, and her cheeks were ashen and hollow. Perhaps it was the injuries that made her look more vulnerable. Whatever it was, Reed knew he had to do something. He'd been holding back, had wanted to do it ever since she'd first called him early this morning. But when he'd picked her up from the crash site, he'd been so worried about her injuries and the state of the car, his professional side had taken over, making him brusque and efficient. And in the hospital, they'd been surrounded by nurses or other patients. But now...Now they were alone.

He sat down beside her and gathered her gently into his arms. And just held her. Careful not to squeeze too tight in case he hurt her ribs. At his touch, Sierra tensed, but then quickly melted into his arms. He heard a tiny sigh escape her lips. She was wearing a zippered fleece today that hugged her body more than the normal oversized hoodies she preferred. She was thin beneath his biceps, he could feel the bones of her shoulders digging into him.

They sat like that for many long moments. He liked the feel of her in his arms, small and fragile, but there was a strength inside her as well. What they were doing here was not sensual at all. It was quiet and life-affirming. Intimate.

Finally, she stiffened slightly, and he knew their peaceful interlude was ended. "Thank you," she said softly. "I needed that." He got the feeling it'd been a long time since she'd been held.

"There's plenty more where that came from." He gave her a quick smile as he gathered himself and stood up.

He hated to say this, but reality was still calling. "I have to go back to work for a few hours."

"Oh. Of course you do. I didn't mean to be so selfish." Sierra went to stand, and he laid a steady hand on her shoulder.

"But you're going to stay here, where I know you'll be safe. I'll be home in a few hours. You will stay here, won't you?" He phrased the last bit as a question, but he wanted to growl it out, demand that she stay so he knew where she was.

Sierra hesitated for a fraction of a second. "Okay. If you're sure you don't mind." He thought a flash of relief showed in her eyes before they darkened again. "I've got something I need to tell you about, anyway."

"Yes, there are lots of things we need to talk about," he said gravely, thinking back to her car, smashed by the side of the road. He hadn't said anything to her yet, didn't want to traumatize her even further. And he'd need to get confirmation from the wrecker. But it looked to him like the lug nuts on her wheels had been tampered with. Loosened. It was the only explanation for the way her right wheel was only just hanging onto the hub. Her left wheel was loose, too.

Someone had meant for her to crash. The same person who'd killed her chickens, if his hunch was right. And that hunch was also telling him it was the same person who'd broken into her house and stolen her laptop. They had to be all connected, but he wasn't sure how, or why, yet. But he would figure it out. And he wasn't letting her out of his sight until he did.

"I'll organize to get your car towed."

She glanced up at him. "I know I sound like a broken record, but thank you, Reed." His chest expanded at her gratitude. It was nice to be able to do something to help her. It alleviated some of the guilt about not going to her right away this morning. Some, but not all.

"I'll get you a spare sweater. That one's got blood on it." He pointed at the drops of blood from her head wound. She glanced down in surprise, as if seeing them for the first time.

"That would be good."

As he rummaged in his closet, his phone beeped in his pocket. Another text coming in. It would be either Eric or Don trying to track him down. Time to get back on the job. He found the sweater he was looking for, a dark-blue, zip-up hoodie, exactly how she liked them.

"I'll be home by dinnertime, I promise," he said, handing her the sweater. "Just make yourself at home. There's food in the fridge, and tea and coffee on the counter." He dithered by the doorway, unsure if he should leave her alone. She was hurt. Injured. And he wanted to stay with her.

"Go, Reed. I'm a big girl. I'll be fine." She finally gave him his first proper smile for the day. The one where the corner of her mouth lifted a fraction, giving him the crooked smile he'd become intrigued by and he knew she would be okay. For now.

He grabbed his police jacket from the peg in the hallway and shut the door behind him. Fumbling for his phone, he tried to put the jacket on at the same time as reading the first text. There were four from Eric, each one becoming more urgent. He stopped mid-stride. Damn, this wasn't good.

He punched in Eric's number and held the phone to his ear.

"It's Reed. What's going on?" he said, dispensing with any niceties.

"You need to get back to HQ. The Sarge's asked us all back there ASAP." Eric's normally jovial drawl was tight and tense as he snapped the words out. "Those bloody mainland cops have just arrested Tom Hubbard. Said they got a tip-off from the public that he had photos of kids on his computer. They're getting a warrant to search his house as we speak."

"Damn," Reed muttered into the phone. This island community was starting to show the strain of a missing girl and now the discovery of the bones of another dead child. He'd seen it happen before. They were beginning to implode, starting to look suspiciously sideways at their neighbors and friends. They needed to do something to nip this in the bud, before it became full-blown hysteria with everyone accusing everyone else. Reed didn't know Tom Hubbard, but he remembered he was the head of the volunteer SES brigade. He'd been coordinating all the search and rescue efforts.

"Do we know if there is any truth to the allegations?"

Eric's voice was low, and Reed could imagine his face looking a little like a beaten puppy. "I hate to say it, but there may well be. We'll know more as soon as we get the warrant. You need to get back to the station. Now. The Sarge wants at least one of us to be in on the interview when the mainland boys bring him in."

"On my way." Reed ended the call and unlocked his police vehicle. Could it be that easy? Had they found a pedophile on the island? The pedophile? Wasn't it always the way, these people put themselves forward as a pinnacle of society, painted themselves as irreproachable, while underneath that facade of integrity they were really just monsters? Could this possibly be the guy who'd taken Jessica?

Reed sucked in a breath. No point in getting ahead of himself. He knew better than most not to judge someone until they had all the facts.

* * *

Sierra woke with a start. Where was she? She'd fallen asleep on a couch, and was slumped at an awkward angle, half-sitting, half-lying.

Then it all came back to her. She was at Reed's place. She lifted a hand and touched the side of her head. It was sore, she'd need some more painkillers soon. The clock above Reed's TV said it was nearly five. She must've fallen asleep almost as soon as Reed left. But she was feeling a little better after her three-hour nap.

Stretching gingerly, she tested the soreness in her ribs. She could barely lift her hands up above her head. She was going to be stiff for a few days to come yet. The ice pack had slipped off her knee during her nap, and she reached down to pluck it off the floor, before getting up to her feet. Wow, her whole body ached. Shuffling to the kitchen, she flipped the kettle on and searched for a mug. A hot, sweet cup of tea was in order. As she waited for the water to boil, she checked in Reed's refrigerator. He'd said to help herself. She couldn't believe how much she'd relied on him today. Needed him. She wanted to thank him for all his help. As her gaze roamed over the sparse food in the fridge, an idea took hold.

The very least she could do was to cook him a nice dinner, he had said he would be home by then. It was a start to show how much she appreciated his help.

Sierra glanced out the window. The glow of the setting sun was lighting up the high clouds with a tinge of pink. Drakes supermarket was only a five-minute walk from Reed's place.

She could be there and back before it got truly dark. Drakes also stocked a lot of local produce from the island, and they would have the ingredients she needed for the dish she had in mind. And a walk out in the fresh air would do her good, perhaps loosen up some of the stiffness in her legs and body. She remembered Reed had told her to stay put, but surely that didn't mean she wasn't allowed to pop down to the market for a few minutes? Now where did she leave those painkillers the doctor had given her?

Ten minutes later, Sierra entered the glass sliding doors of the supermarket, happy to be out of the biting wind. At first, she'd had to force her legs to move. They protested for a few minutes before she got warmed up and moving. Her knee still hurt, and she couldn't quite hide the limp, but on the whole, she was glad she'd decided to get out.

She headed straight for the wide, glass-fronted, deli section, eager to see if they had any venison in stock. There was one local deer farm on the island, and their products were just scrumptious.

"Sierra, fancy seeing you again." The familiar voice came from behind her left shoulder, and she tensed before turning around.

"Blake," she replied woodenly, taking an unconscious step away from him and crossing her arms in front of her chest. "Twice in two days. Imagine that." Her heart began to thump in her chest. Surely this was just a coincidence. Nothing more. Of course, he wasn't following her. This was a small island; she was bound to run into him occasionally. She stared up at him. He really was handsome, tall, blonde, blue-eyed, with a square jaw most men would kill for. Sierra searched for any kind of reaction within her body at the sight of him. Nope, not a thing. Instead, an image of Reed, shirtless, played in front of her mind's eye.

"Yeah, imagine." His mouth quirked into a wry half-smile.

But the smile didn't quite meet his eyes. "Not under the best of circumstances, though. What's going on? I thought I was moving to an island haven, away from all this kind of shit they get on the mainland." He shook his head, his shaggy, blonde, surfer locks swinging into his eyes. Then his eyes widened as he noticed the bruising on her face.

"Are you okay?" He reached up, as if to touch her face, and she moved away even farther.

"Don't touch me." The words were out before she could stop them.

He narrowed his eyes and lowered his hand. She hadn't meant to offend. But he didn't have a right to touch her. Not anymore. And after all the strange things that'd happened to her in the last little while, she had a right to be wary. Didn't she?

"Oh, your car. Something happened to your car today."

"What?" How the bloody hell did he know about her car? Sierra drew farther away until her butt came to rest up against the edge of the deli counter. How could he possibly know about the car accident? If he knew, then...Did he have something to do with it?

"I saw a car being towed into the auto shop as I drove into town this afternoon. I thought it looked like yours. Was it your car? Fuck, Sierra, were you in a car accident?"

She studied his face carefully. There seemed to be genuine concern hovering in the questions behind his eyes. But it was getting so she didn't know what to believe anymore. She couldn't even trust her own judgement.

"Yes," she admitted slowly. Was that true? Had he seen her car being towed? Or did he know something else? Did he have something to do with her accident? With her chickens? No, surely not. She was just being paranoid. Again, her mind conjured up the way he'd glanced at her yesterday out at the crime scene. Spitefully. As if he did indeed harbor some kind of animosity for her. There was no hint of that look today. His good-looking features were carved with anxiety.

But there was no way she was going to tell him the truth. "I ran off the road on my way into town today. Ended up in a ditch. Silly really." She tried to make her voice light, as if it hadn't been that big a deal. As if she was some stupid woman who got easily distracted when driving.

"Well, thank God you're okay. I mean, you look okay. Are you?" He seemed suddenly uncertain, that boyish charm gone now. She felt a tug of self-reproach. She was being unkind to him. But right at this particular moment, it was the only way she knew how to handle him. To keep a cold, aloof distance between them.

"I'm fine," she said, giving him a half-smile. She just wanted him to leave. An awkward silence gathered between them.

Finally, Blake said, "Look, I get it, Sierra. You're not interested. I must admit, part of the reason I applied for the job on KI was because of you. I thought…Well, I guess it was obvious what I thought. But you've made it abundantly clear how you feel." His last words held a note of bitterness. And that sly lift of his eyebrow was back. The one that made her blood run cold.

Sierra wondered if it was all just talk. She wanted to believe him. But with all the strange stuff going on at the moment, she was finding it hard to trust anyone. Except Reed, a small voice at the back of her head kept repeating.

"Look, Blake…" What did she say? How to make this as painless for both of them as possible? "You're a great guy. But —"

"Yep, whatever," he interrupted quickly. "See you round." Turning on his heel, he strode back down the aisle, effectively dismissing her. An air of disquiet hung around her like a dark cloud and she suddenly wanted to get her shopping done as quickly as possible and get back to Reed's house.

She hadn't given it a second thought when she left Reed's place, but perhaps she'd made a mistake coming here on her own. It was only a short walk back to his guesthouse, but it was nearly dark now. It suddenly hit her that perhaps she should be worried. If it was true, and someone had gone to the trouble of sabotaging her car, what else were they capable of? Was she safe walking the streets of Kingscote by herself anymore?

She quickly gathered the ingredients she needed, hurrying though the supermarket, casting a glance behind her every now and then. There were lots of people here, after a pint of milk, or like her, ingredients for tonight's dinner. She had no reason to be afraid. And there was no sign of Blake now. But a small voice kept asking, was one of them her stalker? Her hand shook as she handed the cashier the money, and he gave her a curious glance as she tossed everything on top of each other into her shopping bag.

Dashing out between the glass sliding doors, she wasn't looking where she was going, and hurtled straight into a man standing on the pavement. She let out a tiny scream before she could stop herself as a pair of arms came up to steady her.

"Hey, luv, you're in a Godawful hurry. You need to slow down. You nearly knocked me over."

Sierra let out a whoosh of breath as she recognized the bearded man holding on to her. Evan's familiar face stared at her, his beady eyes showing confusion behind his glasses.

"Sorry," she apologized. Drawing a couple of large, calming breaths, she almost laughed out loud. She was being silly. There was no one hunting her through the aisles of Drakes. What on earth had taken hold of her?

"Are you all right, luv?" Evan was still holding her, his stout fingers clamping onto her upper arms. "What are you doing here? It's late to get home, isn't it?" He glared at her in much the same way her father might've. "I didn't see you out with the search group today." Now his tone had gotten a tad accusatory. "I've been out helping them all day, you know."

"Oh, yes, I've been...busy." She searched around lamely for an excuse.

"My dear girl, what have you been doing?" Evan must've seen her face for the first time and now he was staring at her bruises, turning her side-on so he could examine her more carefully, still holding her by the shoulders.

She couldn't think quick enough, couldn't come up with a reason for the injuries, so she said, "I crashed my car today. But it's all good. Well, my car isn't too good, but I'm fine." She offered up a wan smile, taking a step back at the same time, out of his embrace. She could stand on her own two feet now her panic had subsided.

"That's no good. Was it one of those pesky roos, jumping out in front of you? They are a menace, you know." His neat beard bristled at the thought. His eyes suddenly became sharp and bright as he waited for her answer, more astute than they should've been, as if he were weighing up her next answer.

"No, it wasn't a roo. It was...just a silly accident." She wasn't going to tell him the truth. "But my car is totaled." She gave a small sigh. She loved that car. It'd been her pride and joy. Her insurance would come through eventually and she'd be able to buy a new one. But she'd have to go and see about a rental car tomorrow. KI was definitely one place you couldn't survive without a vehicle.

Her head had started to ache again and the cold wind was finding its way inside her coat, leaving icy trails down her skin. She gave a shiver.

"How are you going to get home then? Without a car, I mean."

"I'm staying with...a friend in town tonight. I was just

about to walk back there."

"Well, the least I can do is give you a lift. You look all done in." The normal, jovial Evan was back, his smile firmly in place. Perhaps she'd imagined the slightly scathing tone in his voice. "My car is just over here." He pointed to an aging, white, four-wheel-drive parked by the curb a few cars down. "I'll save you the walk. Are you limping?" he added, as he looked down at her knee. "Let me drive you. I want to make sure you get home safely."

Yes, her leg was sore. It seemed to have swelled a little from her walk. And her head ached. Perhaps walking down here hadn't been such a good idea. Just then, it started to drizzle. A light rain that was cold and unwelcome.

"Ah...Okay, that would be nice. Thank you, Evan."

His face split into a grin. "Good. Very good. Yes, that's a good plan. I'll take you." He picked up two shopping bags at his feet and turned to hurry toward his car. "To your friend's place," he added, almost as an afterthought.

He was a strange man. Harmless, she decided, but definitely a little strange. Reed's place was only a two-minute drive from here. It'd save her hobbling up the street. Why wouldn't she accept a lift from him, a respected member of the community? He was practically running toward his car now, in such a hurry to open the door for her. An awkward gait, as his stout legs pounded down the pavement with the shopping bags banging by his sides. All of a sudden, he tripped, nearly falling. One of the bags went flying, spilling its contents over the pavement. Evan took a few stumbling steps forward, and managed to recover himself just in time.

"Are you alright?" she asked, quickening her pace.

"Fuck. Bloody hell," he swore loudly, startling a young couple crossing the road nearby.

"Let me help." Sierra crouched down and began to pick up the grocery items strewn all over the path.

"Leave it. Leave them alone," Evan shouted, using the same rough tone he'd cursed in. "I'll get them. Just leave them alone." She recoiled away from the things she'd been about to pick up. What the hell? She was only trying to help him. Was he so embarrassed that he had to yell at her? His behavior was beyond baffling. One second as nice as pie, the next like a snarling junkyard dog. Perhaps accepting a lift wasn't such a good idea, after all.

"Sierra," a deep, male voice called from behind them.

She whirled around to see Reed striding down the sidewalk toward her. Relief flooded through her body. He looked so good in his dark-blue police uniform. Like he could save the world. Or at the very least, save her.

"Reed." She wanted to run up and hug him, but managed to stay standing in the one spot, waiting for him to approach.

"What are you doing here?" he asked. "I thought I told you to stay put." He frowned at her, but his tone was forgiving. "I was worried when I got home, and you weren't there."

Evan finished picking up the last of his groceries and turned to greet Reed. "Evening, Officer Kapua." He nodded at Reed, but kept his distance. Sierra couldn't read his expression properly. If she hadn't known better, she would've sworn he was glowering at Reed.

Sierra could see Reed sizing up this man, probably wondering who he was. "This is Evan, he owns the newsstand in Penneshaw. He offered me a lift home."

"Any news on the missing girl?" His eyes darted to Reed's face.

"No, I'm sad to say we still don't have any leads."

"Oh, that's not what I heard. I heard you arrested someone this afternoon." Evan glared openly at Reed now, and Sierra's interest was piqued. They'd arrested someone? She was itching to ask who.

Reed pursed his lips. He probably wasn't used to the

public knowing things until he was ready to tell them. It was different out here. Everyone knew everything about everyone else.

"So, it seems that Kangaroo Island's finest haven't been asleep on the job, like we all thought. Or was it the cops from the mainland who nabbed this guy?" Evan was outright smirking now, and Sierra felt a sliver of dislike run through her.

"Right. Thanks, Evan. But I've got it from here." Reed took the shopping bag from Sierra's hand and turned on his heel. "Let's get you home, where it's warm."

"Thanks again, Evan," Sierra said, shooting him what she hoped was a grateful smile.

But he didn't smile back, just watched them with lowered eyebrows. "Enjoy your night with your *friend,* then, Sierra," he muttered so low she almost didn't hear him as she followed after Reed.

CHAPTER FOURTEEN

Reed clenched his teeth together to stop himself saying the words that were rolling around on his tongue. He'd asked her to stay put, and what had she done? Calmly wandered down to the local Main Street, as if there wasn't a crazed madman out there somewhere. Did she not realize how much danger she could potentially be in?

By the time they got back to his little flat, he'd managed to calm down. When he'd first come home to find Sierra missing, he'd been irritated. But that irritation soon turned to growing fear. What if her stalker had found her here at his place? Reed hopped back in his car and searched the surrounding streets with growing trepidation.

Then he'd spotted her, talking to some plain-looking guy on the street. Even though Sierra seemed to know the guy, and assured Reed he was all right—owned a business on the island, and all—he hadn't liked the vibe he was getting from the man. He was shortish, stout almost, but not fat. All muscle, he obviously kept himself in shape. With that neatly trimmed beard and those heavy-rimmed glasses you could easily dismiss him. A memory tugged at his mind, of a man hailing Sierra as she drove off the ferry the other night. It looked like the same guy. He was uninteresting and plain.

Yet, he was obviously captivated by Sierra. The way he looked at her, with hungry eyes. The jealous glance he'd shot at Reed when he thought he wasn't looking. But then again, who could blame the man? Sierra was a sultry beauty, and he wouldn't be surprised if half the male population of the island had a thing for her.

And then there'd been that guy yesterday. The ranger. There was something going on between him and Sierra, an undercurrent he hadn't been able to decipher. The ranger had been good-looking, if you liked the surfer type. And young. Much younger than Sierra, if he wasn't mistaken. Reed didn't like it. He'd already asked a mate of his, a cop back in his old unit, to take a discreet look at the Ranger for him. He was way too busy here with the missing girl to be following up leads on people that looked at Sierra wrong. But that didn't stop him calling in a favor.

"Sorry if I scared you. I should've left a note." Sierra seemed to read his mind. Was it that obvious on his face?

She limped into his flat and he followed, putting the bag of groceries on the kitchen counter.

"I wanted to cook you something nice for dinner. To say thank you for all your help. That's all." She leaned back against the laminate, her chocolate eyes alight with contrition. The bruises on her temple and forehead had turned darker since he'd last seen her, and were now a vivid shade of purple. There were tiny lines around her mouth as she pursed her lips. She was in pain, he could tell. But it wasn't just physical pain. There was an emotional pain there, buried deep. He'd seen flashes of it before. Perhaps now that she was vulnerable after the car crash today, it was able to manifest into something stronger he could finally discern. He went up and stood close to her, so close she couldn't escape, the bench trapping her. Raising a finger, he traced the lines around her mouth. Her eyes widened at his touch, but she didn't pull away.

His lips met hers gently, one hand slipping around her slim hips to pull her closer. He liked her wearing his sweater, it looked good on her, much better than it did on him. Her arms wrapped around his neck as she nestled into his chest, their kiss deepening. Her lips were both soft and firm against his and she opened for him, so he could slip his tongue inside. A burst of heat charged through him like a firework going off, and his cock stirred. God, she was beautiful. And God, he wanted her. And if the urgency with which she was kissing him was anything to go by, she wanted him just as much. They could forego dinner and move onto dessert. Dessert being her. *Slow down*. He needed to stop thinking with his dick for a second. He broke their kiss and she stared up at him with those unfathomable eyes, her lips slightly parted and slick from kissing him.

"How about I cook dinner? You go and sit on the couch and tell me what to do. I'm pretty good at following directions."

She looked dazed for a second, pulling herself back from the depths of the kiss. Finally, her eyes focused on him. "All right. If you think you can manage. I might go and sit down." He could see how much it cost her to admit defeat, she was used to fending for herself. He playfully slapped her on the bottom as she made her way toward the couch. It was round and firm beneath his hand. He was starting to like the way she wore these tight leggings more and more. They afforded a great view of her pert rump, as well as allowing ample access to her curves.

He turned toward the counter, hoping to hide the growing bulge in his pants. "Fire away, what should I do first?" he asked, rummaging through the shopping bag, pulling out some kind of meat, and a couple of delicious looking cheeses, a bunch of baby carrots, some fresh beetroot, and a bottle of red wine. Reed prided himself on being able to cook healthy, wholesome meals. But this looked like it might be more gourmet than he was used to.

"Don't look so worried," she laughed. It's all very easy. It's just oven-baked veggies, grilled venison and a red wine jus. I bought a bottle, I wasn't sure if you'd have any, being at a guesthouse, and all." She sat in the single lounge chair so she could watch what he was doing, easing her hiking boots off and resting her socked feet on the coffee table. "You won't need all the wine for the dish. There's enough for a glass each if you like."

He poured them both a glass and took hers over. Her dark eyes followed his every move as he chopped and peeled the vegetables, and then prepped the frying pan. He liked it. He liked the way she sipped her wine, savoring the taste, even while her gaze never left him. He couldn't remember the last time he'd cooked for a woman. It was probably for Penny, when he'd lived back in Ballarat. Such a long time ago. This felt cozy and intimate, in his little rented flat. A kind of energy buzzed between them, a heightened awareness.

"I told you my life story the other night. Now I reckon it's your turn. What about you? Have you ever been married?" Her eyes widened as a thought seemed to occur to her. "I never even asked, but I assume you're not married now?"

He chuckled as she stared at him, waiting for his answer. Eventually he put her out of her misery. "No, I'm not married. Now." He took a deep breath, the knife hovered in mid-air. He found himself blurting out the words before he had time to think. "I was married once, though. We were both really young. Bit of a shotgun wedding. Penny was pregnant." This wasn't something he shared with most people. But something about Sierra made him more at ease. He forced his hand down to continue chopping the veggies.

"So, the marriage didn't work out, then? Does your child

live with your ex-wife now?"

His fingers tightened on the knife handle. "No. The baby was still-born." He wanted to say more, to make his voice light and flippant, but his traitorous throat had closed up all of a sudden.

"Oh, Jesus, Reed. I'm sorry."

He looked up finally, wondering what he might see; scared of what he might see. Condemnation. Rejection. Pity. The bruising on her face stood out against her pale cheeks, but there were none of the emotions he feared would be there. Instead, he thought he saw…understanding. Awareness. Empathy.

He gulped in a couple of deep breaths. "It was a long time ago," he said, in explanation.

Silence descended, as she stared at the wine sloshing lazily in her glass. But it was a familiar silence, not awkward and Reed didn't feel the need to break it. The recipe was indeed as simple as Sierra said it would be. With the veggies in the oven he got down to making the red wine sauce—or jus, as she called it. Reed shook out his leg surreptitiously. It was aching again, and he really needed to sit down to give it a break. All this extra walking—and sometimes running—as well as standing for hours on end, was taking its toll. He should really ice it at some stage tonight, but that might not happen with Sierra staying here.

"What did Evan mean when he said they arrested someone?" Sierra asked over the rim of her wine glass.

He was glad she'd decided to change the topic. Reed raised his gaze to the ceiling. How did he put this? His gut told him this man wasn't involved in the missing girl case, or the newly uncovered bones. But it was just a feeling, a hunch. The mainland cops were all over this guy. Interrogating him hard.

"I suppose I can tell you; it'll probably be on tonight's

news anyway. They arrested Tom Hubbard."

"Why? Whatever for? Tom's a good guy. I know him. He's in our walking group. He wouldn't…" She trailed off, staring at him.

"They found kiddie porn on his computer. Lots of it."

"No," she whispered, almost to herself. A small shudder ran through her. "Shit. It goes to show how much we really don't know people like we think we do. This is going to cause an uproar in the community." He watched her swirl her wine, digesting the news, brow furrowed in thought. "Oh God," she whispered. "Tom is a member of the Friends of The Glossies."

Reed raised an eyebrow at that information.

"It means he knows about the nesting areas. How secluded they are." Then she speared him with that investigative gaze. "What do you think? Do you think he's involved in Jessica's case? Or the bones we uncovered?"

"I'm not sure." Reed shook his head, stirring the sauce slowly. Then he looked up and met her eyes. She deserved the truth. "No, I don't think he's involved. They've turned his house upside down, and apart from the photos, there're no other indications he's ever taken his sick obsession any further than online. Of course, we've been checking the child sex-offense registry and this guy, Tom wasn't on it. I wouldn't be surprised if this case uncovers more people like him on the island. Hiding in plain sight, keeping their sick fantasies under wraps."

"So, you're saying there could be more pedophiles here on the island? Or murderers? You don't still think Jessica just wandered off anymore, do you?"

Reed shook his head. "No, I don't." He didn't add that he'd always had a bad feeling about this case, right from the very first phone call he received. He just hoped they'd followed all the correct procedures, done all due diligence where the investigation was concerned. For the little girl's sake, as well as their own. Their reputations as police officers were on the line over this. "I think it's the growing consensus among the other detectives as well." And that was an understatement. Behind closed doors, they were scrambling. Calling in more experts, calling in favors to get lab results back quicker. Don looked like a walking zombie, with the lack of sleep and the high amounts of stress he was dealing with. Reed hoped the man could handle it. Don would still be at the station, poring over reports, looking for that proverbial needle in a haystack. Reed should be there too, but his priority had shifted after Sierra's accident today.

"I checked on your car. It's at the wreckers. Sorry, but they said it was a write-off." He looked at Sierra beneath lowered brows. She grimaced, but didn't seem too upset by the news.

"I kind of already knew that," she admitted. "I saw the damage."

"Sierra." He waited until she looked at him, until he had her full attention, before he continued. "I had a good look at it. And I will wait till Fred from the wrecker confirms it. But I don't think your accident was actually an accident."

"I know." She sat up straighter in the chair, and he saw her fingers tighten on the wine glass stem.

In two strides, he was around from behind the bench and crouching in front of her, ignoring the stab of pain as he knelt down. He grabbed her free hand with his. It was cold and he held it in both hands against his chest.

"I already came to the same conclusion. I saw how the right front wheel was hanging off. I checked the left one before you came and picked me up and it seemed really loose, too. And not in a way that would've been caused by the crash," she said, voice shaky.

Her hand was small and delicate inside his. With his stomach resting up against her knees he was suddenly aware of their proximity. His body reacting before he could stop it, that tingling recognition spreading over his skin.

He had to say it. Had to warn her how much danger she might be in. "I don't know if this is connected to those letters you're getting, but I have a hunch it is."

"You and your hunches," she said, with a half-hearted smile. He didn't respond. This was serious.

"But we also can't discount anyone else at the moment, either."

Sierra narrowed her eyes. "What do you mean?"

"I mean, how well do you know your neighbors? You live in a pretty isolated spot. They're the first people I'd be looking at."

"You're kidding." He could tell by the glint in her eye she actually thought he was joking.

"No, I'm not, Sierra."

"Well, that's just ludicrous. I count Sam and Debbie amongst my dearest friends."

"I know this sounds far-fetched, but in my experience, crimes, especially something as personal as this seems to be, can often be linked to the people closest to a victim."

"No," she breathed.

He plowed on, needing her to understand. "You must know yourself, after all your experience reporting on these things. Sometimes the sickest crimes are committed by the person you least suspect."

"Are you saying that Sam might be a suspect?"

Personally, Reed didn't believe he was. He'd only met him the once, but he prided himself on being able to take a person's measure pretty quickly. He'd also learned the hard way, never to discount anything.

"I won't believe that. He's a good man. A kind man."

"Okay," he said, but in a tone that made it obvious he didn't believe her. "What about your other neighbors?"

She turned her head to survey her glass of wine, her long ponytail swinging on her shoulder. "Terry is the only other person who stays out there regularly. But he's harmless, a little weird, perhaps..." Her words trailed off as she considered this guy, Terry. Then her gaze came back to his, her face somber, lines of worry arching over her forehead. Good, now perhaps she was starting to get the picture. Until they found whoever it was who'd tampered with her car, everyone was a potential suspect.

"What?" he prompted.

"I wasn't going say anything, but now you've mentioned it..." She stopped and bit her lip. Damn, he wished she wouldn't do that. It was sending his mind to places he shouldn't go right now.

"That guy out at the bone site yesterday. The ranger, Blake."

He nodded. Here it came. The story he'd wanted to know.

"He and I dated for a while, about two years ago. It was nothing special and he went back to the mainland to finish his PhD." Her eyes became unfocused as she stared at nothing over his shoulder.

"Mmhmm," he encouraged.

"He wanted to pick up where we left off when he came back recently. But I told him no. And he's been phoning and texting me ever since. I don't think he'd want to hurt me. I don't think he's capable...But I thought you should probably know," she finished, taking a large gulp of her wine.

He wanted to tell her to stop being so naïve, that everyone was capable of violence, given the right motive. Could this Blake be responsible for the things that'd happened recently to Sierra? Reed was going to make damn sure he knew the answer to that question before he let Sierra out of his sight again.

It was time to put his foot down. Demand she do as he say.

So he could keep her safe.

"I want you to stay here, with me, until I sort this out."

* * *

Sierra couldn't say anything at first. Did he realize quite what he was asking of her? This was becoming way too complicated. She couldn't stay here. With him. Could she? Here he was, telling her she could be in mortal danger, that he wanted her to stay with him so he could keep her safe, and all she could think about was him. Sleeping under the same roof as him. Being alone in his house with him.

Because if she did stay, all this simmering sexual tension would surely boil over. There was no way she could share this small flat with him all night and stop herself from crawling into his bed.

Would that be such a bad thing? It'd been a long time since Blake had left the island. And there had been no one since Blake. A long time to go without a man in her bed. And Sierra wanted Reed in her bed. Wanted desperately to see him naked. The image of him with his shirt off was still etched deeply into her mind. Just the thought of it had her insides squirming with lust. Oh yes, she wanted him. Badly. The ache between her thighs intensified as his grip on her hand tightened. He was still wearing his cop uniform. The color set off his black hair and equally dark eyes. Made his coffee-hued skin stand out so that she wanted to run a finger along the length of his square jaw.

"I think your jus is burning," Sierra said. He lifted one eyebrow, but he didn't move right away.

"Will you think about it?" he asked.

"Yes," she conceded, then watched as he got stiffly to his feet to go and rescue his sauce. Was he limping? It was slight, but she was sure he was favoring his left leg.

At least she was feeling better now, the red wine was doing the job. It added a nice mellow feeling to the pit of her stomach. Should she go and help him with the jus? No, she liked the view from right here. Who cared if the sauce was a little overdone? It was more than nice to have a man cook for her. Even Jake had never done that. He was more of a re-heater of leftovers, if he was ever required to cook. Sierra liked watching Reed's strong hands and his deft fingers as he put the venison into the pan to fry and then bent down to check the oven. Mmhmm, even better. His butt looked just about perfect in those long pants. A low hum throbbed through Sierra, as her gaze followed his every movement. How could she be so attracted to this guy when the rest of her world was falling apart—the rest of the island was falling apart? But the tension in the room was almost palpable. A thread of connection running between them that couldn't be broken.

It only took a few minutes for the venison to cook, and then before she knew it, Reed brought two plates to the small dining table in the corner, and was refilling her glass.

"Dinner is served, my lady." He gave a gallant bow and offered her his hand to help her out of the armchair. He sat down opposite her and they clinked glasses before she cut into her meat. It was good. The table was so small, they bumped knees often. Every time they touched, she felt a jolt race up her thigh, until finally Reed moved his leg and purposefully left it resting against hers. Her palms became sweaty as a thrill of excitement ran through her.

"You've done well," she said raising her glass in his direction. It was delicious; he'd cooked the venison to perfection, still pink and juicy in the middle, but she hardly tasted each mouthful, her nerve-endings were on fire with him so close, her brain perceiving him and nothing else. Finally, she lay down her knife and fork, her meal forgotten, and watched him over the rim of her glass. Normally, she wouldn't have more than one glass of wine, and the second glass was going to her head, leaving her inhibitions somewhere far, far away.

"Yes, I will stay with you tonight." They both knew she wasn't referring to her own safety.

"That's good." He swallowed hard, and she watched his Adam's apple bounce up and down. "You can have my bed. I'll sleep on the couch."

She smiled. "Okay, if that's what you want. But I had another arrangement in mind." Leaving her glass on the table, she got up and came around the table, sitting herself in his lap. His eyes widened, then darkened as the irises flared. She knew she was behaving shamelessly, but so be it. Let her forget about her problems tonight. And hopefully he might forget about his. She needed this. Needed him.

"Are you sure?"

She covered his mouth with hers by way of an answer. Oh, yes, she was sure. Without a word, he lifted her off his lap, took her hand and led her into his bedroom, flicking on a small lamp by the bedside. It gave the room a soft light. All concerns about her sore knee and ribs were drowned under her growing desire. She couldn't feel any of her injuries right now, it was like they didn't exist.

Even before they'd got all the way into the room, her fingers were fumbling with the buttons of his uniform, desperate to see that wonderful, chiseled chest she knew lay beneath. He helped by undoing his belt buckle and loosening his pants, then kicking off his shoes. She jerked his shirt down over his shoulders and watched as he pulled it the rest of the way off.

Reed was just as spectacular as she remembered. That gorgeous, honey-colored skin, so delicious she wanted to lick it. Dark nipples stood out on his rock-hard chest, and lines of abs rolled down towards the top of his pants. That amazing tattoo that covered all of his left shoulder. It was striking, made him look just a little bit menacing and warrior-like. Her stomach quivered at the sight. She would ask him about it. Later.

His black eyes fixed on her as he tugged on his waistband, shimmying them down over lean hips, revealing... everything. Sierra liked what she saw. He could be model material, he looked so good. Her gaze travelled down the length of his nicely-shaped legs, taking in his muscled thighs and tapered calves. Her stare caught on a litany of scars covering his left calf, reaching all the way up to his knee. She'd noticed him limping slightly a few times before, and now she had an answer as to why. She'd have to ask the *how* later.

"Your turn," he said, but made no move to help her off with her clothes. She thought she might be shy when it came to it, but all she wanted was to get naked, so she could press her skin up against him, absorb him into her. This was no sensual striptease, she pulled her clothes off as fast as she could, hungry to get back to him. Her bare feet hit the chilly floor, and now she was as exposed as he was.

It was cool in here, the warmth from the little heater in the living room not permeating this far, and gooseflesh raised up all over Sierra's body as the cold air brushed over her bare skin. But her thoughts were only of Reed, as he closed the distance between them. His lips came down to meet hers, and one hand traced up the side of her body, starting at her hip bone and finally coming up to cup her breast. A small sound escaped her lips at his touch. It felt so good.

Before Sierra knew what happened, Reed pushed her slowly backwards and her spine came to rest up against the wall, but she didn't stop kissing him, savoring the taste of his lips, firm and plump, demanding. Her arms locked around his neck and he lifted her so that her legs locked around his hips as he jammed her up against the wall. The solid heat of his erection pushed against her and she felt her bones liquefy. It'd been so long since she'd had a man inside her, her body ached for that feeling. For him to fill her up completely. She lifted her gaze and broke their kiss, looking for the bed. They needed to get to the bed.

He smiled, a hot, sexy smile, as he read her gaze and turned away from the wall, carrying all of her weight towards the middle of the room. But as he took a second step, he stumbled and she grabbed his neck tighter, worried they were going to fall.

"Bloody leg," he muttered. She flashed back to the scars she'd noticed. "Don't worry, babe, I won't drop you." His hot gaze came back to hers, and she quickly forgot all about his leg as he lowered her gently onto the bedspread and then covered her with his own warm body. All thoughts of missing girls, stalkers hunting her, crashed cars, and newspaper articles disappeared from her head. There was only here and now, with Reed. Nothing else existed.

CHAPTER FIFTEEN

Reed lay propped up on one elbow, staring down at Sierra. Soft, dawn light seeped into the room between the curtains. He needed to get up, he was already running late. The Sarge had requested he be at the station by 6 A.M. sharp. But he couldn't stop staring at her beautiful face.

There were tiny lines around her mouth and fanning out from the corners of her eyes, but otherwise her complexion was smooth and creamy. Which was quite amazing considering she'd told him she was thirty-eight last night. Perhaps it was her Middle-Eastern heritage that kept her looking so young and sexy. He liked the feel of her in his bed last night. The heat of her back against his chest as he pulled her into his body after they made love. Liked the feel of her soft curves as he lay a protective hand on her hip.

They had talked last night, while they lay together, satiated. She'd asked him about Penny and the baby, and he'd told her everything. How devastated he'd been, but how he tried to hide it for Penny's sake. How Penny couldn't cope, had blamed herself for their loss. It was the first time he'd really opened up to anyone about those years of his life and afterwards, he'd slept like a baby in her arms.

His eyes traced the curve of her cheek then up to her

temple, where the small scar split her eyebrow. Wincing as he took in the dark purple bruising around her forehead, he had to stop his finger coming up to trace the injuries. The old scar that ran along her hairline was exposed this morning, with her hair falling back onto the pillow. Where had it come from? He wanted to know more about this woman, wanted to know what made her happy, and what made her sad. They'd talked a lot about his past, but not about hers. He wanted to understand her history, so he could understand her present.

Sierra stirred and her eyes flickered open. Then her lips curved upwards in that delicious, lop-sided smile.

"Morning, sleepyhead."

"Morning," she replied, voice husky with sleep.

"You're so beautiful."

She lifted a wry eyebrow at that, as if she didn't believe her sleep-ruffled self to be at all attractive first thing in the morning.

He let his head drop and met her lips with his, kissing her gently. His heart stuttered in his chest, and it took him a moment to realize what the emotion flooding through him was. This felt so right, kissing her as she awoke. He wanted to keep doing it. Wanted to do it forever. This is where she belonged. In his bed. And in his life.

At last he lifted his head, but continued to stare down at her. "What is this scar?" He used his index finger to lightly trace along the jagged line on her forehead.

Her eyes shuttered for a second, her lips pursing, and he thought perhaps he'd crossed the line. But after what they'd shared last night, what they'd done together, he wanted to know it all. They shouldn't have any secrets.

"It's a reminder," she said at last.

"Of what?"

"Of what I lost."

Okay, so she was being cryptic. But he knew about loss.

And he knew what it did to a relationship. After all, he and Penny hadn't been able to survive her miscarriage. He was still stung by grief every time he thought about her. And the baby.

"Are you sure you really want to know? It was a long time ago, but it had a huge impact. It changed me as a person forever. It's the reason I left Adelaide and moved to KI."

Wow. It was early in the morning, and perhaps the wrong time to be diving so deep into Sierra's past, but he couldn't stop now. He needed to know.

"Yes," he said, careful to keep his voice low and compassionate. "It obviously forms a big part of your life. It matters to me." He wanted to say *you* matter to me, but stopped himself just in time.

Sierra averted her gaze, let it rest on the ceiling above instead.

"Not many people on KI knows about this." She drew in a shuddering breath. "I don't tend to talk about it. I've only told Sam and Debbie, and that was only the most basic details. Even Kylie and Rhianna don't know."

He already knew she was an intensely private person, so it made a certain kind of sense she would keep it to herself. Much like she'd kept the story of her stalker to herself.

"I was involved in a car accident, ten years ago. I hit my head. I was in a coma for two weeks afterward." She was trying to keep her face devoid of emotion, but a small twist in her mouth gave her away.

"Jesus," he whispered. He took hold of her hand, calming her fingers that'd been nervously picking at the edge of the sheet. He hoped she might feel some of the empathy he wanted to pour over her like a balm coming through his touch. He hated to see her in such emotional turmoil. Wanted to help heal it.

Images of the crash he'd been involved in morphed into his

head. It'd been bad. He'd been chasing a felon who'd staged an armed robbery and then stolen a car. The accident hadn't been his fault—not really—but he didn't particularly want to relive it, either, so he understood her reticence. He remembered the woman in the other car, screaming and screaming. A purely animal sound that sometimes still plagued his dreams. Funny, but his accident had been around ten years ago as well. The world was full of coincidences.

"But that's not the part that truly haunts me..." She hesitated and her eyes flicked quickly to his and then back to the ceiling. But it was enough to show him a glimpse of the terrible pain she carried inside. He held his breath, not sure he wanted to know anymore. "My daughter was killed in the accident. She was only nine months old. They said I was in the wrong, that I should've heard it. But I didn't, I swear I didn't. They said it was an unmarked cop car, but it had its lights and sirens blaring. Everyone else stopped. They all heard it. Why didn't I?"

Reed's blood stilled in his veins, frozen to ice. He stopped breathing. Sierra wriggled her hand in his as his grip became vise-like, and he released her with a start.

But she didn't seem to notice his distress, still lost in her own memories as she kept talking. "I didn't even get to go to Grace's funeral. Jake said they weren't sure when I would wake up, or even if I would wake up, and they couldn't wait forever." Her eyes had glazed over as she continued to look at the ceiling.

He stared at her, watching her lips move, yet paralyzed, unable to move or talk.

"Jake and I didn't last long after that. I think he blamed me, even though he denied it. That's when I moved to KI, to get away from all the people and—"

"Where did it happen? Where was your crash? Exactly." Reed ground the question out between clenched teeth. His body had gone rigid, all muscles so tightly tensed he thought he might snap in two.

"What? What do you mean?"

"I need to know. Can you tell me the name of the intersection where the crash happened?" His voice was a low growl, sounding rough, like a crazed bear.

"Why?" Her gaze finally refocused and came to rest on his face, bewilderment slowly replacing torment.

"Please, just tell me."

"It was on the corner of Morphett and Anzac in North Glenelg." She sat up, pulling the blankets to cover her breasts. "Why, Reed? What does it matter where it was?"

Reed swung his legs over the side of the bed and put his head in his hands. A low groan escaped his throat.

No. This couldn't be. It couldn't be right.

"Tell me what's going on." Her tone had taken on a high note.

He stood up, unable to sit still a second longer, and started pacing across the room. Should he tell her what he suspected? What he feared? What would it do to her? To them? He'd wanted to take those few seconds in time back for so long. Had revisited them over and over again, wishing them into oblivion. He'd been driving an unmarked police car when he'd gone through a red light. Sirens blaring, blue-and-red lights flashing. All the cars had stopped for him. He'd checked. Double-checked. The other car had come out of nowhere. Her car. They'd told him a baby girl had died in the crash. Died on impact. When he heard that he'd wanted to howl like a wounded animal. Like the sound the woman had made trapped in the car, trying to get to her dead baby.

Was it Sierra?

Was she the woman in the other car?

Had he killed her daughter?

He stared at her, eyes wild, wanting to run from the room.

"Tell me what's wrong, Reed. You look terrible. Like you've seen a ghost."

He owed her something. An explanation. How did he start?

"I think…" His voice came out hoarse and croaky, like he'd swallowed a toad. He tried again. "I was driving an unmarked police car that day. I hurt my leg in an accident." He pointed to the scars on his calf. "At the intersection of Morphett and Anzac."

She got out of the other side of the bed and backed away from him, ignoring the cold and the fact she was completely naked.

"What?" she whispered through bloodless lips. "What are you saying?" She shook her head wildly, her long, dark hair falling in untidy waves across her face. "You can't be the one… They would never tell me the officer's name. And I didn't want to know anyway. Knowing wouldn't bring back my daughter. But you can't be him. You can't!"

"I don't know, Sierra. I'm not sure." But he was sure. He reached out a hand toward her. This couldn't be happening. Surely this wasn't true, they could figure it out. The two of them.

She recoiled from his hand in horror.

"No." Her voice was a ghost of a declaration. Dark eyes stared back at him, wide with fear and confusion. Then she started scrabbling around on the floor, gathering up her clothes they had tossed heedlessly around last night. God, was it only last night they'd made love? He'd felt so alive, so overjoyed. Such tenderness and warmth. All of it gone in the blink of an eye.

"I need to get out of here." Taking her jumbled clothes, she fled to the bathroom.

"Fuck." Reed ran a hand through his hair and began pacing across the room again, ignoring his own nakedness.

The names of the victims of the crash he'd been given were S. Cumberland and her daughter, G. Cumberland. That must have been Sierra's married name. What had she said her husband was called? Jake? She'd introduced herself as Sierra Goldstein on the ferry. Probably reverted back to her maiden name after she divorced.

The Senior Sergeant had advised Reed against finding out too much information afterward. Said it was better to leave it to procedure. It didn't help to dwell on the details. If he wanted to move on, continue to do his job as a cop, then he had to drop the guilt, leave the past behind him.

There had been an internal investigation after the crash, of course there had. Reed was laid up in hospital for three weeks afterward, and then there was months of rehab after that. The SAPOL internal investigation unit had grilled him over and over, and Reed had answered them truthfully, over and over. Yes, his sirens had been on. Yes, his lights had been on. Yes, he'd slowed at the intersection. Yes, he'd checked to make sure the traffic was all stopped.

Then she'd just taken off, without any warning. Plowed straight into him, while all the other cars sat obediently waiting for him to pass through.

After talking to witnesses at the scene, the investigation concluded Reed was not to blame for the crash. He'd been carrying out his sworn duty, that was all. Chasing down a fleeing felon, who'd just stabbed an innocent attendant at a nearby gas station. And he'd taken all due precautions before heading through the red light.

There had been an outcry from the public, as there always was when something tragic like this happened. A call for police to stop high-speed pursuits. Reed could understand the public's view. It was a terrible tragedy, and all they saw was a little girl, dead. But they didn't see the other side of the coin; how many felons the police had stopped that day, that week, that year. How many other people's lives had been saved by putting these criminals behind bars where they couldn't hurt anyone. What were they supposed to do? Let the criminals go? If the underbelly of society knew police weren't allowed to take part in pursuits, then they'd all start doing it. An easy way to evade the cops. Things would descend into anarchy.

Something sharp ripped through Reed's gut, and he nearly doubled over with the pain. Guilt. Guilt and regret sliced through him. Oh God, Sierra. He'd been responsible for the death of her baby. He hadn't been able to forgive himself when it happened, not truly, no matter how much people told him it wasn't his fault, that it was a sad repercussion of doing his job. But now that he knew her, knew how much she'd lost, the guilt was unbearable.

What to do now? A shiver racked his body, and for the first time he noticed he was still completely nude. As if on auto-pilot, Reed grabbed a pair of jeans from his closet and an old sweater from a drawer and dragged them on.

Sierra emerged from the ensuite bathroom, avoiding his gaze as she skirted around the bed and out the door.

"Sierra, wait. We need to talk about this."

But she quickened her pace, rushing down the hallway.

He couldn't let her go, not like this. Running after her, he managed to grab hold of her arm just as she reached the front door.

"Let go of me," she snarled, whirling around, her face a mask of fear and rage. "Don't touch me."

He let go as if she'd burned him, and she flung the door open and ran out of the flat, her long legs taking her around the corner and out of his sight. Where was she going? She had no car. He went to run after her, but stopped after only a few strides. That look on her face. She despised him. Hated him.

There was nothing he could do to help this. Not right now, not until she calmed down.

He thought about Penny and his unborn son, and the words, *if you let yourself love someone, you're bound to get hurt*, churned around in his head. Sierra had just proven those words correct, yet again. Not that he was in love with the woman, but even the idea he might be falling for her should be warning enough for him to step away. It was a reminder not to get too involved.

His phone buzzed from the table inside, and he hung his head. He was already late for work. Lifting his head, he stared in the direction Sierra had disappeared. If he couldn't help her right now, then he may as well expend his energy on finding the lost girl. Dive back into work headfirst. Perhaps that would help to ease the terrible tight band around his chest. The one that was threatening to choke off all his air.

CHAPTER SIXTEEN

The streets were quiet; it was still early. Sierra didn't much care which direction she went in, her feet stumbled first down one road and then another. All she cared about was getting as far away from Reed as possible.

She wandered in a daze, her mind refusing to focus on anything as it shied away from the terrible truth.

Kingscote wasn't that big and after a while she found herself walking along The Esplanade, with the ocean stretching out, sullen and dreary before her. She came across a bench seat, set on a grassy knoll, facing the water, and sat down, suddenly too exhausted to keep going. Staring blankly out to sea, she held the tears at bay. She was too numb to cry.

How long she sat there, Sierra wasn't sure, but when she looked up, the sun was much higher in the sky. She couldn't sit here all day. Her car was a wreck, and she had no immediate way to get home. An idea formed in her head. She'd go to Kylie's. It was the first place that came to mind. She would be safe there. She could think there.

Her phone had been buzzing in her bag ever since she left Reed's place. She didn't need to look at it to know they were messages from him. She didn't want to read them. Not any of them. Nothing he could say would ever make this right. She turned her phone off. It was better that way.

Kylie's house was only five minutes back up The Esplanade, and then two blocks inland. Sierra knocked on the front door, but there was no answer. Where could she be? Her discombobulated mind took many minutes to process the answer. Today was Monday. Kylie would be at work, and her kids would be at school. Sierra knew where the spare key was kept, so she headed around to the backyard to retrieve it from the special rock hidden in the garden.

Kylie wouldn't mind if Sierra let herself in, she was a good friend. That's what good friends did. Sierra made it as far as the brown leather couch in the living room. She lay down gratefully and curled into a ball, pulling her long legs up into her chest.

Reed.

Oh no, Reed.

It couldn't be. He couldn't be the one. Her mind refused to believe it. But somewhere inside she knew it was true. If only he hadn't been chasing that speeding car. If only she hadn't had the music up so loud. If only she'd picked Grace up five minutes earlier, like she was supposed to. If only she hadn't met him. She wished she'd never met him. This pain was like losing her daughter all over again.

Sierra curled even tighter as the sobs began to rack her body.

The sound of a key rattling in a lock woke Sierra hours later. She sat up and looked dazedly around the room. Kylie walked in, her hands full of shopping bags, her two boys following behind her. They all stopped and stared at Sierra sitting on their couch.

"Sorry," Sierra said, getting painfully to her feet. All her muscles felt like they were made of molten lead, still painful and aching from the crash. "I hope you don't mind. I didn't know where else to go."

Kylie dumped the bags on the kitchen counter and made her way to the couch, shooing the boys toward their bedrooms as she did so. "No probs, honey. You know you're welcome anytime." A worried frown lined Kylie's face, belying her easy words. "I've got a bottle of wine in one of those bags. Shall we open it?"

Sierra wasn't sure if she wanted alcohol, but she nodded mutely and followed her friend back into the kitchen.

Kylie turned to study her and gasped, "What the hell happened to your face?"

"I crashed my car yesterday," she replied, and gave Kylie the short version of events.

Sensing that Sierra didn't want to go into detail just yet, Kylie chatted brightly about her day while she prepared dinner, and Sierra sat on a barstool on the other side of the counter watching as she sipped slowly at her wine. This was the second time in less than a week Sierra had come to Kylie for help. She owed her friend big-time. Kylie waved away her offer to help cook dinner in her efficient way, her short blonde bob swaying as she moved, and told her to stay put and chill out. Kylie was petite and athletic, everything about her exuded proficiency and competence. She worked as an administrator at the island's only accounting firm, and was dressed in a classic pencil skirt and matching navy jacket. There was nothing flippant about Kylie, and that was one of the reasons Sierra liked her so much. Every now and then Sierra caught Kylie eyeing her speculatively, but she didn't ask the questions that were hovering on her lips. Sierra knew she owed her a more in-depth story, especially after she'd used her friend's house as a crash pad. Twice.

"Have you heard about Tom?" Kylie stopped what she was doing and turned to stare at Sierra, confusion and worry creasing her face. "I can't believe it. Maureen told me this afternoon at the supermarket. They've arrested him, but they're not saying why yet. Do you think he's a suspect in the missing-girl case?"

Sierra froze. She wasn't sure what to say. Reed had told her in confidence about Tom Hubbard's arrest for having kiddie porn on his computer. But they were yet to file any charges, and so the public hadn't been told the details.

She decided to play innocent. "No, I hadn't heard."

Kylie continued, "God, what if they find out Tom has been keeping her prisoner in his basement, or something equally depraved?" Kylie pursed her lips as she glared out the window, considering. "Nope, I won't believe it. Tom isn't capable of something like that. Jesus, we all know the man. Trust him. He's a pillar of the community. Why would he do something as stupid and sordid as that? He wouldn't. He just wouldn't."

Sierra silently agreed with Kylie. She didn't think Tom had anything to do with abducting a child, but he couldn't be completely discounted, especially if he had those pictures on his computer.

After dinner, when the boys had gone to their rooms to do homework, Kylie could no longer hold her tongue.

"So, honey, what's going on with you?"

Sierra leaned back in the couch and stared at the floor, unable to meet her friend's gaze. Where to start? After a moment's consideration, the beginning seemed like the best place. She'd never told her friends about her car accident, or losing her baby. At first, it was because she didn't want to burden them with that kind of sob story so early in their friendship. Afterwards, it had never seemed like the right time to bring it up. And part of her wanted her friends to see her as normal. Well, as normal as possible, anyway. She didn't want them looking at her with pity or even condemnation in their eyes.

Sierra sucked in a deep breath. "You know I moved to the

island around ten years ago, right?"

"Yes, you wanted to get away from your ex-husband, after a bad divorce." Kylie reached over to top up her wine and waited for Sierra to continue.

"That's true. But it's not the full story." She glanced behind her to make sure the boys were still safely tucked away in their bedrooms. "I wasn't just escaping my ex, I was also recovering from a bad car accident."

"Oh, honey. That's terrible." Kylie put her glass carefully down on the side table, so she could give all of her attention to Sierra.

Sierra clenched her hands together tightly as she continued, "My baby daughter was also killed in that accident."

Kylie's face blanched. "Holy shit, Sierra."

Sierra held up her hand to stop Kylie saying any more. She needed to get this out now, or she might run out of courage. She kept talking, letting the words tumble out in a torrent, while Kylie stared at her with a look caught between horror and heartbreak. Sierra told her how she and Jake couldn't survive. How Jake blamed her for the accident. How she blamed herself for the accident. And that's why she'd moved to the island. Then she told her about Reed. About meeting him on the ferry. About staying the night with him. And about his revelation this morning.

When her words finally ran out, Kylie gathered her up in her arms and she wept into her friend's shoulder. Later, once her torrent of tears had run dry, Kylie persuaded her to stay the night. Sierra gratefully accepted. There was no way she wanted to go home to her cold, empty house tonight. Not with her heart so raw and exposed. And not with Reed's words of warning still ringing in her ears.

After a not-so-quick phone call to Debbie to ask her to feed her cats—for the second night in a row—Sierra lay down on the couch under a soft blanket and stared out the front window of Kylie's house at the stars appearing in the sky. Debbie had been shocked when Sierra told her about the chickens, and she was still terribly worried about Sierra, wanting to know who would do such a terrible thing. Debbie informed her that Sam had wanted to bury her girls for her, so she wouldn't have to see their poor little dead bodies. But Sierra told her that Reed would send someone out just as soon as they could, because after her crash, it was now considered a crime scene. It took a lot of persuasion and calm discussion to finally get Debbie off the phone. But it left Sierra with a warm feeling in the pit of her stomach. Her neighbors cared deeply for her, and she was lucky to have them. There was no way Sierra was ever going to believe Reed's theory that everyone around her was a suspect as her stalker. At least, not where Sam was concerned. He was a good man. She knew it right down to her bones.

Her crying fit with Kylie had left her feeling drained and empty. But also strangely peaceful. As if a tsunami had washed through her. That was twice now in two days she'd cried her heart out.

Now it was the middle of the night, and as Sierra lay on the couch her mind was clear for the first time that day. Unable to sleep, she started to go over the past few days, trying to make sense of all that'd happened. The break-in. Her chickens. Her car, which'd been tampered with. Reed had confirmed her suspicions. Who would want to hurt her? Was it her stalker?

She thought about running into Blake last night at the supermarket, and the spooky feeling he left her with. Could it be Blake? No, he couldn't be her stalker, those letters had started twelve years ago, when she'd published the exposé. She hadn't even known him then. But could he have done the other things? Killed her chickens and sabotaged her car in a fit of spite? A spurned lover? He had admitted half the reason he'd accepted the job in KI was because of her. Blake was hot-tempered and impetuous, but surely he wasn't capable of murder. Was he?

Her thoughts flittered to Evan, and running into him as she careened out of the shop. He'd seemed genuinely worried about her. He'd even spilled his groceries, he was in that much of a hurry to give her a lift in his car. But then Reed had appeared, and she'd been so relieved to see him. A vague memory tugged at the corners of her mind. Of bending down and retrieving some of Evan's fallen items, of him yelling at her to leave them alone. What had she picked up again?

Sierra sat up in a hurry, her hand flying up to cover her mouth.

Shit.

It was all coming back to her now. At the time, she hadn't thought much about it, with Reed calling her name and Evan yelling at her.

The things she'd picked up and handed back to Evan. One was a packet of caramel candies. The other was a light blue cap. Like a baseball cap. But it was small, way too small to fit on Evan's head. It was meant for a child.

A child's hat.

And a packet of caramels.

The same brand they'd found at the alleged abduction site.

A shiver ran all the way through Sierra's body.

Was it a link?

Normal people were allowed to buy candies and hats. Right?

The thing was, Evan didn't have any kids.

Were they for a friend's kid?

And then there was the information she'd gleaned from the detective the other day, the small detail not many people knew about. The small detail that'd been discounted because there wasn't enough evidence to link it to anything. The small detail she'd wanted to tell Reed last night, but hadn't gotten around to it. That a caramel wrapper had been found near where the first girl had been taken in the Adelaide case. Was it relevant to Evan? Could they match it to him somehow?

She knew Evan was unmarried, with no children, through their talks at the news agency. Evan liked to talk, a lot. Sierra used to think he was probably lonely. The very first time she'd gone into his shop, just after he took it over eighteen months ago, he'd struck up a conversation with her, had seemed genuinely interested. And he'd seemed harmless enough. He was always fascinated in her and what she had to say. The least she could do was return the favor. She often quietly thought to herself he might even be gay. With his neat and tidy appearance, his clothes always clean and squared away.

But now that she was looking at him in a different light, she began to wonder if he was that attentive to all his customers. Or was it just her? She shuddered.

Her immediate thought was perhaps she should call Reed and let him know. Then she remembered who he was, what he'd done and she discarded that idea. If she was going to call anyone, then it would have to be the Sarge.

Surely this was crazy? She couldn't go tattling on someone to the cops just because of a crazy hunch. Could she? Then she'd become just like every other scared and near-hysterical member of the island community. Ready to rat out a friend at the slightest provocation. There was no way Evan had anything to do with the abduction of a child, she was sure of it.

Just as sure that Tom Hubbard hadn't liked kiddie porn? She should leave this be. The police had a man in custody already. They knew what they were doing. Most likely they had the right guy, and it was only a matter of time before the truth came out. Before Tom confessed to abducting that little girl.

But then why were her guts churning like she'd swallowed a colony of ants? Sierra couldn't sit anymore, her legs were trembling, so she wrapped the blanket around her shoulders and got up and walked over to the window to stare out at the street. It just didn't feel right. How could Tom have lived for so long in the island community without raising any red flags? If he was the pedophile responsible for taking Jessica, then this would be his first offense, because there was no way he could've gotten away with something like this before. Not in this close-knit island community.

But Evan, on the other hand. Well, he'd only moved to the island less than two years ago. No one really knew anything about his past. Where he came from, what he did before he bought the newsstand. The more she thought about it, the more questions she had about Evan.

One feeble light cast a dim glow, but the rest of the street was in darkness. Everyone tucked up in their beds, asleep, like she should be in the wee hours of the morning.

Her journalistic mind began to mull things over. What if she did a little bit of investigating on her own? It couldn't hurt, could it? No, she shook her head, she'd given up on all that ten years ago. It'd all seemed so unimportant and petty after she lost the only truly significant thing in her life. Jen had tried so many times to talk her back into writing more articles, doing some freelancing for *The Advertiser*. But Sierra wasn't interested, she'd shoved that part of her life into a small compartment and that's where it'd stayed. Sure, she still did the occasional piece for *The Islander*, but they were fluffy pieces, nothing with any real grit or relevance. But that itch behind her eyes, that small buzz of excitement running through her was so familiar, it made her want to grab a piece of paper and start writing things down. Putting the puzzle pieces together. That was what she'd been so good at, after all. It wasn't the story she was after. No, she was well past selling herself out for a story. If she found anything, anything at all that even smelled slightly like Evan might be involved then she'd call the Sarge straight away. It was about the chase, matching wits with a foe. And winning.

Evan owned the small one-bedroom flat attached at the back of the shop. It'd come as a package when he bought the business. But Sierra knew he also owned a property over near Hog Bay, around twenty minutes away. He'd told her once he was going to build on it soon, when he'd gained a bit more capital from the shop. He was proud of his property, had big plans for it, but at the moment, it only sported a couple of run-down sheds.

Sierra had never been there, but his descriptions had been pretty detailed. She thought she might be able to find it. Would Kylie lend her her car? Normally, Kylie walked to work. And the boys rode their bikes to school, unless it was raining, and then Kylie would drive them. Sierra searched the dark sky. No clouds covered the stars tonight. The forecast was for a clear, but cold, day tomorrow.

A plan began to form in Sierra's head.

The terrible lethargy was still there, her heart still hurting from the truth of Reed's declaration. But now she had something else to think about, something else to distract her. It wasn't a remedy for her problem, it was a diversion and nothing more. But anything that helped her forget what Reed had done, to help bury those memories back down deep, where they belonged, was a good thing.

She'd ask to borrow Kylie's car tomorrow. Rental cars were in high demand on the island from the single rental company, and Sierra might have to wait days for one to become available. Kylie would understand. Sierra bit her bottom lip. Should she tell Kylie where she was going? Yes, she didn't want to lie to her friend, and if anything did happen to her—which was highly unlikely—then at least someone would know where she was. She might be stupid enough to go off on some half-baked plan, but she wasn't stupid enough to do it without telling someone. Kylie might take a little convincing, but she would argue that if she found anything, anything at all, she'd let the police know.

She still hadn't turned her phone back on. Wasn't sure she was ready to look at all of Reed's texts that would be there waiting for her. Would he be asking for forgiveness? Because if he was, she wasn't going to grant it. Or would he be worried about her? Especially since he wanted to protect her from the stalker, and she knew he'd probably be feeling helpless and frustrated with her lack of communication.

Should she at least send him a text to let him know she was okay? A guilty conscience warred with grief and betrayal inside her head. Maybe she'd get Kylie to send him a message tomorrow. That way, she wouldn't have to talk to him, but she could also assuage her guilt. Sierra wasn't sure she ever wanted to talk to Reed again.

She went back to the couch and lay down. There were still a few hours before daylight, and she might be able to catch a bit of sleep before she had to get up for the day. Now that she had a plan in place, her churning mind was quieter. It felt good to have something solid to do.

CHAPTER SEVENTEEN

Reed tapped a finger on the front counter. It was mid-morning, and the Sarge was coming in to the police station to meet him in half an hour, then they were going to have a debrief with all of the mainland officers. Jessica had been missing for four days now. Hope was fading quickly of finding her alive. The media were becoming downright nasty in their growing condemnation of police handling of the case. They needed a breakthrough soon, and Don hoped that by going over everything again, they might find something they'd missed.

The problem was, Reed's mind was no longer on the case. He spent most of his time worrying about Sierra. And those thoughts had him oscillating between anxious agitation and outright anger. Worse, he couldn't decide which one to settle on. She wasn't answering her phone. What if the stalker had re-appeared? What if he'd managed to finish the job he'd started? Sierra could be in imminent danger. And Reed was more than partly to blame.

He began pacing back and forth across the small reception area.

Where had she gone yesterday morning? He'd gone in search of her. Thrown his police uniform on, jumped into his car, and driven up and down the nearby streets. The town wasn't that big, how had she just disappeared? She must've run far and fast on those long legs of hers. But then the Sarge had phoned, asking where the hell he was, he was already half an hour late. They'd been completely inundated all day by the media, and Don asked him to help him with another press conference to try and keep the wolves at bay. It hadn't worked, the media kept demanding more answers, calling Don out, asking him if he thought he was fit to head this investigation. It was exhausting, and a tiny part of Reed wished Sierra had been there to help.

Any spare second he got, he would send her a text, pleading with her to let him know she was okay. There was no way he had time to drive out to her house, to see if she'd somehow managed to get home, so he'd called her next-door neighbors—the ones he'd met at the fire station the other day, Sam and Debbie—and asked them to check on her for him. They told him that apart from a phone call from her asking them to feed her two cats last night, they hadn't seen Sierra. At least they confirmed she stayed with a friend, which allayed some of his fears.

More and more people were joining the search for the missing girl, and Reed helped Eric coordinate with the SES. The coroner had removed the human bones they'd found on Saturday, but he had many questions that still needed answering. Reed had been out to the burial site twice in the past two days. A hotline had also been set up for the hundreds of leads pouring in, people claiming to have seen the missing girl, Jessica, or to have a pertinent piece of information. Reed had worked late into the night, combing through some of the more promising leads, with no result. Then he'd stumbled home a little after midnight to try and grab a couple of hours' sleep. But sleep eluded him as the scene with Sierra that morning played over and over in his head.

But the longer it went without any contact from Sierra, the angrier Reed became. At first, he thought it was built on his fear for her safety. But in the end, he knew it was a lot more than that.

He was angry at her because she blamed him for the accident.

When he'd first made the admission, he'd wholeheartedly agreed with her. Wasn't that the exact reason he'd been wracked with guilt for the past ten years, because deep down inside, he still believed he could've done something to stop it?

But she hadn't wanted to listen to him, to hear his side of the story. He needed to explain himself, to get her to understand, try and ease the burden of guilt, even just a little. But she'd looked at him like he was the devil incarnate. And that hurt.

He'd wanted to shout at her then, that everyone else had heard his sirens, knew there was a police car coming, and stopped to let him through. Why hadn't she? Wasn't she also partly to blame for the accident? The idea was irrational and perverse, but nonetheless, he couldn't shake the anger boiling up from deep inside at the way she'd treated him.

His cell vibrated on the counter and he reached for it. Was it Sierra, finally replying to his numerous texts? He hesitated when he saw the caller ID. It was his father. It probably wasn't the right time to talk to Nikau, but on instinct, he took the call.

"Hi, Reed."

"Hi, Dad." It was good to hear his father's voice. "Sorry I haven't called you. It's been a little hectic over here." In different circumstances, Reed would've enjoyed talking to his father. They had a solid relationship, built on trust and respect. His father's relaxed demeanor and unfailing faith in his son's ability might help to calm the growing fear gnawing through Reed's guts right now.

"So, things aren't as quiet as you thought they'd be on your sleepy little island?" chuckled his father.

"No," Reed agreed. "As soon as I can get some leave, I'll come home to see you all." His parents had hoped he might be able to go home for a week or two before he started his new job, but it hadn't been possible, Don had needed him to start ASAP. He would've liked to go home and spend some time with his family, see his grandparents, as well. Both sets of grandparents were still alive and going strong. When this was all over, when this mess had finally died down, he'd ask for a much-needed break.

"That'd be great. We'd love to see you. Your mum especially, you know she worries about you."

Yes, he did. But he knew Shelly's worrying about him was her way of showing how much she loved him. Reed wondered how Sierra and his mother, Shelly, would get on. Both were very strong, opinionated personalities. He mentally drew himself up short. Why was he even considering such a meeting? That would never happen, not now, not after what they'd discovered about each other.

And he couldn't blame her.

Whatever the fledgling hope that'd built in his chest the other night, as she lay in his arms—the soft sound of her inhaling and exhaling as she slept tugging at the very core of him—it was no use anymore. If he'd thought there might have been a future for him and Sierra, it'd been destroyed by one terrible mistake ten years ago.

"It's hectic over there, you say. I'm sure it's nothing you can't handle, though. You're a damn good cop, Reed, and don't you ever forget it." There was a note of curiosity in Nikau's voice. "I did hear something on the news the other night about a missing girl. Is that in your neck of the woods?"

Wow, it must be big if it was making it onto the nightly news in Auckland. Reed stifled a sigh. The media were certainly pointing a spotlight onto the small island, at the moment. But he probably shouldn't expect anything less of them. They all wanted the girl found.

"Yes, Dad. I'm involved in that case." It was all he was prepared to say, even to his father.

Nikau gave a low whistle. "I can see why you're busy, then," he muttered. "But I have no doubt you will find her. It's what you do, Reed."

"Thanks, Dad." It was stupid how a few words of praise raised a lump at the back of his throat. He wasn't a gangly teenager anymore, needing his father's admiration. But it still felt good, even as a grown man, to know his father had faith in him. "I've gotta go. The boss is due in a few minutes."

"Sure. Oh, Reed, before you hang up. Have you met anyone nice over there? I'm only asking because your mother has been nagging me for the past week to ring and find out. She would kill me if I didn't ask now."

Reed laughed. It was so true, and he could hear the fear in his father's voice at the thought of what Shelly would do to him if he hung up with nothing to report. What to say, though? On the spur of the moment, he decided to go with the truth.

"I'm not sure, Dad. Maybe. I'll let you know as soon as I do. She's a very interesting woman. But also very complicated." Sierra was all that and much more, but he wasn't about to go into the nitty-gritty details with his dad right now.

"Bah, all women are complicated, son. Haven't you learned that by now?"

Reed was a little surprised at the vehemence in his father's voice.

"But if she's worth it, then you'll find a way to get around those complications. And believe me, I know. Your mum's one of the most complicated women on this planet."

"Got that right," Reed agreed. "But this is different. Sierra…Well, she's been hurt. And she's looking for someone to blame." He didn't add, *and that person is me*.

There was a second of silence on the other end of the phone line. "I won't pretend to know the full story, but when someone's hurting, they usually just need time to work stuff out. Give her a bit of space and understanding. But don't give up on her. She'll come around in the end."

"Mmhmm." Reed made a non-committal sound in his throat. He wasn't so sure any amount of space and understanding would heal Sierra's wounds.

"It's about time you let someone into your life again, Reed. You've been alone too long now. It's time you fell in love."

He was shocked by the forthright words, especially coming from his father. "Ah…thanks, Dad. I'll think about that."

"Good," Nikau replied, voice gruff. "All right, off you go, and find that missing child."

"Bye," Reed said down the phone, but his dad had already hung up.

Well, that was an interesting conversation. His father had never voiced his opinion on his son's love-life quite like that before. Not even when he was grieving for his stillborn son. Or when Penny left him.

Life had always taught him, if you let someone in, let yourself have feelings for them, then all you were doing was opening yourself up for them to hurt you. Love wasn't worth it. But the conversation with his dad had suddenly turned things around in his head.

A message pinged on his phone and he looked down. It was from a number he didn't recognize. Reed frowned as he opened the text.

Hi, this is Kylie. You don't know me, but I'm a friend of Sierra's.

His eyebrows slowly lifted. It wasn't from Sierra herself, but this might be the next best thing.

I'm so sorry for not getting in touch with your sooner. I got caught up with the boys and then my boss was in a pickle at work. Anyway, never mind.

Was this woman ever going to get to the point?

Sierra asked me to contact you. She wanted me to tell you she is okay. She stayed with me last night.

Reed let out a small puff of relief. Thank God. Then he narrowed his eyes at the phone. Damn woman, why didn't she have the decency to talk to him herself? Why did she have to get a friend to do it?

Sierra also asked me to tell you that she borrowed my car, and is headed out to some place called Hog Bay, and to please not worry about her anymore. That's all. Bye, from Kylie.

He ground his teeth together in frustration, fighting the urge to hurl the phone at the wall. Anger warred with growing anxiety in his gut. The last thing he needed today was to be chasing Sierra all over the island. Especially when she most likely wouldn't even talk to him. His father's words came back to him. *"Give her a bit of time and space and she'll come around."*

Reed grunted and stood, walking over to the large map of KI hung on the wall behind the reception desk. With his finger, he traced the road to Hog Bay. It was isolated. Why would she go all the way out there by herself? Something wasn't right. The more he looked at the map, the more it set his stomach to churning. There were no search sites over in that direction, not as far as he knew, anyway. So, she couldn't be out with an SES crew. What the hell kind of clue could she possibly be chasing over there?

Kylie's text had told him not to worry, that she was only letting him know as a courtesy. But something told him he needed to get over there.

* * *

Sierra sat in the idling car, staring across the gravel road at the partly hidden driveway. It was pure luck she'd spotted the small turnoff. This was the third time she'd made a pass down this section of the road, and had been just about to call it a day, turn around and drive back to Kylie's. Could this be Evan's place?

A wire fence straggled along the side of the road, falling down in some places and in severe need of repair. Tall weeds grew high and gangly along the fence, and Sierra could just make out some old pastures on the other side, but they looked unused and unkempt, no animals had grazed here in quite some time. As she peered through the windshield three gray heads popped up over the top of the weeds, and a small mob of kangaroos stared thoughtfully back at her. Well, no domesticated animals grazed these paddocks. This small patch of land was at odds with the two farms on either side. As she'd driven down the road, she'd seen well-tended fences, and fat sheep filling a couple of the green paddocks. Evan had said his land had once been a small farm, more of a hobby farm, really, but they'd raised some goats and a few cows for milk. Now it was completely run-down and unkempt. Ripe for his plans to re-build and renovate it.

She put the car into reverse and backed it up a hundred meters or so, until she came to a large stand of eucalyptus trees. Pulling the car off onto the side, she slid it in behind the trees, nose in against the falling-down fence. Grabbing her bag and coat, she locked the car and walked back up the road. She checked her phone was in her bag, and noticed she was getting some weak reception, which was good if she needed to make a quick phone call.

Instead of walking back to the overgrown drive, Sierra looked for a spot where she might get through the fence. Why announce herself by boldly walking straight down the driveway? She would take a more circumspect route and hopefully take a look around without arousing too much suspicion. Sure enough, there was a gap in the fence where one of the wooden posts had rotted away. She squeezed through, and then had to fight her way between the tangled long grass and weeds until she came out into the clearing and the slightly shorter pasture. As she stepped into the open, numerous sets of eyes swiveled her way. A whole mob of kangaroos stared belligerently at her, as if annoyed their peaceful breakfast of grass had been disturbed. She took a couple of steps towards them and they took off, bounding in great, lazy hops away from her, toward a patch of thick scrub at the other side of the clearing. The overgrown driveway skirted along the edge of the pasture, heading in the same direction, so she decided to follow the roos' lead.

It was now mid-morning, but in typical KI tradition, the clouds hung low, threatening rain, and the day was gray and dismal. The long grass was damp with raindrops from a previous shower, and her pants were soon saturated up to her knees. Thankfully, she had on her hiking boots, so at least her feet would stay dry.

The branches crowded down low and thick as she came to the end of the pasture. This area hadn't been cleared, or even had a fire through here in a long time. The trees lined up like dank soldiers in front of her and there were places where the undergrowth was so thick, she had to go around rather than beat her way through it. An aura of disquiet settled in her abdomen, urging her to turn around, go back to her car, forget about her little escapade. But she stiffened her spine. There was nothing to be afraid of here. She'd walked all over KI, through dense scrub and over sparse, coastal heath, she knew what she was doing. Was a pro at this. All she wanted was to take a quick survey, get the lay of the land, and then get the hell out.

Evan had mentioned the property had an old, ramshackle cottage, mostly falling down and definitely not livable. Then there were two or three sheds, Evan thought they were used for housing the hobby-farm animals once, long ago. Sierra assumed they would be at the end of wherever the winding driveway led. She glanced over to her left and could just make out the meandering road as a shaft of sunlight broke through the clouds. If she kept it on her left, walked parallel to it, then she could remain hidden in the bush and hopefully approach the place unseen.

After fifteen minutes of hard slogging through the forest, Sierra was out of breath and wishing she'd brought a bottle of water with her. This property went back farther than she thought. She was suddenly grateful for her long legs and glad she kept her fitness level up with lots of walking and swimming. Her bruised knee was beginning to ache with every step, however, and she stopped to give it a rub, ease some of the pain out of the tendons.

This place was really out of the way. Someone would have to be looking hard to find it. She thought the trees were thinning a little up ahead, and after another few more minutes, she was rewarded by a large clearing, and the square shapes of buildings morphing out of the forest.

Sierra stopped just inside the edge of the tree-line, and surveyed the structures in front of her. There were three of them, all huddled together a short way away. Long grass romped around the base of the buildings, and they looked deserted and uncared for. It was gloomy in here, surrounded on all sides by towering eucalyptus trees. Some people might like it, this closed-in view of wild scrubland and nothing else. A tree change, some might call it. But personally, she liked to be able to see the sky, and the ocean, the feeling of being unconfined.

She stared at the small farm for many long moments,

looking for movement, signs that Evan might be here somewhere. There was no car parked nearby that she could see.

It would do no good standing here all day, so in the end she decided to move forward, head around the back of the first building, which looked to be a small tin shed, rusted through in many places. Her steps were quiet and precise. Stealthy, stalking toward the structure. What was she expecting to find? Did she really think she was going to come across a clue? Something to point to the fact Evan was a child abductor. That he had taken Jessica? It was preposterous. So why was she being so covert? She had no idea, really. All she had was a gut feeling, and her gut had been right in the past.

A circumnavigation of the small shed did nothing to enlighten her as to its contents. There were no windows, and only one small door, locked with a big padlock. The ground around the shed looked undisturbed, as if no one had been near it in a long time. Sierra found a small hole and put one eye to it, to try and see inside. It was dark and dingy, and from what she could see, completely empty. Nothing moved in there. It was all hushed and still. Not even the scuffle of a fleeing rat, or a bird tweeting.

Actually, the dead silence was starting to unnerve her. It was creepy. Sierra felt as if there were eyes boring into the back of her neck. She turned suddenly, and stared back the way she'd come. Then she gave a quiet laugh. There was nothing out there, she was being stupid. Nevertheless, she scrabbled in her bag and got out her cell phone, checked for reception. Shit, it wasn't good, it oscillated between one bar and nothing. Mostly nothing. But she kept the phone in her hand.

"Hello, Sierra."

She jumped and nearly screamed before she could cover her mouth. Then her hand flew up to press against her heart, which was about to beat right out of her chest.

"Shit, Reed, you bloody scared me," she hissed, forgetting for a second that she was mad at him.

Reed stepped out from behind the corner of the shed and gave her one of those laconic grins, the one where the dimple in his chin showed. Had he been hiding from her? Stalking her? Her heart lurched at the sight of him, standing all tall and manly. Dark and dangerous. And very, very tempting. But then the terrible memories came crashing back down on her. She crossed her arms and took a step away from him. His grin evaporated as fast as it'd appeared.

"What are you doing here?" Her voice had regained some composure and was now cold, her tone slashing at him like a knife. And if her words weren't enough, she also shot daggers at him with her eyes, warning him not to come any closer.

"I could ask you the same question." His dark eyebrows lowered as he gave her one of his cop stares. Oh, no, he didn't. He didn't get to pull his cop card on her. Not now. Not ever.

"None of your bloody business," she replied, jutting her chin at him in defiance.

"Well, actually, it is my business. You seem to be trespassing on someone else's property."

How did she get rid of him? The last thing she needed was Reed here, upsetting her equilibrium, so she could barely think straight. He was getting in the way of her investigation, was going to ruin it.

She glared at him, willing him to leave her alone.

"I got a text from your friend. Kylie, was it? I was worried about you, Sierra. Actually, I was scared shitless. I thought…" He didn't need to finish his sentence, she knew what he thought. He was worried the stalker had got hold of her. He took a step toward her and she flinched backward.

"Don't. Don't you dare touch me," she snarled with such

force that he recoiled, as well. Good. She didn't want him anywhere near her. Didn't trust herself. If he touched her, all of her carefully constructed walls and excuses might crumble. She might even want to forgive him. And that wasn't going to happen. She was never going to forgive him.

"Sierra, I…" He raised his hands, palm upwards, but she continued to glare at him. He sighed and looked away. But not before she saw the pain flash through his eyes. Too bad. She told herself she was glad he was hurting. Because it couldn't be nearly as bad as how she was feeling.

"You may as well tell me what you're doing here, because I'm not leaving until you do." His voice was harsh now, all signs of the pain she'd seen before gone. The proficient cop was back. And he almost sounded angry. He had no right to be angry at her.

Shit. She could leave. She could turn around and storm back the way she'd come, toward her car and the road. But then she'd never know if her gut instinct had been right. And she was here now.

The bare minimum, that was all she'd tell him, no more. Then, as soon as they were sure there was nothing out here, she was getting the hell away from him. She glanced at him and then away. Her chest ached every time she looked at him. Because, for a second, she forgot what he'd done and her fingers wanted to go and tangle in his hair, pull his firm mouth down onto hers and have him kiss her.

But that was not going to happen again. Not now. Not ever.

"This place belongs to Evan, the guy who owns the newsstand in Penneshaw," she began, not bothering to keep the begrudging note out of her voice.

Reed squared his shoulders, his gaze fixed on hers, intelligent eyes taking in every word she said.

"The other night, when you found me talking to him near

the supermarket, I remembered he dropped a packet of candies."

"Mmhmm," he encouraged.

"They were caramels." Sierra wanted to roll her eyes when he didn't immediately twig to what she meant, but she kept her face deadpan. "The same kind as the wrapper we found on the edge of the road that day. And there was also a child's hat in the bag. Evan doesn't have any kids."

Finally, his eyes widened with surprise, then quickly became shrewd and thoughtful. "Do you think he had something to do with Jessica's disappearance?"

"I don't know," she replied huffily. "I didn't want to go around accusing a poor, innocent man if he'd done nothing wrong. I knew he owned this place, so I thought I'd come and check it out."

"You should have informed me, or Don," he said.

"Yeah, well, I'd have phoned if I found anything in the least bit incriminating."

"You know there are right and wrong ways to conduct a search. And this is definitely the wrong way." He frowned, but she didn't care about his protocol, or needing a warrant, or whatever it was he was thinking. She was sick of this conversation, and wanted to get on with her search. He could follow her if he wanted, there wasn't much she could do to stop him. She turned around to get her bearings.

The old cottage was next, separated from the shed by a patch of bare earth, filled with rutted potholes. The glass in all the windows was smashed, and most of them had been covered up with wood. The steps up to the front veranda were broken and sagging. It was made of wood, had been here a long time, and had never seen any tender, loving care. What the hell did Evan see in this place? it wasn't friendly at all, and the buildings certainly weren't worth keeping. The whole lot should be scrapped. Bulldozed. Start again. Sierra didn't dare go up the steps onto the veranda, scared she might fall through the rotten boards.

Instead, she skirted around the outside, having to fight her way through piles of junk stacked up against the external wall. Reed said nothing more, but followed a few steps behind her. She knew he was right behind her, the tiny hairs on her arms raised to attention, awareness flooding her body.

There were old pieces of machinery, wire, metal piping, rotten boxes, amongst many other things. She wanted to go up and look in one of the two windows facing out on this side, but they'd both been boarded up. And she couldn't get near enough because of the garbage, anyway. She kept going, pacing slowly and determinedly around to the back of the house, trying to block out the sound of Reed moving behind her. A single door was closed tight, with two steps leading up to it. Sierra went up and tried the door, but it was locked. She tried again, and let out a grunt of frustration. For an old, ramshackle place, it sure was hard to get into.

"You should let me do that," Reed said from behind her.

She ignored him and kept going, right around to the other side of the house. Here, there were two more windows, staring blank and forbidding back at them. At least they weren't covered over. She could see nothing from here; it was dark inside the cabin. Stepping gingerly over some broken slabs of concrete, she finally made it to the wall. If she stood on tiptoe, she could just see over the windowsill. It took a few seconds for her eyes to adjust to the deep shadows and dim corners. Nothing. There was nothing in there. Not a stick of furniture; the room was completely bare. This was nothing more than a dead end.

Reed came up beside her and took his own look into the house. He gave a quiet curse when he saw it was empty and then said, "You know, if we find anything, it will be inadmissible in court. We shouldn't be here. Why don't you let me—"

"Then why don't you just leave?" Sierra snapped back at him.

She put her head down and returned to the back door. A strange relief flooded thorough her. Whatever she'd been expecting to find, it wasn't here. Thank God. There was still one shed left, but she knew that would be empty, too. It'd all been a wild-goose chase. She and Reed could return to their prospective cars and drive away and never see each other again.

Then she noticed scuff marks in the grass, a few boot prints in the mud at the edge of the step leading up to the door. Someone had been here. Recently. Otherwise the rain would've washed the prints away. Was it Evan? Most likely, he did own the place after all. But what would he be doing in a run-down place like this? Then she looked up, gave the back door a closer examination. And noticed a new lock had been installed. That was strange. She pulled on the door again, making the door frame rattle and shudder, but the door wasn't going to give. It was shut up tight. With a huff of annoyance, Sierra stood back and stared at the door. What should she do now?

"If you go in there, it would be considered breaking and entering," Reed sighed from behind her. She wanted to turn around and tell him to go to hell.

But a noise, like a small bird, broke through Sierra's anger. She lifted her head, tilted it to the side and listened intently. There it was again. This time, it sounded human. A young, high voice, belonging to a child. A girl.

"Hello?"

Sierra froze. Turned around to see Reed also rooted to the spot, listening.

"Hello? Is that my mum? I want my mum." the voice called, thin and tremulous.

Holy fuck.

Was that Jessica?

They needed to get inside. She cast around for something to break the door down, and found a long metal pipe. Both she and Reed bent down to pick it up at the same time.

"I wouldn't do that if I were you."

Sierra spun around at the sound of the voice. Reed was a little slower to turn, his hand going to his hip where his Smith & Wesson sat.

It was Evan, and he had a gun pointed at them.

CHAPTER EIGHTEEN

Bound up like a fly in a spider's web; that's how Reed felt as he struggled against his bonds. Evan had been brutal and rapid with the rope that now held Reed captive. He'd tied it so tightly, Reed would lose circulation in his legs and arms sooner, rather than later. He wanted to yell in frustration, but the only sound he could make was a muffled grunt through the gag Evan shoved in his mouth. Fuck, he was such a dumbass. He'd let the guy sneak up behind them. He'd been so worried about Sierra, about what she was feeling, and how hollow and wretched he felt every time he looked at her, he hadn't been concentrating.

And now, he was trussed up like a Christmas turkey. But what else could he have done? He couldn't risk Sierra's life. Or the little girl's.

Sierra's hunch had been dead right.

Evan had the girl.

And he needed to rescue her. How he was going to do that was unclear at the moment, but he would come up with a plan, somehow. He had to. Reed glanced over to the dark corner, where Jessica curled in on herself, watching him with wide eyes through long, dirty hair which fell over her face. He needed to get control of himself. He knew he was frightening her with his useless struggles to free himself. Was she okay? Had that monster hurt her? A red-hot rage roared through Reed at the thought. If that mongrel had hurt her, he would kill him. Plain and simple.

They were in one of the rooms in the cottage where the windows had been boarded up. A small bed took up one corner, with Jessica huddled on top. She'd been chained to the bed frame by her ankle—the fucking bastard—but the chain was long enough so she could walk around a little. A low table took up the center of the room, an empty plate and cup on top. At least it looked like he'd been feeding her. What was he planning to do with her? Reed's skin crawled at all the possibilities. Most pedophiles panicked when they realized what they'd done and usually killed the child within the first few hours. To get rid of the evidence. Which meant Evan wasn't most pedophiles. The girl hadn't come near him, had stayed huddled in the corner, as far away from him as possible. Maybe she viewed him as just another form of nightmare monster in this skewed world she suddenly found herself in. If only he could get rid of the gag, he might be able to convince her he meant no harm. Reed let his gaze rake over the rest of the room, looking for anything that might help him escape. But apart from the bed and the table, the room was empty. And he was empty of ideas, too.

The sound of the back door opening stopped his struggles, as he strained to hear what was going on.

"Hurry up and get in there." That was Evan's voice. Then Reed heard a murmured reply and sagged with relief. That monster still had Sierra with him. Which meant she was still alive. After he'd hog-tied Reed and shoved him into the corner of the room, he'd prodded Sierra outside with the gun, saying they needed to move the fucking police car out of sight, before it attracted too much attention.

Sierra entered the room first, and Reed met her eyes. She

was scared, he could see it in the pinch of her tight lips. But her back remained straight and shoulders up. She wasn't letting this asshole intimidate her. Her hands were tied in front, but her legs were left free so she could walk.

"Hello, sweetheart. How are you doing, my love?"

What the...? Was Evan talking to Jessica? Yes, his gaze had left Sierra and was resting on the girl. Sierra, too, stared at Jessica, probably trying to discern if Evan had hurt her. It sickened Reed to hear him treating her like she was some kind of beloved pet. But it also told Reed that perhaps Evan meant to keep the girl alive. That he liked her. Jessica shrunk even farther back into the corner, becoming almost invisible in the dim light.

"Sit down over there," Evan waved the gun at Sierra, and Reed flinched at his blasé use of the weapon. The man was a walking enigma. He looked like butter wouldn't melt in his mouth. So plain, so boring, so blah. Like he wouldn't have the gumption to abduct a child, much less hold a policeman captive at gunpoint. But wasn't that often the way? They liked to blend in, to look harmless and innocent. Hide their seething immorality under a patina of righteousness. Sierra lowered herself down into the other corner a little awkwardly because of her bound hands, not even glancing in Reed's direction, keeping her eyes lowered, as if she were cowed and beaten. But Reed knew better.

The pair had been gone over an hour, and Reed wondered whether Evan had said anything. Revealed anything about himself or what he planned to do with the girl. What had they been up to? Evan mentioned moving his police car. But where had he put it? And what had happened to Sierra's car? Sooner rather than later, Reed's presence would be missed. How did this man think he was going to hide a cop, as well as a grown woman and the child?

"You've posed quite a problem, the two of you. Thrown a

wrench in the works, that's for sure. How am I going to get rid of two bodies?" Evan mused, almost as if to himself. "We need to get off this goddamned island."

Reed stiffened at his words, and out of the corner of his eye, he could see Sierra did the same. Fuck, so he was intending on killing them both. Not good.

"You won't get away with this," Sierra said in a low voice.

"Don't be too sure about that, luv. After all, I've done it before. I'm getting pretty good at covering my tracks." Evan gave Sierra a smarmy smile, more suited to a first-grade teacher than a murdering pedophile.

What was he talking about? What had he done before? Abducted a child? Or killed a cop? Reed heard her sharp intake of breath at his words.

"Besides, I know you won't try anything, not with gorgeous little Jessica here." Goosebumps ran down Reed's spine at the way the guy nearly purred as he said the girl's name. The fucking sicko. "I know you too well, Sierra, you won't risk her life to save your own. You'll stay here and try and protect her. Not so sure about Mr. Brave-and-Courageous Cop here, though. The jury's still out on him."

"Who the hell do you think you are? You don't know me at all, you—" Sierra shot a look at the small girl, who made a whimpering sound and folded even deeper into the bed at the sound of Sierra yelling, and she stopped talking abruptly.

Evan had no such compunction about upsetting the girl, however, and he kept talking. "But that's where you're wrong. I do know you, Sierra. I've known you for a long time. Some might say I'm obsessed with you, but that would be inaccurate. I like to think I studied you, like a connoisseur might study a fine wine. I learned everything I could about you. I believe that like a fine wine, your personality has improved with age. You're no longer the impetuous, star journalist who forged her news articles, regardless of anyone else's feelings or of the consequences. Now, you're more considerate, and, I have to say, withdrawn. Losing your daughter definitely changed you. For the better, I think."

Realization hit Reed hard and fast. This guy was Sierra's stalker. He snapped his gaze toward Sierra. She wasn't moving, it was as if she were made of stone. Oh yes, she'd figured it out, as well.

* * *

This was the man who'd been sending her all those poisonous letters for so long? Who'd been haunting her life? Sierra squeezed her hands into fists by her side, wanting to smack that smug look off his face. But what did he have to do with abducting Jessica? Sierra was confused, and couldn't make sense of all the information flooding into her brain.

Evan had been stalking her every move since she'd written that exposé. About the missing children. But why would he care about that? Unless...Unless he was involved, somehow.

"Holy fuck," she whispered.

"I see you're starting to put the pieces of the puzzle together. Finally. It's taken you long enough. You're not nearly as smart as you think you are."

"Who...?What...?" Sierra couldn't form coherent words. She could feel Reed's tense presence to her left. He must be as shocked as she was.

"I changed my name when I left the police force a couple of years ago. Thought it might be better that way. I used to be called Damien Nicholson." Evan said the words with glee, watching her face animatedly for a reaction. But he didn't lower the gun that was still pointed directly at her.

Damien Nicholson. The name sounded familiar and she searched her memory banks for some kind of recognition. Then it came to her. He was one of the cops who'd worked the very first child abduction case, back in Port Pirie. Had been on the frontline of the investigation. One of the cops she'd accused of misconduct during the case. Of making mistakes and mishandling evidence.

Was that because he'd been involved the whole time?

The magnitude of this man's deceit was only now beginning to dawn on her. He was a police officer. A cop was supposed to protect the innocent. But he'd used his position of power for evil. Used it to cover up his own tracks. And Sierra had come too close to the truth. That's why he'd started the hate mail, to try and lead her away from the evidence.

Sierra felt sick, as if she was going to vomit. She wretched. She cast a horrified glance at Reed, and he stared back at her, wide-eyed. He began to struggle against the ropes Evan had tied so cruelly around his hands and feet, and Sierra wanted to go to him. To help him. So they could escape this madman.

Her memory kicked up the image of her on the pathway with Evan, about to get in his car when he'd offered her a lift home. Holy shit. What if Reed hadn't come along then? What if she had gotten into his car? Had he planned to abduct her that day, too? To get rid of her once and for all?

And Evan had helped with the search for Jessica. But it'd all been a ruse, a ploy to make him seem innocent. One of the many concerned citizens who only wanted to find the little girl, bring her back to her mother, safe and sound. How could he possibly live with himself? He was pure evil.

"You know you shouldn't keep so much cash in your house, Sierra," Even berated in that horrible teacher's voice she was coming to hate.

"What?" Then it dawned on her what he meant. "It was you?" The extent of this man's reach was beginning to frighten her.

"Yes, I broke into your house. I took the money to make it look like a normal old burglary. But I got what I really went for. Your computer. I needed to see if you were writing more articles. You should really choose a better password, though. *Jon Snow* was just too easy." Evan gave a high-pitched giggle, and Sierra was struck by the edge of hysteria in it. Was he having a breakdown? Or was he permanently crazy and just very good at hiding it?

"The good thing about owning the post office? You get to take a peek at everyone's lives, through their letters. And deliveries. It's really interesting what you can find out about a person by opening their mail." He'd been tampering with her mail? Was he opening other people's mail as well? "I know that bitch back in Adelaide sent you a box of files on those missing kids. She wanted you to do another exposé, didn't she? Fucking bitch, why is she always interfering?" It was now starting to make a horrible kind of sense.

"The two girls who were abducted in Adelaide. That was you, too?"

He gave another evil chuckle, but ignored her question. "Stealing your laptop was a piece of cake. And there wasn't too much incriminating on there, I have to say." Evan's eyes glazed over and he glanced back at the little girl. "But then things happened. Things that were out of my control. Jessica came into my life. And I knew I had to have her. It wasn't planned, but there she was, just waiting to be rescued."

Sierra knew. Knew what he meant. He'd found Jessica standing by the side of the road, looking for her beloved kangaroos. This abduction had been a spur-of-the-moment thing. Like an addict, he'd seen the little girl all alone, and couldn't resist temptation.

"I needed time to let the heat die down. Before I could move her. And I needed you not to poke your interfering nose in where it wasn't wanted. Killing your chickens was more satisfying than I could've imagined. I would've loved to see the look on your face when you discovered them." A grin split his face, like a fissure opening up across his repulsive features. "Pity my little plan to disable your car didn't work so well."

Before she knew what she was doing, Sierra was up on her knees, bound hands raised in front of her face. She was going to kill him.

"Oh, don't be so melodramatic, luv," Evan said in his high, nasal voice. "And you, stop trying to be the hero." He slowly moved the gun around so it was pointing at Reed. Reed stopped endeavoring to free himself, but glared at Evan, pure hatred in his eyes. Sierra froze, as well.

"Stop it." A high-pitched wail started from the dark corner. "Stop it. Stop it. Stop it." Jessica was sitting on the bed, rocking back and forth with her hands over her ears. The poor girl was terrified. Her wail got louder and louder, so high it felt like needles going through Sierra's brain. Sierra half-rose up on her haunches. She almost forgot about Evan and his gun in her need to go to the girl. That mothering instinct to soothe.

But Evan beat her to it. He was on his feet and bending over the small child, patting her on the shoulder like she was some kind of frightened pet. It was obvious he didn't have a clue what to do. And it was also obvious this girl was special to him. In his sick, twisted mind, he'd become attached to her, and she'd become his property. He'd kept her alive for this long, after all.

It came to her in a flash. He wasn't going to kill the girl. He wanted to keep her. Earlier, he'd said, *we need to get off this island*. She hadn't twigged at the time, but now she thought she knew what he meant. He was going to try and smuggle Jessica off the island. Take her to the mainland, and then disappear. Perhaps wait till the investigation had died down. There were many ways to get off the island unseen. He could charter a small boat. Or he might even own one, himself. But now that Sierra and Reed had interfered, he would have to change his plan. Move more quickly.

Evan was still hunched over the girl, and in that split second, Sierra made her decision.

She cast one more, despairing look toward Reed, praying he'd understand what she was about to do. Hoped that he didn't just think she was saving herself. Because that's not what she was doing. She glanced at the door, which stood wide open, and Evan with his back to it.

She sprang up and in two long strides was out the door and down the short corridor to the back door. The door rattled on its hinges as she barged her shoulder into it, then took off like a startled gazelle toward the nearest trees, one hundred meters away. Running was harder with her hands tied in front, but she still made a good pace.

Her panting breath and pounding feet were the only sounds to break the silence. Until there was a loud crack, and she heard a buzzing noise over her left shoulder. A bullet. She increased her speed. Fifty meters. She zigged, then zagged, not daring to look back. Willing her sore knee not to buckle underneath her. Another bullet hummed past, closer this time. Twenty meters. She daren't look back to see if he was coming after her. Ten meters.

She dived into the long grass beside a large tree like she was a world-class baseball player diving for first base. Damp clods of earth crumbled under her hands and she lay panting for a moment. Was he chasing her?

"Come back, or I'll shoot the little girl." Evan's words stabbed her to the core, but she could hear the hysterical note in his voice. And she knew. Knew he wouldn't shoot the girl. Knew he'd come after her. He couldn't afford to let her get away. Couldn't take the chance she'd betray him to the police. But also, his ego wouldn't allow it. He *had* to come after her. It was the only way her plan was going to work. Biting down with her teeth, she worked at the knot around her wrists. It was too tight and she grunted with frustration. She got up onto her hands and knees and began an unwieldy crawl though the undergrowth, needing to get farther away.

"Come back, or I'll shoot lover-boy cop." Evan's words drifted to her over the growing distance. She faltered, mid-crawl. Reed. She couldn't let Reed die. She turned around.

No, she had to keep going. Forcing her hands and feet to move again. If she kept going, Evan would follow, she had to believe that. If she went back now, they were both as good as dead. It was the only way.

"You stupid fucking bitch, get back here." Evan had lost all pretense of playing the refined guy. "You're going to ruin everything."

Yep, that's exactly what she hoped to do.

Stopping for a second time, she worked at the rope knot again. This time she felt it loosen. He hadn't bound her as tightly as Reed. He needed her to drive the cars, to put them out of sight, while he held a gun to her head. Then, when she'd done the deed and locked the cars away, he'd really only tied her hands as a precaution. Probably he'd meant to bind her up properly once they reached the cottage.

She chanced a glance backwards, toward the clearing and the cottage. She could just make out Evan, standing on the top step of the back door, staring out at the tree-line, hatred snarling across his face.

Come on. Come on, she pleaded silently.

He took a step down and then another. Then he started to jog toward the spot where she was hidden. With one final tug, the ropes fell free. Sierra stood and began to run again, drawing him closer, reeling him in like a fish on a line. Towards her and away from Jessica and Reed.

* * *

Reed had never felt more helpless in his whole life. Not even when Penny had miscarried their baby. Not even when he'd been involved in the crash that'd claimed Sierra's daughter. He needed to get out of these bindings. Now. Sierra was out there, putting her life on the line, with a madman trying to kill her, and he had to get out there and help her.

All that lay between them seemed to be of no consequence right now. The huge gulf that'd opened up when he discovered he'd been the one driving the other car was gone. He knew, without a shadow of a doubt, he needed Sierra to stay alive. So he could tell her. Tell her how he felt about her. The anger was gone. Evaporated in a puff of smoke. His feelings right at this very moment were crystal-clear. He was falling in love with Sierra. With her sultry beauty. With her willful, stubborn streak. With her fragile heart that she kept hidden from the rest of the world. With her courage. The courage it took to lead Evan away, to be the bait, leaving her faith in Reed that he would save the little girl. They could work this all out. He knew it. There was something between them that just couldn't be ignored.

A shot rang out and Reed froze. Fuck, the crazy bastard was shooting at her. Then Evan shouted something, and there was a pause and then another gunshot. Reed was going to internally combust if he didn't free himself soon. In desperation, he looked around the room. He needed something. Anything. To get him out of these ropes.

Jessica was snuffling quietly in the corner, not looking at him, huddled in a tight ball like a cat on her bed, her hands clamped over her ears.

Poor little thing. She must be absolutely terrified, but he couldn't even go over and comfort her, protect her, trussed up as he was.

Then Reed narrowed his gaze. She was his only chance. Could she help him untie the ropes?

How was he going to convince a terrified five-year old to do that?

Reed was already lying on his side after his thwarted struggles to free himself. He had to get over to the bed somehow. His hands were tied behind him, and his legs tied all the way from ankle to knee. He began to curl and uncurl, pulling his knees into his chest and using his shoulder, hip, and legs to shuffle forward over the dirty floorboards. He was moving, but slowly, much too slowly. Sweat trickled freely down his back and into his eyes. Another shot sounded from outside, this time muffled and farther away from the cottage. It galvanized him into even more desperate movements. If Evan was still shooting, it meant Sierra was still running. Which he hoped was a good thing.

After what seemed like an eternity, Reed made it all the way to the other side of the room. He lay breathing heavily through his nose for many precious seconds, the gag preventing him from gulping lungful's of air as he wanted to do. With a huge surge of energy, he managed to sit up. But that was as far as he got. He couldn't kneel, let alone stand up, the ropes were just too tight. But it was enough to bring his chin level with the edge of the bed.

Jessica's tear-stained face peered at him from beneath her elbow. She must've watched his progress across the floor, wondering what he was up to. How did he communicate his need to her? How did he let her know he was one of the good guys? That he wasn't here to hurt her, but to help her.

All he had was his eyes, and so he stared at her beseechingly, making little grunting noises which he hoped sounded calming rather than plain maniacal. Smiling was impossible with the rough, cloth gag in his mouth. The girl stopped sniffling and stared back at him, blue eyes wide and fearful, but she didn't move.

Reed wracked his brain for something to convince her. Then he had it. Shuffling around slightly, he lifted himself as high as he could off the ground and shoved his left shoulder up at her, tilting his head sideways and grunting, trying to get her to look at what was on the side of his dark blue uniform. It was the South Australian Police badge. Would she recognize it? Would a five-year old even know what it meant?

Jessica moved, slowly sitting up, and drew her small hand across her face, scrubbing away the tears. Her hair stood out in great snarls and tangles, and her face was all big eyes and a small, rose-bud mouth. And Reed was filled with the urge to smash that pedophile's face into a pulp. She was so small and helpless, and that bastard deserved nothing less than castration.

Shoving the rage back down his throat, he concentrated on the girl, holding his face up towards her, in a mute request for her to pull the gag out of his mouth. Finally, she moved, crawling towards him, and plucked at the dirty rag. As she pulled, Reed used his tongue to help work it out of his mouth, until it eventually fell on the floor with a soft thud.

Thank God. He could breathe now, and he sucked in two, three, four deep breaths.

Quickly composing his features, he smiled. "Thank you, Jessica."

She said nothing, just withdrew a few inches. He couldn't afford to scare her. He needed her help.

"You know I'm a policeman, don't you, sweetheart?"

She nodded, her ratty hair falling down over her eyes as she did so.

"And I'm here to take you back to your mum and dad."

Her eyes light up at his words, a small lift of her lip the first sign of hope she'd shown so far.

"I also know how brave you are."

He wasn't going to mention Evan, or anything to do with the abduction, in case he scared her back into that comatose state. But she straightened a little at his praise. This might work, after all.

"Do you think you can help me? If we can get these ropes of my hands, then I can take you straight home."

She looked at him speculatively for a few seconds, then nodded again. She wasn't speaking to him, obviously badly traumatized, but that was okay, all he needed was to get them out of here. The rest could come later.

He shuffled around farther, so she could access his hands behind his back and then prayed to whatever God was listening that her tiny fingers could undo the knots Evan had tied. She hopped down onto the floor, light as a bird, the chain clanking as she moved. Reed gritted his teeth when he heard it, quelling another urge to hurt that man so badly he'd never walk again.

He could feel her small movements against his wrists, which'd been rubbed raw from his struggles. She spent many minutes behind his back, and he held as still as he was able, hoping against hope she could free him. Free them both.

At first, he thought he was imagining it. But then he knew. The ropes were loosening. He wriggled his wrists and could feel movement now.

"Good girl, you're doing great, sweetheart. Your mum's going to be so proud of how brave you're being."

"I want my mum," Jessica said in a small voice, sniffling, her fingers stopping their fluttering behind his back.

"I know you do, Jessica. And if you keep doing such a good job with these ropes, I'm going to take you to her." At last, he felt her fingers attacking the ropes again. He tested them and felt something give, and all at once, after a few more tugs and twists, his hands came free.

She'd done it!

Slowly, he brought his arms around to the front and shook his hands out, rubbing them together. They were numb, and he'd need a few minutes before they would work properly.

Just then, another gunshot rang out, frightening Jessica,

who scuttled to his side, huddling into him, whimpering. Reed's own heart rate skyrocketed. Oh God, please let Sierra be all right. But he couldn't let his fear show. One thing the shot told him was that Evan was moving farther away from the cottage, which was a good thing.

He draped a protective arm around her. "Shh, sweetie, it's okay. I won't let him hurt you again." Damn right he wouldn't. He leaned forward and began attacking the knots that bound his legs, careful not to bump Jessica, who still clung to him like a rag doll.

At last, his legs were free as well. He jiggled them up and down to get the blood flowing, while at the same time he reached around and drew Jessica closer under his arm.

Evan had removed his gun belt, and taken it with him when he and Sierra went to move his car. So, he had no gun, taser, or baton. He'd also taken his phone and smashed it to smithereens on the front step. So, Reed was weaponless and unable to contact anyone for backup. But his main priority was to get Jessica to safety. Even though his heart was urging him to go after Sierra, to track down that bastard, he had to do what was right.

Getting up gingerly, he placed Jessica on the bed and stamped his feet on the floorboards, wincing at the pain of the pins and needles as the blood rushed back to his toes. The chain tying her to the bed might be a problem. The bed was old, a rusty, metal frame with a dirty mattress piled on top. Evan had chained her to one of the long metal bars at the end of the bed. It would be much too hard for a small girl to break free. But a large, strong man on the other hand…

He lay down on the bed and kicked at the bar with his booted foot. After a few good blows, the rusted metal gave way with a clang. There wasn't much he could do about the shackle clamped around her ankle, but he could deal with that later.

"Come on, sweetheart, let's get out of here." He lifted her up onto his hip, gathered the chain up in one hand, and stalked toward the door.

CHAPTER NINETEEN

Sierra watched Evan—or Damien, or whoever he was—move through the thick scrub. He probably thought he was being stealthy, but he was making enough noise for her to follow his path. But then what did he really care? He had the gun, after all.

She was crouched down behind a big, old sugar gum that reached its tall branches far above her. What to do now? She couldn't let the murderous bastard go back to the cottage, she needed to protect Reed and Jessica. So, she had to somehow distract the man, overpower him if she could. And try not to get shot at the same time. It was only mid-afternoon. No one would be looking for her, yet. Kylie wouldn't start to worry that she hadn't brought her car back until she got home from work, which was still a few hours away. How long till someone started looking for Reed? She had no idea what excuse he'd given Don so he could come out here and check on her. And even if Don was getting irritated about his lack of attendance, it didn't mean they knew where Reed was. She was on her own.

Sierra still couldn't reconcile the Evan she knew from the newsstand with this man. A dirty ex-cop. A serial stalker. And a serial pedophile. Her brain was having a hard time

222

believing such a mild-mannered man could do all those horrible things.

Evan turned away from her, following some non-existent trail through the long grass. He was going the wrong way. She was going to have to do something to draw him back toward her, otherwise he would miss her completely and probably give up and go back to the cottage.

Staring up into the branches of the tree, an idea began to form. She was good at climbing, did a lot of it while checking on the Glossies' nesting sites. Admittedly, she was usually roped up for safety when she did. But with her long arms and legs, she was sure she could climb this sugar gum with ease. A quick search around on the ground turned up a few good-sized, small rocks she could use. Then she spied a large, dead branch lying in the grass, and knew it would make another good weapon.

A minute later, she was perched on a branch three or four meters off the ground. Evan was still going the wrong way; he'd be out of sight in a few seconds if she didn't do something now. Taking one of the rocks she'd stashed in her pocket, she threw it with all her might, so it landed with a plunk halfway between her and the pedophile. He turned sharply at the sound. She threw another rock, this one landing a little closer to her tree. Evan raised his gun and crouched lower in a hunter's stance. Sierra wondered if he knew just how silly he looked. But then she reminded herself he was dangerous. She shouldn't underestimate him. He was an ex-cop. Just because he looked innocuous didn't mean he couldn't handle a gun. And look how he'd broken into her house. Spied on her. Killed her chickens and tampered with her car.

He came closer. She'd have to time this just right. She gauged the distance to the ground again, and her eyes raked over the bit of wood she'd leaned against the trunk of the tree. Evan came closer still; he was going to walk right underneath her branch.

She drew in a deep breath and froze, not moving a muscle, getting ready.

She counted down silently in her head. Three. Two. One. Go.

She leaped, landing on Evan's back, knocking him down to the ground. He gave an involuntary shout, and then she heard a whoosh as the air was knocked out of him. She landed on her butt, the shock of the impact dazing her for a second.

Evan got to his feet. "What the fuck?"

She scrambled backward on her hands and feet, like a crab. The gun. The gun was missing from his hands. He must've dropped it when she jumped him.

Her back hit the tree trunk and she used it to lever herself up. Without taking her eyes off Evan, she felt around behind her for the stick. It wasn't there. Had she knocked it over?

He was coming at her. Fast. With a wild roar like an enraged bull. She ducked at the last second and bent under his swinging arm and he careened into the tree. But he turned, much quicker than she would've thought. She would be no match for him on the ground and unarmed, even without the gun. He was heavier than her, although not faster. But he knew how to handle himself, how to bring down a felon. She caught sight of her stick, still leaning against the tree, just farther around than she thought. But Evan was now between her and her weapon.

"You little bitch. Just give up now, we both know how this is going to end." As he spoke, his gaze darted around on the ground behind her, and it took her a few seconds to figure out what he was doing. Looking for the gun. Where was it? Should she turn around and try and find it? Or keep to her plan of using the stick to overpower him?

Evan was studying her now, crouched and ready to spring, but not diving in like he had before. His little piggy eyes screwed up in concentration behind his glasses, which'd been knocked askew. If this wasn't so real, she might laugh at how comical he looked.

She took a step backward. Then another one. Quiet and slow.

"Stay where you are, bitch," Evan snarled. He took a menacing step toward her just as she went back another one, like they were dancing in some macabre, slow-motion scene. He didn't want her to get out of range; if she ran, he wouldn't be a match for her. Not unless he found his gun again.

With a burst of speed, she feinted left and then surged forwards, dodging right past him, shocking him with her choice of direction. He was bigger and stronger than her, but she had speed on her side and so she used it, darting past him to the tree. She grabbed the large bit of wood with both hands, already swinging it in a wide arc as she turned to face him.

The stick glanced off his shoulder as he lumbered to keep up with her and turn around. It wasn't enough to disable him completely, but it was enough to knock him off balance. As he stumbled to the left, she gathered up her strength and swung the club again. A yell left his lips a split second before the stick collided with his chest, knocking him backward.

Shit, why couldn't she hit him in the head? That's where she was aiming, but she couldn't seem to connect. She danced around him in a semi-circle, trying for a better angle. Before she could lift the stick above her shoulder to take another swing at him, Evan charged at her. She got in a glancing blow, but not enough to stop both of them going to the ground in a heap. The broken branch spun away from her.

She used all her might, fueled by a kick of adrenaline, to twist away, try and get out of his grasp. She managed to crawl a few feet before a vise-like grip took hold of her ankle.

"You ain't getting away from me now, Sierra. I've been dreaming of this day for twelve years. Ever since you wrote your namby-pamby news articles, pointing your finger at the police. At me. Making up those lies. Who do you think you are? If you got people looking at the cops, raking through our investigation with some kind of commission, well, that would've been no good. No good at all. I had to leave that plum job in Port Pirie because of you. Move into a stinking big-city station, just to get away from all the prying eyes your new article left behind."

Sierra was being dragged backward by his hand on her ankle, and she kicked out at him with her other foot, trying to dislodge his hold. But he gave an almighty wrench on her foot, twisting it, trying to flip her over, and she felt something snap. She screamed in pain. Her fingers tore at the long grass, looking for something, anything to grab hold of as he dragged her slowly toward him. It was useless. Her mind was shrieking at her to give in. She sobbed as knives of agony sliced up her leg every time she moved. Had he broken her ankle? It sure felt like it. Evan had hold of her other foot now, and she had nowhere to go.

She drew in a deep breath. There was only one option left to her. And it was going to hurt like hell. She flipped over onto her back, at the same time sitting up and landing blows on his hands, trying to dislodge his clasp, screeching at the top of her lungs at the torment of her broken ankle. With a grunt, Evan let go one of her legs and swung a fist, catching her on the nose. She let out a howl of pain. Blood gushed down her face, and she threw both of her hands up to staunch the flow. His weight on her legs got heavier as he hauled himself toward her, his chest now pinning her feet, his glowering face coming closer to her. The torment from her ankle was excruciating.

No. He was overpowering her. Turning her hands into talons she began to rake at Evan's head and face. Her nails dragged through his skin, leaving deep scratches. He yelled loudly, but didn't release his grip, inching up along her body, until, with a grunt, he lunged forward, head-butting her with his forehead. He hit her right on the scar from her old accident, and pain shattered through her head as her sight blurred and briefly went dark. She closed her eyes, trying to shut it all out.

Evan planted his weight on her stomach, and she opened her eyes to see him sitting on top of her.

"This is going to be fun." Evan smiled down at her, leaves and small bits of dirt clinging to his normally neat beard, giving him a deranged look. She'd misjudged him. Badly. And now she was going to die.

She let out an involuntary whimper.

"Good, you should be afraid. Once I've finished with you, I'm going back to get rid of your boyfriend. Then me and my little angel are getting off this Godforsaken island." His clammy hands closed around her throat. And began to squeeze. Both of her hands came up to pluck uselessly at his arms, as his grip tightened. And tightened.

She couldn't breathe.

Her right hand left her throat and began to flail around wildly in the grass behind her head. Searching for a rock, a branch, anything she could use.

Her fingernail tinged against something metal. She reached farther back. No air. She needed air. Any second now, she was going to pass out.

Her finger brushed against cool metal. It was the butt of the gun. Evan stared down at her, giving small grunts of exertion as he pushed on her windpipe, his face going red with the strain of strangling her.

With the absolute last of her energy she stretched

backwards. Her fingers closed around the gun. And she brought it up, pulling the trigger.

* * *

With Jessica on his hip, Reed hunkered in against the wall of the shed. They'd escaped from the cottage without any sign of Evan, but Reed wasn't taking any chances. He was carrying a precious package, and he would do nothing to jeopardize it. Even though he wanted to run into the bush and search for Sierra. He couldn't. Instead he was crouched next to the larger of the two sheds on Evan's property, a few hundred meters away from the derelict cottage. He listened intently for a few seconds, then peered cautiously around the corner. No sign of movement. Sierra had done her job well, led Evan deep into the surrounding scrub. Away from him and Jessica.

Reed made his way to the small high window and took a quick glance inside. He nearly let out a whoop of joy. He'd been hoping against hope, and his wish had come true. They had moved his police vehicle and Sierra's car and put them both inside the shed. Out of sight for a while. Of course they would be found soon enough, when the police started to swarm the area. But Evan would have planned to be well-away from here by the time that happened. And if his plan had succeeded, the Sergeant and his team would be finding Reed and Sierra's bodies. He hugged Jessica tighter to him. Thank God they'd found her. Thank God Sierra had found her.

He made his way around to the front of the shed. Damn. Evan had padlocked the double doors.

"Hey, sweetie, I just need to put you down for a second. Is that okay? Can you stand up for me?"

She nodded at him, eyes wide.

"Good girl." He put her down gently, laying the chain still around her ankle on the ground, and picked up a half-brick from a small pile of rubble beside the shed. "Cover your ears," he told her. "I'm going to make some banging noises." Which was a bugger, he hoped the noise didn't attract Evan's attention. With a couple of well-aimed hits, the padlock fell away, but Reed was too busy scooping Jessica up to be thankful. They slipped inside, and Reed went straight to the police Land Cruiser and opened the door. As he thought, Evan had smashed the police radio, but Reed had an ace up his sleeve. He kept a back-up cell stashed under his seat. He prayed to God it was still there, and still charged.

Putting Jessica onto the front seat, he rummaged around underneath, his fingers finally closing around the small phone. He turned it on and waited.

"Are we going for a ride in your police car?" Jessica said, voice still tremulous, but obviously impressed as she stared at the dashboard.

"I will take you for a ride as soon as I can." He promised. "We can turn the lights and the siren on, too, when we do."

"Thank you," she whispered in awe, her face breaking into a smile. The first one he'd ever seen on this tiny little girl's face. That smile broke his heart. Such a small thing to make this gorgeous child happy. After all she'd been through. He wanted to kill Evan all over again. Slowly.

The phone pinged to life and Reed's stomach did a somersault of triumph. He was going to get Jessica out of this alive. Thanks to Sierra. But could he say the same about her?

He dialed 000 and spoke urgently into the phone.

* * *

The Sarge stood a few feet away from the Land Cruiser, his back to Reed, talking fast and furious into his phone. Yet another police car careened down the dirt driveway, lights flashing, and screeched to a stop in front of the cottage, joining the two others already there. Two officers leapt out of the car and made their way over to the Sarge, who put his hand over the phone and barked out some orders. Immediately the officers drew their guns and fanned out, searching for Evan. And Sierra. There was already another uniform stationed near the cottage, standing guard, gun drawn, eyes scanning the surrounding bushland. In case Evan came back. But Reed thought that was highly unlikely.

Reed sat in the back seat of the Sarge's car, Jessica by his side.

"Your mum will be here soon," he said quietly, trying to keep her calm. Her big, blue eyes had gotten wider and wider as more and more cop cars and police officers arrived, and she clung to his arm as if he might disappear at any second. Poor little thing, she probably didn't have a clue what was going on, and he was the only solid thing she had to hold on to right now. He desperately wanted to get out of the car and run into the bush with the rest of the officers. To look for Sierra. It was killing him, not knowing where she was. If she was alive. Or dead. He had an urgent need to see those seductive lips curl up in that half-smile she seemed to keep only for him. The secretive one that said she remembered what they'd shared together the other night. How much she'd liked it. Her come-to-me-smile that drew him in. Made him want to land soft, butterfly kisses on the corners of her mouth.

Fifteen minutes after he'd made the 000 call, while he waited for Don and Eric to arrive, he'd heard a single gunshot. It chilled him to the core. Was it Evan? Had he shot Sierra? Killed her? Was he coming back for them? But there was nothing he could do about it. His only goal now was to protect the little girl, with his life if he had to.

After he'd made the call and directed Don to Evan's farm, he'd taken Jessica and hidden in a thick bit of scrub behind the house and near the driveway, so he could see when Don arrived, but was also out of sight if Evan returned. Then they'd waited. Ten more agonizing minutes, before he heard the sirens, and saw the car speeding down the road. The look of relief on Don's face was a sight to see, and probably matched his own when he ran out to meet them. Then he hopped into the car with the girl while Don and Eric swung into gear and called in the cavalry.

Where were they? Where was Sierra? And Evan? Another police car, a sedan this time, belonging to the mainland cops, raced down the driveway. Reed watched, only half-interested now. The rear door opened, and a slim, blonde woman stepped out. Jessica's mother. Sweet relief swept through him.

"Look who's here," he said, gathering Jessica up in his arms and stepping out of the car, striding toward the mum, Heather, who broke into a run as soon as she saw them. She tore Jessica out of his arms and hugged her small body to her chest, completely ignoring Reed. Ignoring everything and everyone except the one thing that mattered more to her than the world.

"My sweet baby. My baby. You're fine now. Mummy's here." Heather crooned the words over and over into her daughters' ear still crushing her to her breast. Jessica burst into tears in her mother's arms, tears of joy and rage and sadness. Reed's throat thickened as he watched the scene unfold before him, his eyes prickling with heat. This was the outcome they'd all been hoping for. It was the whole reason he did his job. To make sure the innocent stayed safe.

Finally, Heather looked up, fixed her gaze directly on him. Tears streamed down her blotchy face, her eyes red.

"Thank you." It was only two words, but she didn't need to say anymore. Reed could see her unspoken gratitude etched into every line of her face. He took her by the elbow and led mother and daughter over to the Sarge's car, helping her to step up into the four-wheel-drive because there was no way she was releasing her grip on her child.

"You'll be safe here. The Sergeant will be over soon to talk to you. He'll take you back to town." Then the whole family could be reunited. The father and older daughter were waiting back at their accommodation. She only nodded her understanding, too busy whispering softly in Jessica's ear. The little girl kept her head hidden in the curve of her mother's shoulder, not looking up, burrowing in as close as she could. Reed didn't blame her, in fact almost envied the little girl's position, safe and secure once more.

But at last, Reed was free to go and help look for Sierra. If only he knew she was safe and secure, too. He strode in the direction he'd heard the gunshot go off. He could see movement just inside the first row of trees at the edge of the clearing off to his left, a dark blue uniform flashing through the gaps in the branches—it might be Eric—warily searching as he probed deeper into the scrub. Reed veered to the right and dived straight into the undergrowth. This was all natural, uncleared bush, left to grow thick and luxuriant, and Sierra and Evan could be anywhere in here. But something pulled Reed in this direction. A strange sense he'd never felt before, but nonetheless didn't question.

A faint kangaroo trail threaded its way through the long grass in front of him, and he followed it. "Sierra." Her name formed on his lips before he could stop it. He shouldn't call out. If Evan was still out there somewhere, he might make himself a target. "Sierra, where are you?" Protocol and his own safety be damned. He called her name again, longer and louder this time. "Sierra." Oh God, please let her be alive. He wanted to run, but the branches cut across his path, whacked him in the face and pulled at his ankles. It would do neither of them any good if he fell over and hurt himself. He forced his legs to slow to a walk. As quickly as he could manage, as he battled his way through the thick undergrowth.

"Sierra." His voice carried high into the surrounding bush,

mixing with the leaves of the tall trees and running down the slope of the hill until it got caught in the stocky bulk of a small tree. A bird called quietly from a branch above him and he glanced up as it flew away. Was he even going the right way? He'd followed some sort of inner intuition leading him in this direction, but he wasn't even sure why now.

"Sierra." Could she hear him? How far into this blasted bush had she led the maniac pedophile? They could be searching out here for days. Sweat began to bead on his forehead, even with the cold, winter air pooling around him.

There was a sound. Was it the bird again?

His feet stopped moving even before he was aware they'd done so, and he tried to calm his breathing so he could hear better.

A noise that wasn't a bird echoed off the tree trunks around him. A voice. A woman's voice. Faint. But dead ahead of him. He kept going, this time running as best he could.

"Sierra." He stopped, craning his neck to hear a response.

"Reed. Help." It was her. She was calling for him.

"I'm coming. I'm coming. Keep calling, Sierra, so I can find you." He slowed his headlong rush, listening for her calls, which got louder as he worked his way between two large tree trunks and down a small incline.

Then he saw her. Sitting on a fallen log a hundred feet or so ahead. Her face and the front of her hoodie were covered in blood. But as he raced toward her, she looked up and caught his gaze, and he thought his pounding heart might explode. She was alive, and she was the most wonderous thing he'd ever seen. Even though blood spattered her face, and ran down over her lip, and streaks of mud covered her cheeks. Even though her hair was a mess of tangles and leaves and dirt. Even though her dark eyes were wide and haunted. She was the most beautiful woman he'd ever seen.

He wanted to scoop her up into his arms and never let her

go.

But then he saw her face up close, and it was wracked with pain. Her left leg was stuck out straight in front of her, her foot at an odd angle. So instead, he knelt down next to her, put a hand on her shoulder.

"Thank God, Sierra. Thank God." They were the only words he trusted himself with at that moment.

CHAPTER TWENTY

Sierra sat in her hospital bed and stared out the window. The little health care unit on Kangaroo Island was lucky enough to be situated on the main road through Kingscote, directly across from the strip of beach and the ocean. Sierra stared at the ocean, not really seeing it. Her mind kept replaying those last five seconds of her encounter with Evan. Over and over.

His fat fingers tight around her throat. Gasping for air. No air in her lungs. Black spots in front of her eyes. She was going to pass out. To die.

Her fingers finding the gun. Grasping the barrel and swinging it up in an arc above her head. Firing the gun. The sound had nearly deafened her, left her ears ringing for hours afterward.

Blood. All over her. Splattered across the tall fronds of grass around her head. Evan's weight landing on top of her. His fingers loosening their grip. She could breathe again. Sweet, clean air poured into her lungs as she gasped and gasped.

Then the horrible reality of what she'd done sunk in and she'd screamed, pushing and clawing at the hideous heavy weight of the man on top of her, pinning her down. All she knew was she needed to get away from him, away from this place.

But when she tried to get up, to walk, a pain so great she nearly vomited, shot up her leg. Her ankle. It was probably broken. So instead she crawled on hands and knees. Away. Away from him and his sick twisted reality. Away from what she'd done.

She didn't know how far she crawled—it felt like a hundred miles, but was probably only a few hundred meters —before she came upon a large fallen log and could go no further. So, she sat there and waited. Waited for either Evan to come and get her, to end this once and for all, or for rescue. She wasn't sure which would happen first.

Finally, Reed had come. Like a bright beacon into her dark world. And she'd cried like a baby on his shoulder.

The gunshot sounded again in her head, like the ringing of a bell. A bell that sounded the end of everything.

"Hi, darling. You're finally awake."

Sierra swiveled her head and watched her mother hurry into the hospital room. Aileen came over and kissed Sierra's cheek.

"You've been asleep for hours. But I didn't want to wake you. Sleep is good. It's a healer." Aileen smiled at her daughter, but Sierra could see the lines of worry deepening around her mother's eyes.

"Hi, Mum." She smiled, a warm, welcoming smile. It was good to have her mother here.

"How's your leg this morning? Better?"

Sierra thought about that for a second, her eyes going to the series of lumps under the white blankets. The cast went all the way from her toes right up to her knee. She gave her toes an experimental wiggle. Yes, it was feeling good this morning. Probably something to do with all the drugs the doctor had prescribed. "It is better, yes," she replied.

"That's good, because the doc said he was going to

discharge you today."

"Great." But Sierra wasn't sure if she really felt great about that bit of news. Did she want to go home? Was she ready to go home?

As if reading her mind, her mum continued, "And I'm going to stay for as long as you need me, so don't worry about coping by yourself. I'm going to do lots of lovely home-cooked meals. We need to fatten you up."

Sierra opened her mouth to argue. And closed it again. It was a bad habit of hers, always wanting to be so independent. So alone. It was lovely to have her mother here, and Sierra admitted it might even be nice to have someone pander to her every need for a few days, at least.

"Thanks, that would be great."

Aileen had arrived late last night, on a chartered flight from Adelaide. When she'd appeared at the hospital, Sierra almost wished she hadn't come, because at first she'd been beside herself with worry, constantly asking strings of inane questions, frequently leaning in to touch her daughter, as if to make sure she was real, and refusing to leave when a nurse or doctor wanted to consult with Sierra. But she knew it was all because her mum had been terrified. Terrified of what Sierra had done. Terrified of what the outcome might've been.

"Hi, Sierra." The hesitant voice had both women turning their heads in unison to see who was standing at the door.

"Blake. Hi." Sierra kept her tone cool, but she could hardly ignore the huge bunch of roses the young man held in front of his chest. There was an awkward silence as Blake continued to stand in the doorway, which her mum finally filled with her usual chatter.

"Blake, is it? Nice to meet you." She reached out and beckoned him into the room, but not before pursing her lips in Sierra's direction and lifting an eyebrow. "Let me take those." Whipping the flowers out of his hands she almost pushed him closer to the bed. "I'll go and find a nice vase to put these in." Then she was gone, leaving her alone with Blake.

"I heard what happened…What you did. Jesus, Sierra, look at you. You're…" Blake seemed to search for the right words, but couldn't find them and instead shoved his hands in his pockets. "You're a hero. Did you know that?"

"Don't be ridiculous," she retorted with a snort. She was no such thing.

"Yes, you are. But that's not actually why I came. I wanted to make sure you were really okay."

"Thanks, Blake," she replied, voice softening. He was really worried about her; she could see it in his furrowed brow. How could she have thought he might ever want to hurt her? He was just a young guy who was passionate about his work and passionate about life, and he liked to wear his heart on his sleeve. That was all. She was stupid to have thought otherwise.

"And I also wanted to apologize. I realize I might've been a bit over the top with my…ah…advances." He wouldn't meet her gaze, and glanced behind himself quickly to make sure they were still alone. "I guess I just didn't want to take the hint that you weren't interested in me."

"It's fine, Blake—"

He cut her off. "No, I mean it. It was a blow to my ego, when you wouldn't go out with me. I had this stupid dream that I would come back to KI, and you would fall straight into my arms, and life would be amazing. But I can see now, it would never work."

Now she felt really guilty, because while Blake continued to stare at her with serious, blue eyes she knew that *she* owed *him* the apology. She'd thought the worst of him. How wrong could she have been?

"Blake, I'm really sorry. I probably didn't handle it right.

But you know…"

"I found one," her mum chirped loudly as she bustled back into the room, a glass vase in one hand and the flowers in the other.

"Thanks, Mum," Sierra said, with a sigh.

There was another awkward silence as Aileen fiddled with the wrapping around the flowers, and began to arrange them in the vase by her bedside.

"I'd better be going," Blake said, already backing out of the room. "Hope your leg gets better soon." She could see there was a lot more he wanted to say, but it was all too late now.

"Thanks, Blake. And thanks for the flowers," she added belatedly as he disappeared around the doorframe.

"He was lovely," Aileen said, still fiddling with the roses. But Sierra could hear the question in her voice. She hadn't mentioned Blake to her mum when she'd dated him two years ago. It was probably a little late to try and fill her in, now. Sierra let her eyes drift to the window again, as Aileen finished arranging the flowers and went to sit in the chair by the bed.

"Morning, ladies." Sierra whipped her head around at the familiar, deep baritone. It was Reed, and she drank in the sight of him as he stood in the door. His broad shoulders nearly filled the doorframe, the deep-blue police uniform looking fresh and clean on him.

"Sorry, I didn't get a chance to buy flowers." His gaze drifted over the extravagant bunch of roses. She wanted to tell him they meant nothing to her. His presence was worth more than ten bunches of flowers. One hundred, even. She didn't need flowers from him. Her heart rate skipped higher as his dark eyes settled on her, a question hovering in their depths. Reed ran a hand through his short black hair, and Sierra was startled by a sudden need coursing through her. A need for him to put his hands on her, run them through her hair, caress her neck. Strong hands. Tough hands. But also tender, knowing just where to touch her skin to get the greatest response.

"Officer Kapua, nice to see you again," her mother replied, before Sierra could untie her tongue. "How are things going out there? Have the media left yet?"

It seemed to take him some effort to tear his gaze away from Sierra and concentrate on her mum. "Unfortunately, not." Reed grimaced. "The vultures are still circling."

"I bet they are," Aileen replied with a rueful tilt of her mouth. "But still, Sierra would understand better than most of us how these things work. You know she used to be a journalist?"

"Yes, she mentioned that," Reed replied. He drew in a deep breath, which sounded like he was fortifying himself for something to come. "Sorry, Mrs. Goldstein, but would you mind if I talked to Sierra in private for a few minutes?"

"Oh." Aileen turned to stare at Sierra, hesitating. And Sierra was suddenly unsure if she wanted to be alone with Reed. But she'd have to face it sooner or later. Have to tell him the truth. She owed him that much. Sierra knew why her mother didn't want to leave. All she wanted to do was protect her youngest daughter. She was terrified this new trauma might tip Sierra over the edge, put her back into that pit of misery and despair she'd fallen into after Grace's death.

But Sierra knew she was stronger than that. She would be fine.

"Sure." Sierra nodded toward Reed. "Mum, would you mind getting me a coffee from that vending machine in reception? I'd kill for one right now." Sierra made shooing motions with her hands, trying to convince her mother with her eyes that she would be fine. She didn't need her mother hovering over her like she was a wounded bird. Her mum mumbled something incoherent, but did as she was asked, looking back over her shoulder once or twice as she walked down the corridor.

"How are you?" Reed came to stand next to her bed, tall and solid. His hand reached out and covered her own. It was warm, and Sierra wanted to close her eyes at the feeling of reassurance and intimacy that touch gave her. She thought she might pull her hand away, but instead, she gave into her impulse and entwined her fingers between his. He winced as he got a good look at her face. "You wouldn't look out of place in the middle of a rugby game with that shiner." His lips twitched in a half-smile.

Sierra resisted the urge to reach up and feel her face. "Yeah, the doc said my nose was broken, but they re-set it last night while I was under, so it should heal fairly straight."

"You're still beautiful," he said.

She stared at him, expecting a wink or a smile of amusement, to make light of the situation. But was clearly deadly serious, and her chest suddenly tightened. He honestly thought she was beautiful, after everything she'd been through? It was as if he was seeing through all the scrapes and bruises on her face and body, straight through to her soul. She needed to change the subject; she wasn't ready for his conversation after all.

"Is he still alive?" she asked flatly, locking her gaze back on the ocean outside, removing her hand from his grasp.

"Yes, he's in an induced coma."

Sierra hadn't managed to kill Evan—or Damien, or whatever the hell his name was—after all. She'd shot him in the head, and the bullet had cracked his skull and grazed his brain. But when Reed got to him yesterday—that seemed like eons ago now—he'd still been breathing. They'd flown him by medi-vac helicopter straight to The Royal Adelaide Hospital. Sierra didn't know how she felt about it. Did he deserve to die? Probably. Did she want his death on her conscience? Probably not.

"Oh." Perhaps things might've been easier, more clear-cut, if he had died. At least then Jessica's parents might have some closure. But now, if he never woke up, the monster might never face charges, and might never pay for what he'd done.

"You'll need to answer some more questions," Reed continued quietly.

The Sarge had already asked her the basic stuff, just before they put her under the anesthetic so they could re-set her broken ankle last night. But she knew there would be many, many more to come before everyone was completely satisfied.

"But I think it's all pretty well cut and dried," he continued. "You won't be charged. If anything, you're already being hailed a hero by the locals."

"Really?" She looked up, surprised, and found his gaze locked onto her.

"Sierra…" His voice broke as he said her name.

She didn't know if she was ready to hear what he was about to say.

He tried again. "Sierra, we need to talk. About…you know…your daughter, and—"

"I'm back," her mum called as she hustled into the room, carrying three coffees in a cardboard take-out tray. "I got you a coffee, too, Officer Kapua. I thought you looked like you could do with one."

Saved by the bell. Yes, she agreed with Reed, they needed to talk. But she didn't think he was going to like what she had to say. She could see it in his eyes. She saw hope there. Hope that perhaps she could get past the terrible thing he'd done—they'd done—back in Adelaide. But his hope was wasted. Because even though Sierra wanted him desperately—wanted him to wrap his arms around her. To kiss him. To lie with him, be cocooned in his strong arms. Feel the strong connection between them. Stronger, perhaps, than anything she'd ever felt for another man—it would never be enough. For her to forgive him.

* * *

Reed tamped down his sudden urge to frog-march Sierra's mother straight back out of the room. He needed to finish this conversation. But he couldn't blame her, Sierra's mother was only trying to protect her child from what she saw as a threat. If not a physical one, then the one to her mental well-being. And it wouldn't do to alienate her. If anything, Reed needed Aileen on his side.

He'd met her last night, when she rushed from Adelaide to be at Sierra's side. It was he who had called her, to let her know what'd happened. It was the least he could do. And she'd been eternally grateful to him then. But now more of the details were emerging, she was starting to look at him with circumspection in her eyes. There were certain similarities between mother and daughter, he could now see where Sierra got her tilted nose and high cheekbones. But their personalities were very different. Sierra was all cool calm and control, while Aileen flapped around like a startled chicken, letting her emotions show for everyone to see.

He glanced at Sierra, but her poor bruised face was a blank canvas, and he knew he'd get nothing more from her at the moment.

"I'll come back and see you later," he said, laying his hand back over the top of Sierra's, not caring if her mother raised her eyebrows at him.

Sierra opened her mouth, but before she could speak, Aileen cut in. "They're discharging her today. I'm going to take her back to her place and look after her for a few days. She needs some peace and quiet to recuperate from all this… trouble." The stern look on Aileen's face made it clear she would brook no argument.

Reed stifled a sigh. By the look on Aileen's face he understood Sierra had already told her who he was; what he'd done. No wonder she was being overly protective.

Sierra still hadn't said a word, just watched the interplay with hooded eyes.

"I'll come and visit you soon," he said, emphasizing the words and ignoring the glare he got from Aileen. "Look after that ankle." He glanced at the lump under the blankets and then back up to her face. He couldn't help himself, he reached up and stroked a gentle finger down the uninjured side of her cheek. Her eyes widened at his touch and he thought he saw a flare of yearning there. "And that beautiful face." There was so much more he wanted to say. Wanted to do. He wanted to take her into his arms and hold her. She looked so small and alone in that big hospital bed. Diminished, somehow. The bruises on her temple from the car accident a few days earlier were turning a deep shade of purple, but were competing with the new, lighter bruising on the bridge of her nose and down her cheekbone, where that bastard had head-butted her and broken her nose. He knew she was a strong woman, that she would recover from this, just like she'd recovered before. But he wanted to help her. He could be there for her this time, if only she'd let him in.

The anger he'd felt towards her yesterday—was it really only yesterday?—was gone. His father's words replaying over and over in his head had replaced the emotion with something softer and more malleable. His father was right; she had every right to be angry at him. Just as he had every right to be angry at her. But perhaps, as his father had said, given time, Sierra might start to change her mind. And he wanted to be the one to help convince her. After what they'd been through together yesterday, it was more than obvious they shared a connection. She'd been prepared to forfeit her life for him. And for the girl. That was huge. He owed her a debt. Plus, he wanted to explore that connection, to find out if it was as strong as he hoped. Because, as his father had also pointed out, it was time he tried to find love again.

Reed turned away quickly, before he got so lost in her eyes he couldn't leave. "I'll let Eric know you're going soon. He's out front, keeping all the media hounds at bay. He can give you a ride home in the police cruiser." He turned his gaze toward Aileen, so she understood his next words were for her. "And make sure you go out the back door, if you don't want to be swamped by those vultures." He tilted his chin towards the main road, where he could see part of the large contingent of journalists who were still camped out near the front door of the hospital. Sierra might've been one of them before, might be good at answering their questions, but now was not the time or place. He could see the vulnerability in her eyes, and the vultures would see it, too, and swoop in for the kill. Aileen would perceive that, and at least her protective instincts would come in handy where that was concerned.

"See you both soon," he said over his shoulder and walked down the corridor. He would be going out the back door as well. No need to give the media any more fodder today. The Sarge and himself had already fronted two press conferences. One last night, and then another again this morning. Giving them the basics to start with, as their investigation was even now still catching up with everything that'd happened. Don told the press that Jessica had been found alive and well. It was the main point, and the Sarge repeated it over and over, like a mantra. They had successfully rescued the girl. It was truly the one thing that mattered, at least to Reed. A young life had been saved. He also told them a suspect was in hospital, under police guard and they would give out more details as they came to light. Of course, it was never enough for the media, and they fired questions at him about Sierra's involvement—how they found out about that Reed didn't know.

Reed still couldn't believe the incredible story they were piecing together.

He'd been on the phone earlier this morning, talking to Senior Sergeant Mike Delaney, head of the Port Pirie precinct. Mike had only been at the station for five years, and knew very little about the case from twelve years ago. But he and his team had spent the night combing through the archives, scrambling to pull together the clues.

"I'll be damned," Mike had said in his guttural voice. "Damien Nicholson was indeed an officer here; worked here for a total of seven years. He was on track to becoming a detective, back then. Had a spotless record. Go figure," Mike had said, sourly.

Reed grunted, but not wanting to interrupt the Senior Sergeant, had said nothing.

"One of my officers pulled out the evidence from child abductions, and now, looking at it with fresh eyes, it does seem like everything that could go wrong, did. Little things like communication documents going missing or calls not being logged, certain witnesses not being questioned. Right up to big things, like destruction of evidence. There are some DNA samples that seem to be missing." Reed could hear the discomfort in the other man's voice after that admission. They both knew without having to say, that an internal investigation would take place. And the Port Pirie station would once more, come under intense scrutiny. Back then Sierra had blamed the police for the way they handled the investigation. And that's why Damien had started to threaten her, to try and keep her quiet. Because her shining a light on the gaps in the investigation might've opened Pandora's Box. And pointed straight to him.

Mike continued, "But Damien Nicholson wasn't dumb. He took a job at a precinct in Adelaide, just as soon as he possibly could, to get away from the spotlight. But it was as a lowly traffic cop, so he would've lost any promotion he might've been angling for here."

Probably something else Evan blamed Sierra for, Reed thought with a grimace.

"Have you got anything to link him to the girls' abductions?" Reed asked. It was the question on everyone's lips. Reed knew in his heart that Evan was responsible, but they still needed to prove it. He was sure some of that missing DNA evidence would've linked Damien to those first crimes.

"Not yet," Mike answered. "But we're throwing everything we've got at it."

It was terribly frustrating that the pedophile was in a coma. The only way they could ever know for sure would be a confession. He needed to wake up. Otherwise they may never be able to corroborate his story, and there would be no chance of finding those poor little girls' bodies.

Nothing much else had come from his call to the Senior Sergeant and so he had hung up with more questions than he had answers.

Reed made it to the police Land Cruiser, parked down a side lane next to the hospital, out of sight of the media pack. He turned on the ignition and started the car, but his mind was still caught up in the bizarre case of Damien Nicholson.

Preliminary DNA testing had come back on the bones found near Sierra's precious bird-nesting site last night as well. It looked like they belonged to that of a six-year-old girl who went missing in Adelaide two years ago. Reed remembered Sierra had mentioned she'd also started following up on the case of two missing kids, Marley and Kasey, from three years ago, because her ex-editor had been convinced that they were somehow connected to the ones from twelve years previous. And it seemed the editor's instincts might've been spot on. Police were now trying to link those more recent missing cases to Damien, as well. It was likely that he'd brought his second victim, Kasey, over to the island to hide her body. Perhaps that was when he'd decided to stay. Because it was reported he'd moved to the island a little less than two years ago, bought the shop and set himself up as a respectable, innocent citizen.

Why he'd decided to abduct little Jessica was still a mystery. He had a new life, was laying low, keeping off the radar. He'd obviously hoped to escape with her, get away from the island and set up with the girl somewhere safe. Perhaps he thought of Jessica as his last hurrah, the one he would keep, the one who never got away. Bastard.

Reed shook his head put the car into gear. Don needed him back at the office ASAP. He'd let Reed have half an hour to go and see Sierra, to make sure for himself she really was okay, but after that Reed knew he was in for a long day. Filling out paperwork, answering questions. It was possible he'd even have to fly to Adelaide for a few days, to answer more questions with the Senior Sergeant in charge of the case. The elation of getting the girl back safely and of finding Sierra alive was fast wearing off. The next few days were going to be long and hard, and emotionally draining. And on top of that, he needed to find time to go and see Sierra. They needed to talk about what had happened. He wasn't going to let her go without a fight, that much he knew. She was special. What they had was special. But how could he get her to understand that?

CHAPTER TWENTY-ONE

The ocean was flat and gloomy, which mirrored Sierra's feelings exactly. It was Sunday morning and she sat out on the deck, her leg up on a chair, sipping a cup of steaming coffee. Jon was purring on her knee. Aileen was happily bustling around in the kitchen; Sierra could hear her banging pots and pans. Her mum was like a pig in mud, she hadn't had an excuse to pamper her daughter in longer than she could remember, and she seemed to be enjoying every second of it. But Sierra's patience was beginning to stretch. Aileen was driving her quietly and gently insane with all her well-meaning help. She'd decided to leave tomorrow. Sierra would be both sad to see her go, and also perhaps a little relived.

"Morning." Jen pulled out a chair and sat opposite Sierra, blowing on her own mug of coffee. Her hair was a rumpled mess, and she was still wearing her fluffy pajamas. Sierra smiled at her old friend and her mood lifted. There were definitely a few more lines in the mocha skin around her eyes. But apart from that, Jen hadn't changed in the slightest. It was lovely to have her friend here. She'd arrived yesterday, and was going to stay on for a few more days and continue to look after Sierra, which meant Aileen was free to go home as she knew Sierra was in good hands. Jon twitched his

249

whiskers at Jen and gave her the cat death-stare, unhappy to have his peaceful interlude with his mistress broken.

"How did you sleep?" Sierra asked.

"That spare bed of yours is so damn comfy." Jen stretched her hands over her head and gave a loud yawn. "Or maybe it's all this wonderful fresh sea air." Jen glanced down at the cast. "How's the leg this morning?"

"Not too bad. Six weeks on crutches is going to kill me, though." Sierra grimaced. How was she going to cope with no daily ocean swim, and without her tramps through the coastal scrubland? It would drive her crazy, she already knew that.

"Your mum told me she was going home tomorrow. So, it'll be just us gals for a while. Don't worry, I'll take care of you. I'm not a bad cook when the need arises."

"It's so nice to have your here," Sierra agreed. "But you don't need to be looking after me, I'm a big girl, you know."

"Haven't you learned not to be so bloody independent all the time? You need a little bit of TLC. Let someone else do the work for a change." Jen's words were soft, but struck Sierra to the bone. She got the underlying meaning. She'd been alone for so long now, she didn't know how to accept help gracefully.

"Yes, well, thank you," she murmured in reply. "You might give away your TLC for free, but Mum has ways of exacting payment. She wants me to go to Hawaii with her when I'm better. She's worried about Keira. No one's heard from her for a while. Which is not unusual." Sierra sighed as she thought about her older sister, and how unreliable she was when it came to contacting her family. "Mum's already planning the trip."

"That'll be good for you," Jen concurred. "A holiday is just what you need."

"I'm not sure you could rightfully call it a holiday," Sierra grumbled.

"And Hawaii? Woohoo, girl, I hear there're some hot men over there." Jen fanned her face and winked at Sierra.

She tried to raise a smile, but the comment about hot men had her thinking about Reed. He was hot. Damn hot.

"And while we're on the topic, are you going to call that hunk of a policeman soon?"

"That's not *on the topic*," Sierra retorted. How *did* Jen know what she was thinking? Sierra was beginning to suspect she had supernatural powers. "And I'm not sure if or when I'll contact him." She hadn't seen Reed since she left hospital on Wednesday. And she'd been intentionally trying not to think about him. He'd called three times, leaving a message each time. Sierra liked to listen to his voice. Deep and syrupy. Turning her insides to mush. Making her nerve endings tingle, as she remembered how he'd made her feel that night they'd made love. But she hadn't replied. Didn't intend to reply.

"Mmhmm. Well, you know my thoughts on *that* topic."

Yes, she knew exactly what Jen thought. Last night, the two of them had sat up chatting in front of the log fire, each sipping a glass of delicious wine Jen had brought with her. Aileen had gone off to bed to read a book, leaving them alone. That's when Sierra told her the whole story. For once she gave Jen every detail, left nothing out. Starting at the break-in, she talked about the missing girl, the kiss, her dead chickens, the crash. How she spent the night with Reed. Sierra even admitted how close she'd come to falling for him. And then she told her the terrible truth. How he broke her heart with the worst betrayal possible.

The funny thing was, Jen wasn't as quick to condemn Reed as she hoped. In fact, Jen had almost done the opposite. Certainly, she'd agreed that it was a terrible thing to happen, a horrible twist of fate.

But then she said something surprising. "You've painted this picture of an uncaring policeman who rammed into your car in your head."

Sierra hadn't answered, but she knew it was true.

"I remember after the accident, how much you hated everyone on the police force, accusing them of protecting one of their own." Jen continued gently. "And back then, I almost agreed with you. My heart was breaking for you, you'd lost your child." Jen caught Sierra's eye and trapped her gaze. "Then they had an internal investigation, Sierra, and they cleared him of any wrongdoing."

Sierra nodded her head, she remembered it all clearly.

"But you refused to believe them. You kept saying you knew they were hiding something sinister. That the cop had been speeding. He didn't have his lights and siren on, as they insisted. The chase had been called off, but in his arrogance, he'd continued on anyway, the safety of the public be damned. Thank God they kept his name out of the papers, as they wanted him to stay anonymous so he could eventually return to work, because I was actually afraid you might try and take some kind of revenge on the man if you ever found out his identity. And I let you keep saying and thinking those poisonous thoughts because I knew you were hurting, and I thought it was your way of dealing with it."

Sierra watched her old friend as they sat on the couch together in front of the fire. As Jen spoke, the truths she'd believed in so implicitly for so long had become blurred and soft around the edges.

"Tell me, Sierra, now you've met him, is he that evil brute you devised in your head?"

No, he was anything but a brute. He was wracked with guilt at what'd happened. Had been affected just as badly as she was. She'd discovered Reed was a caring, wonderful man. Insightful and funny. Honest and achingly sensual. She wasn't about to tell Jen that Reed was constantly on her mind. That her body ached to have him hold her, just once more. That her soul felt somehow empty when she thought about never seeing him again.

Jen hadn't stopped there, however. "I know you don't want to hear this, but perhaps no one was to blame, after all. Perhaps it's time to stop holding a grudge. To let go of the past, and look to the future, instead."

Sierra went to bed with her head full of contradictions and questions, and hadn't slept well at all.

"Are you okay?" Jen's question pulled her back to the present. There was genuine concern in her friend's voice and Sierra suddenly felt her chest tighten. Nope, she wasn't going to cry now, she'd done more than enough of that last night.

"Yeah, just thinking," Sierra replied, giving her a half-smile.

"That's good. Thinking is good." Jen laughed and there was a slight pause. "So, while you're thinking, I'd like to chat about something else that's close to my heart." Sierra's internal alarm bells started ringing. "You know you're sitting on the biggest scoop of the year, don't you? Biggest scoop of the century, even."

Sierra drew in a sharp breath. Even though she'd known this was probably coming, she still wasn't ready for it. That wasn't the reason she'd wanted to search for the girl. To help save the girl. A journalistic coup was the furthest thing from her mind.

"You know I would never pressure you if I thought it would do you harm," Jen prompted quietly.

Sierra snorted her response. But Jen was right. Yes, she'd pushed her to get back into journalism, but only when she thought the time was right. Just because Sierra had refused, didn't mean the other woman was wrong. Sierra just hadn't been ready back then. But now, she might well be the best person to tell the story. To tell Jessica's story. Her own story. And the story of a monster. Perhaps if she told it right, it might help others. Might help the families of the abducted girls find a little closure. Make sure other families kept an extra vigilant eye on their young children, safe from predators like Damien. Because people like him would never go away, but her story might make them think twice before they acted.

At Sierra's lack of response, Jen sighed and said, "All right, but please, promise me you'll at least think about it."

"I will, Jen, I will think about it."

"Really? That's great." Her friend's face split in a wide grin, teeth white against her brown skin, and Sierra grinned along with her. More at the sight of Jen's bed-head hair that was still sticking up in odd tufts. "You know there's always a job at *The Advertiser* for you. Even if you just want to do freelance stuff. You're way too talented to be doing articles for that little *Islander* piece of fluff that calls itself a newspaper."

Sierra laughed. The sound startled her. It felt good. She hadn't laughed like that for a while. Not since she and Reed…

Better to leave that thought alone. She wanted to get up and wrap her friend in an enveloping hug. To say thank you for being there for her. For kicking her butt when she needed it. But her cast made it too awkward, so she reached over and grabbed Jen's hand, instead.

"You're a real piece of work, Jen," she said.

"Yeah, I know." Jen squeezed her hand tight.

"But I love you anyway."

"Yeah, I know that, too."

They sat in companionable silence, just grinning at each other until the faint scrunch of tires on gravel made Sierra look up. A car had pulled into her driveway. The sound of feet pattering down the hallway reached her, as her mum went to open the front door. Good, Aileen could deal with whoever it was.

"I'm going to get dressed." Jen hoisted herself out of her seat, grabbing her now-cold coffee on the way into the house.

"And brush your hair," Sierra called after her.

"Sierra." Aileen's voice drifted through the house as her mum hurried to the glass door and opened it wide. "Darling, there's someone here to see you."

"Who?"

"It's Reed."

Sierra's stomach filled with fluttering butterflies at the mention of his name. Then her heart plummeted. She couldn't see him. Not now.

"I don't want to talk to him. Can you please tell him to come back another day?"

"Nope. I'm going to let him in, and you are going to talk to him."

"What?" Sierra gasped. She started to protest. "That's not really fair. I'm stuck here like an invalid. You can't make me —"

Aileen cut her off. "I've been watching you mope around these past few days. At first, I thought it was because of what you'd been through. My God, you nearly died." Her mother's voice hitched as she said this and Sierra opened her mouth, but Aileen held up her hand to stop her talking. "But you're strong, Sierra. I can see that. No, it's something else that's got you into such a misery. And now I know what it is. It's this man. I honestly never thought you would find anyone again, after…what happened. I think you need someone in your life, Sierra. And I think he might be good for you, no matter what he did. You need to forgive yourself. It wasn't your fault. And it wasn't his fault. It was a terrible accident. Nothing more, nothing less. You need to give him a chance."

Sierra stared at her mother, openmouthed. She'd always

been very careful what she said around Sierra, especially after the accident; after she lost Grace. As if she were afraid Sierra might break if she said the wrong thing.

"So, I'm going to let him in, and you are going to talk to him." She didn't give Sierra a chance to reply, just turned on her heel and disappeared back inside.

What should she do? She was stuck now. Could only make the best of a bad situation.

Jen materialized at the door while Sierra was still contemplating her next move. She was pulling a sweater over her head, and trying to pat her hair into place. "I'm going to take your mum for a walk. I need to go down and visit that gorgeous little beach."

What the hell? Was this some kind of conspiracy? Jen hated walking.

"It'll be a long walk, so you two take your time." With a wave of her hand, Jen disappeared down the corridor and Sierra heard her voice as she introduced herself to Reed, and then suggested very loudly to Aileen that it was a beautiful morning for a walk.

Calm. Just be calm. Footsteps on the wooden floorboards announced his arrival. Then Reed strode through the open door, and Sierra suddenly found she couldn't breathe. He was glorious. So tall and lean, masculine and strong in a pair of blue jeans and tight, black sweater that showed off his pecs and his broad shoulders to perfection. That chin and his square jaw, a slight one-day stubble roughing up his profile. Then he smiled, showing off his dimple, and she nearly melted into a puddle on her chair. It was not going to be as easy to resist this man as she'd hoped.

* * *

"Hi, gorgeous." Reed leaned in and kissed Sierra on the cheek before taking the seat next to her, ignoring her frown. He'd waited long enough to come and see her, imagined seeing her for days now, and her skin felt good beneath his lips. Even if she kept her gaze cool, he saw her reach up and touch the place his lips had been when she thought he wasn't looking.

"Hi, Reed," she replied. She looked good. Fresh and fit. Stunning. Her long hair was left to flow over her shoulders today, wisps of it curling around her high cheekbones, as the sea breeze tickled the patio. Perhaps having her mum here, looking after her and feeding her was a good thing, after all. The leg in the cast was propped up on a chair in front of her, and there was a cat on her knee. She had on a pair of leggings that'd been cut up the side, to allow for the bulky cast and her usual oversized hoodie. On closer inspection, he saw it was the dark-blue hoodie he'd given her to wear after her car had been sabotaged. The night they'd made love. He smiled, not bothering to hide his happy grin. She was wearing his sweater. It had to mean something.

"How's the investigation going?" she asked, bringing him back to reality. So, she wanted to start with business. That was fine, he was happy to get it out of the way, then he could move on to the real reason he'd come out here today. Reed slipped his hand in his pocket and found his lucky penny. Began to play with it, the warm coin soothing him, like it always did.

With a great effort, he removed his silly grin and replaced it with a more appropriate, serious expression. Professional mask in place, he said, "I've got some things in the car to give you. We found your laptop and your jewelry hidden in a closet at his flat."

"That's good," she said impatiently, and he knew it wasn't really what she was hoping to hear. "Thanks for that."

"And I've got good news, actually. He's awake."

"What?" Sierra's head shot up. "Evan came out of his coma?" A mixture of revulsion and relief crossed her face. He knew how she felt. A small part of him had been hoping the monster wouldn't survive. But he also hadn't wanted Sierra to bear the guilt of knowing she'd taken a life. Even if it had been a man who didn't deserve to live.

"Yes, he did, and you won't believe what he's told us. He's been singing like the proverbial canary."

"Really," Sierra said on a breath, her attention now fully focused on him.

"Yes, I think a bullet to the head has made him even more talkative than he was already. Strange how a brush with death will do that to you."

"Tell me," she demanded, leaning forward. "Tell me everything."

"All right, well, I think you know, or have guessed at a lot of it already. But let me start at the beginning." He drew his chair closer to the table so he could rest his elbows on the top. And to put him closer to Sierra. The black cat on her lap glared at him.

"He confirmed he was indeed the Port Pirie abductor."

Sierra sucked in a loud breath at his pronouncement.

Reed continued, "He gave us all the intimate details, so there's no doubt it was him. The first child he abducted in Port Pirie was six-year old Emily Newman. She was out playing in the front yard with her younger brother, while the mother was inside getting ready to go to the store. The newspapers said that when the mother came out Emily was gone and the boy had a candy in his mouth and said the nice man gave one to him and one to Emily."

Sierra only nodded as she followed along with his story. It was probably all very familiar to her, she'd worked on the news articles for months on the case before she published her exposé.

"It seems that Evan, or Damien as he was called then, planned his crime well. He looked up the sex offender registry and found that Charles Dorkney lived on that street, and Damien knew he would be the number-one suspect if a child went missing. He chose the street because there were a number of young families in the area, and it was quiet. It's scary how cold and calculating he was when he planned this." Reed almost shivered as he remembered reading the deposition taken by the Sergeant in charge over at the Royal Adelaide Hospital.

"And you were spot-on with your suggestions about police getting things wrong. But what no one knew back then, was it was all due to Damien. He did small things to hinder the investigation, like making sure neither of the first teams on the ground interviewed the neighbors by mixing-up orders so they weren't passed down the chain."

"Wow," Sierra said quietly. "I knew there was something dodgy going on. If only I'd dug a little deeper, perhaps—"

"Don't you dare blame yourself. For any of this," Reed growled. He was going to make damned sure she knew this had nothing to do with her. She was a good journalist, with good instincts. As it was, the police had definitely failed on this one, not her.

She frowned, the wrinkles marring her perfect high forehead. "Go on, then," she insisted.

"So, we know the second girl was abducted eleven months later. Seven-year-old Naomi Chadstone had been playing in the local park close to home with her two older sisters. They had a fight and Naomi ran off, saying she hated both her sisters and she was going home. When the two sisters arrived home fifteen minutes later, Naomi wasn't there."

"Yes, I remember all that." Sierra stroked the cat absent-mindedly as she spoke.

"Well, Damien filled in the blanks for us. This was a spontaneous crime of opportunity. Damien had been driving home from work after finishing a shift, and seen the girl crying at the side of the road. He was still in his uniform and driving a squad car. He invited her into the car and offered her a lift home." Reed grimaced as he recounted the story. "What little girl wouldn't think it was safe to get into a marked police car? He was a sick, sick bastard. And it kills me to know he got away with this for so long, and he was right under our noses." Reed balled his fists on the table.

"I know what you mean." Sierra laid her hand over the top of his, easing his fingers apart. "But you are as blameless in this as you keep telling me I am. You weren't even working in Adelaide by that stage. There was nothing you could've done to stop him, either." Her face softened as she looked into his eyes and, surprisingly, she didn't let his hand go.

"I know," Reed admitted, then continued with the story. "Anyway, Damien knew he'd been stupid and lazy, and vowed he'd never do anything spontaneous like that again, it was too easy to get caught. That's why there was such a long hiatus between his crimes. He laid low for nearly nine years, until two more girls went missing."

"Hang on. Back up a little," Sierra interrupted. "Neither of those two little girl's bodies were ever found. Has he…"

"Yes," Reed said. "He told us where they're buried. But I'm going to spare you all the details of their deaths, at least for today."

"Okay," she agreed. "Now, those poor families finally have some kind of answers. Even if it's not the ones they were hoping for."

"Yes. But let me tell you the rest. So, Damien took another job and moved to a police unit in Adelaide shortly after Port Pirie, and he continued to lay low. But then one night, eight-year-old Marley went missing. Her mother admitted at the time Marley was a handful of a child. She had ADD and other learning difficulties, and had even run away a few months earlier, but was found at her grandmother's house. Damien knew about the girl's problems; he was one of the cops originally called in when she first ran away. Knew her schedule, knew where she'd be each day. And pounced on her as she waited for her mother to pick her up from a swimming lesson one afternoon. He told us he tried to stop after Marley, but he couldn't. After three abductions, he'd had a taste by then, and that's when he started planning the next one. Six-year-old Kasey had been walking home from school with her older brother. But he'd got sick of waiting for her, said she was always so slow, and had rushed on ahead with two of his other mates. They were almost home by then, in sight of their house, and the brother thought she would be okay. Damien had been casing the street for days, and he was finally in the right place at the right time. That poor little girl." Reed shook his head as he thought about just how easy it'd seemed for Damien to do his evil deeds.

"Jen tried to tell me the cases in Adelaide were linked to the Port Pirie ones, but at first I didn't believe her. Or perhaps I couldn't be bothered. It takes a lot of time, effort and research to delve into these things. I think perhaps I just got lazy." Surprisingly, Sierra still had her hand wrapped around his. The connection helped. Calmed him, soothed him. But her touch also heated his insides. "So, the bones of the child we found at the Glossies nesting area?" she asked.

"Yes, they belonged to Kasey. Believe it or not, she was alive when he first brought her here on his own private boat. He gave some garbled explanation as to how he thought they could start a new life together out here, where no one knew him. But things obviously didn't work out, because he killed her after only a day or so. Again, I won't go into the details, because they're just too grisly and sad. I will say that he knew about the Glossies' nesting site because of his stalking you. He knew everything about you, spent hours and hours researching everything he could about you online. And that's how he found out about the Friends of the Glossies."

Sierra shook her head and let out a sigh. "I did wonder about that, because Evan was never a member of the Friends."

"Anyway," Reed continued. "Afterwards, he decided to quit the police force and move out to the island for good. He changed his name and identity, grew a beard as a disguise. Perhaps law enforcement started getting a little too close for comfort. Damien is not a dumb man, he knew it was time to disappear, or risk getting caught. He also kept in touch with a mate of his over in his old Adelaide unit. Which is also how he knew you'd started digging around for more information on the Adelaide girls."

"God, how horrible. That he was here, and we never knew." Sierra sighed and finally removed her hand as her gaze drifted out over the ocean. He wished she'd bring it back to his.

"I believe there was more to his motivation than that, however," Reed continued. "I think you were part of the pull he felt towards the island. He knew you were here, and he has some kind of strange fixation on you. It probably started with his letter writing. He was trying to scare you off at first, nervous you would discover the truth. But I think the stalker side of him grew, until he found he was inextricably linked to you somehow."

"Yes. Perhaps if I paid more attention to his letters, instead of dismissing him as some kind of crackpot…"

There she went again, blaming herself for something she had absolutely no control over. It sounded like the story of her life. She had a bad habit of shouldering the blame.

"It seems he had the perfect spot to watch you from, as well. His newsstand faces the ferry dock. That's how he knew your movements the night he broke in and stole your computer. He watched you drive onto the ferry in the morning and when you didn't disembark that night, he knew you must've been staying on the mainland."

Sierra shook her head as she pieced his words together.

"What about Tom Hubbard? I assume he's no longer a suspect?" she asked.

"Not in this case," he confirmed. "But he will still go to jail for that child porn on his computer."

"Strange, isn't it, how you think you know the people around you. But really, you don't have a clue," she mused.

"If you hadn't seen that candy wrapper …" The rest of his sentence remained unsaid. But the sentiment hung in the air anyway. *They might never have found him.* "It's his weapon of choice. Those caramels. They're his calling card. He used them to entice every child he lured away."

"That's so disgusting. I'm never going to eat one of those ever again."

He couldn't help it, he laughed. She was so determined, so resolute. And so beautiful in her unwavering view of the world.

But it was time to change the subject.

"Talking about being enticing, you're a sight for sore eyes. I've missed you over the last few days, Sierra. I wanted to come earlier, but work has been crazy, as you can imagine."

She drew back from him, her mouth puckered in surprise. The displeased cat shot off her lap at her sudden movement and went to hide under the table.

"I beg your pardon?"

"You heard me." He moved in closer, so their knees were touching. And locked his gaze with hers. She arched a fine, dark eyebrow at him. God, she was beautiful. Those sexy lips pursed in an expression of disbelief. Those slim shoulders pulled up in affront at the audacity of him. It all made him want her more. Want to discover more about her, how she worked, both inside and out.

He'd come to a decision over the past few days. In between

all the long hours of work and travel and question after question, he made one, earth-shattering resolution.

He wanted Sierra Goldstein. And he wasn't going to let their past come between them. He'd spent enough time feeling guilty. It was time to get over it and move on. Start living again. And she was the one woman he thought he could do that with.

It wasn't just the searing attraction that boiled between them, although that was definitely part of it, he would never get tired of looking into that alluring face, those voluptuous lips. It was the way she stared at him, through him. She could see into his soul. Touch his soul. The way she shared herself with him so totally and utterly. How fearless she was, even though she was damaged and broken. She'd still picked herself up and carried on. How she was determined to tell the truth, especially back in her journalist days. What had she said on one of her newspaper articles? She was bound by truth.

And so was he. Now he was bound to tell her the truth. Of how he felt about her. Of how they might be together. Make each other stronger.

He grabbed her fingers, which had been tapping nervously on the tabletop and trapped them between his palms. It did the trick, she turned her gaze towards him, but he waited until he knew he had her full focus.

"We'll always have scars from that accident. Both physical and mental." He lifted the corner of his pantleg, revealing the marks on his calf. Then he reached up and gently touched the faint scar running along her hairline, practically hidden now behind all the bruising.

"But these aren't something to be afraid of. Or ashamed of. These scars draw us together. They're a connection, a bond that shouldn't be broken. Shared scars. We shared in a disaster and both of us came out with a truckload of guilt afterwards."

"You got that bit right," Sierra sad so softly he almost missed it. "I think I win on the guilt stakes." She gave a wry, humorless grin.

But he wasn't giving up. "I know you lost the most precious thing a mother could ever lose that day. And I will never take that away from you. You deserved to be allowed to wallow in your grief, to withdraw from the world, if that was your way of coping. I know you will always feel like a part of you is missing. But we can help each other through this, together. Move on and be better, together. I know we can."

Sierra stared at him, not speaking. What was going on behind those deep pools? Was she listening to him? Or was she going to refute him? Send him away without a second glance?

On instinct, Reed swept his chair out of the way and got down on his knees in front of her. Reaching for her hand, he took it up in his again. Now that he was level with her face and he came in as close as he dared, so he could see the tiny flecks of red and gold hidden in the depths of her irises. He wasn't going to beg, but he wanted her to know how serious he was. This might be his only chance to get through.

"Sierra, can you find it in your heart to forgive me? To forgive yourself? Because I want to be with you. To give this thing between us a chance to grow, discover where it might lead us. So, please think about it. Think about moving on from all that hurt and anger and guilt. And choose me."

CHAPTER TWENTY-TWO

Sierra opened her mouth to tell him no. How dare he presume to understand her pain? Understand her guilt. He'd never walked in her shoes. He'd never lost a child.

But she closed her mouth with a click of her teeth.

Yes, he had. He had lost an unborn baby. And he'd been devastated by that loss. He might not understand her particular suffering, but he did understand his own.

It was true, what he'd said. She had done all that stuff. She had wallowed, and she had withdrawn from everyone after Grace died. She'd pushed her husband away, and become less of a person because she didn't know how to handle her loss. But she was entitled, wasn't she?

Should she admit that she'd been thinking a lot over the past few days? Thinking about him. About how she felt when she was around him. How his mere presence made her come alive like she hadn't done in years. How she missed him when he wasn't around. Missed his deep laugh. Missed his smoldering gazes that heated her to the core, like there was lava bubbling beneath her skin.

After her talk with Jen last night, she'd also replayed the car accident over and over in her head. Re-analyzing it, now that she had more information. Looking at it from different sides, all angles. Taking a more un-biased view of it. There was still one single truth to come out of it. Her daughter was dead. She would never see her grow up into a beautiful, strong young woman. Had been denied that luxury.

But denying herself the luxury of love wouldn't change that. It wouldn't bring Grace back.

"I've already booked in to see a psychiatrist here on the island. It's time I addressed all this past shit that's holding me back." Reed was still down on his knees in front of her. Those patient, dark eyes fixed on her face. "I'm falling in love with you, Sierra. And I want to see where it might take us. We'd be good together. I know it. If only you'll give me a chance."

Could she? Could she forgive the man who had been partly responsible for her daughter's death?

It was the hardest decision of her life.

Because if she forgave him, then she'd need to forgive herself, as well.

She stared into his eyes for untold seconds. He never wavered, never withdrew, just waited for her answer.

"Yes." It was time to choose life. "I'd like to try."

His bright smile lit up the entire deck. "Really?"

"Yes, really." She gave him her first genuine smile in days in return. Now that she'd come to her conclusion, her heart felt like it was made of helium balloons. Her whole chest was expanding, and she might just float away. The weight that'd been holding her down like a thousand tons of lead drifted away into the clouds.

"That's amazing. You're amazing." He was staring at her, that silly grin still on his face, as if a little dumbfounded by her words. The dimple was there in his chin, and that crooked nose that she loved so much.

"Perhaps I might go and see that psychiatrist as well. What was their name?" she said.

"Yes, yes. That's a great idea." He removed one of his

hands from hers, and started fumbling around in his pocket as if looking for something to write the psychiatrist's name on.

"Kiss me, you idiot," she said with a laugh.

And he did, his firm lips landing on hers. Enticing, tempting. Drawing her tongue into his mouth. Stoking the warmth between her thighs into a flaring fire. When he drew back, his fingers traced a gentle line over the contours of her face, and she could tell by the slight narrowing of his eyes that he was worried about the bruising on her face; about hurting her.

Her body burned for him and she could hardly believe this man was hers. "Take me to bed," she sighed into his fingertips.

"What about your mum and your friend?"

"They won't be back for a while. Jen will keep Mum occupied. She knows when to give me space."

"Hmm." Reed didn't sound sure, so she pulled his face toward her and kissed him long and hard, until he gave a grunt and swept her up into his arms. "Well, okay, when you put it like that…" He carried her into her bedroom and laid her gently on the bed. "What about your ankle?" He took a step back, as if seeing the cast for the first time.

"It's not sore, if that's what you mean." Then she gave a wicked grin. "And if it gets in the way, we'll just have to get more inventive, won't we?" She beckoned to him with her finger, and he lay down next to her on the bed, tucking his arm under her head and holding himself up on one elbow so he could look down into her face.

"This is not all going to be easy sailing, you know. We might not make it through." She thought she should warn him one last time, before they became so completely lost in each other and there was no turning back.

"We'll make it, I have faith in us." His mouth claimed hers

and she believed him. They were meant to find each other. Meant to save each other. Against all odds. To be bound by truth.

If you liked Bound by Truth and want to hear more of Sierra and Reed's story, then you might like

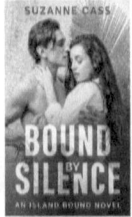

Bound by Silence

Bound by the Stars

The books in this series can be read as stand-alone novels, but are enhanced if you read them together.

Connect with the Author

I really hope you enjoyed reading Bound by Truth. For more action romance info, upcoming release dates, and access to free books join the exclusive Suzanne Cass reader club. As an added bonus, you'll get a copy of my FREE STORY.

Solar Flare

http://www.suzannecass.com/contact/

Or you can stay in touch via my website
www.suzannecass.com

Facebook: www.facebook.com/suzannecassauthor/
Instagram: www.instagram.com/suzanne.cass/
Pintrest: www.pinterest.com.au/suzanne_cass/
Twitter: twitter.com/SusieCass1

Also by Suzanne Cass

NEW

Stormcloud Station Series
(A Stargazer Spinoff Series)
Small Town Romantic Suspense

Clear Skies
Starlit Skies
Crystal Skies

Stargazer Ranch Romance Series
Small Town Romantic Suspense
Combustion: Prequel Novella
Wildfire
Firelight
Snowbound: A Christmas Novella
Snowfall
Cloudburst

Island Bound Series
Mystery Romance (on an Island)
Books can be read as stand-alone
Bound by Truth
Bound by Silence
Bound by the Stars

Colors of the Earth Series
Small Town Romantic Suspense
Books can be read as stand-alone
Shadows in the Dust
Shadows in Deep Blue
Shadows of Red Earth

Romantic Suspense
Single Title
Island Redemption

Glass Clouds
Chasing Bullets

Love in the Mountains Novella Series
Small Town Short Romance
Novellas can be read as stand-alone
Rain on a Tin Roof
Lost and Found
Rescue his Heart

Please Leave a Review
The greatest gift you could ever give an author is to leave a review. You will be helping other people to discover this book and making a difference to me as an Independently Published Author. If you liked this book and want other people to read it too, please leave a review.

About the Author

Suzanne Cass is an Australian author who writes rural romance and romantic suspense abounding with passion and danger.

Her debut novel, Island Redemption, won the Romance Writers of Australia Emerald Award in 2016. Suzanne was also a finalist in the 2019 Romance Writers of Australia RUBY award.

She had always had a fascination with the tough resilience of people who live in our amazing red-dirt outback country. When not writing about the characters that inhabit her head, Suzanne can be found roaming the Perth beaches with her border collie, or encouraging from the sidelines as her two sons play sport.

Visit her website www.suzannecass.com or subscribe to her newsletter via: www.suzannecass.com/contact

Acknowledgements

This book is the first in an exciting new series, where each story is set on a new and intriguing island all in different corners of the world, linked by three siblings, who follow their own journeys. I wanted this to be a global series, and what better way to do it. Bound by Truth is set on Kangaroo Island, just off the South Australian coast. This island has fascinated me for a long time. It is so wild and beautiful and a lot of it is also isolated and desolate. Which got my imagination working overtime. What better place for a crime to take place? At the time of writing this story, the case of Madeline Mccann was also back in the spotlight and it got me to thinking about all the poor children out there who are missing, never to be found. So Sierra and Reed were born, the two characters with problems of their own, who would nonetheless give their lives to save an abducted child.

This book took a whole lot of time to research. It rolled around in my head for many months before I even started writing. But a book also takes a whole village to bring it to fruition.

I need to thank my author tribe, and in particular Jillian, Rose and Rachel. Without you gals there would be no finished manuscript. Thank you. We are all on separate journey's in our writing career, but the best part, is we are sharing those journey's.

There is a team of people who I also couldn't do without, other beta readers (big thanks to Rebecca) and my ARC team, who are essential to an Indie Author like me. Big thanks to my editor, Tanya Saari.

My husband, Gary, needs a special mention. He puts up with my crazy need to hide away in my study, tapping on my computer till all hours of the night. He recognizes we all need to follow our dreams. And to my two beautiful boys (who are soon to be gorgeous men) Thank you for your unconditional love.

I am so very grateful to all the readers who have bought and enjoyed my books and who will continue to do so. Writing for you is what keeps me focussed and motivated.